IANT

Steve Blandford

Print ISBN 978-1-8384289-7-6

Published by
Llyfrau Cambria Books, Wales, United Kingdom.
Cambria Books is a division of
Cambria Publishing.
Discover our other books at: www.cambriabooks.co.uk

Acknowledgements

The story of *Iant* is woven around a few anecdotes about my maternal grandfather, David Owen, who died when I was two. I obviously did not know my grandfather in any meaningful way, but everybody that I have ever spoken to about David Owen talks of a gentle, kind man who disliked conflict of any kind. Ironic, as he was, in his teens, thrust into one of the biggest conflicts the world has ever seen. This novel is therefore partly dedicated to the memory of David Owen who died in 1956 at the age of 59 leaving behind memories, some of which I have been able to use in *Iant*.

The amount written about the war on the Macedonian front is quite small, at least compared to that on France and Belgium, but when writing *Iant* I was grateful for *Under the Devil's Eye: Britain's Forgotten Army at Salonika 1915-1918* (Sutton Publishing) by Alan Wakefield and Simon Moody. The authors helped me to understand, in particular, how forgotten this part of the war tended to be, despite the very harsh climactic conditions and the fierce fighting experienced, especially at the hands of the Bulgarians.

I would like to thank Chris Jones at Cambria for his patient help and support. Most importantly, as ever, I would like to acknowledge the love and support of my wife Mitch Winfield and my two children Sam and Beth Blandford. As well as my grandfather, this book is dedicated to them. Thanks guys - for everything. Beth is in the early part of her life an illustrator and it is has been a real treat to work with her on the cover of *Iant*.

CONTENTS

Part 1

Chapter 1

1916

Iant had read in the Post about Lloyd George encouraging the people of North Wales to 'live up to their past' and join up. He wasn't quite sure what it meant but felt some sense of vague pride at what people like him had done before. He wasn't old enough at first and was turned down by the recruiting sergeant in Corwen. 'Even I wouldn't get away with you son' he'd said. He had always looked younger than he was and knew he would have to wait.

By 1916 it had all changed anyway. They took you much more easily. Supposedly you couldn't be sent abroad until you were nineteen, but everyone knew boys who had gone much younger.

His father grumbled about having to do more work at his age, but his face gave away his pleasure that Iant wanted to go. It was the same primitive thing that had sent his father halfway across the world when he was younger.

The sergeant was scornful of his accent straight away and warned him and the others in their little troop not to 'jabber away in that bloody heathen language'. Iant laughed inwardly. He had been warned that this was the first thing they did, to toughen you up a bit.

By the time they got to the camp at Abergele his resolve was a bit weaker. He had no idea that there would be so many or that they would come from all over. In the huge crowds, the boys from around Bala and Corwen were quickly broken up and dispersed and he began to feel the isolation of someone speaking in an unfamiliar language.

In some ways, he wasn't naïve. He had grown up around the

3

animals, but nothing had quite prepared him for the vast communal showers and the mass of sweaty bodies drawn from all over the cities of the north of England. The thick Liverpool and Manchester accents made it sound as though they were speaking another language altogether, especially to someone used to life in Welsh.

He had never seen a tattoo before and certainly not stood so close to a naked man. He felt puny beside some of these young giants, though he felt disgust at the wobbling beer bellies of some of the older ones. At least he still kept lean chasing bloody sheep over the hills.

They joked constantly about not dropping the soap and keeping your back to the wall. It took him a while but when he began to understand he felt glad that he had kept his ignorance hidden. He understood better now the veiled stories that people told about Elfyn, a cousin from the other side of Llangollen, though he had no idea if the rumours were true.

He listened to stories of girls left behind and, seeing him as a local, he was asked constantly about the "skirt" in the places nearby and whether they were "willing". He said that he thought they were. He felt fleetingly guilty at this, especially as the jokes about Welsh women got more and more extravagant.

A uniform seemed to have an effect on girls that was hard to explain. His sister Gwennie, had gone uncharacteristically soppy when she had seen him dressed up in what seemed to him to be the most uncomfortable clothes he had ever had on and he had been pleased to see Frances, the barmaid of *The Grouse* stare at him a bit longer than usual as he walked down the village.

Quickly he learned of the girls that visited the camp or hung around near the entrances. He got as far as sneaking down there and taking a look from a place behind a tree where he couldn't be seen. In truth they frightened him, these young women, some of them from as far away as Liverpool, who dressed in ways that would have scandalised his mother and sisters and most of the other women in the village.

When they joined up they were all given a leaflet signed by

4

Kitchener himself warning them about the dangers of excess 'both in wine and women'. So far, he hadn't had much chance of either. Looking at the women from a safe distance felt dangerous enough for now. One of them especially caught his eye because of the way she was dressed. She seemed a little apart from the others as they joked and made faces at the men. All the women wore coats as the weather was cold, but most were very skilful at showing flashes of what was underneath; flimsy silk dresses, petticoats and stockings. This one kept her coat buttoned and her hat pulled down over her face. As he watched this first time, he saw men disappear into the fields and woods with a number of the women, but this one hardly moved. A young corporal that he had seen earlier, barking out orders, now looked much less brave as he approached her. Some words were exchanged and they moved off without touching. It was dusk and he couldn't see where they went.

The daily routine was supposed to be harsh, but physically he was a lot more able to cope than those who were from the towns and cities. He hated it, *nonetheless*. The constant barrage of abuse and mock outrage from the NCOs was wearing especially as a lot of it was directed at the 'fucking Taffs'.

There were one or two others from the Corwen area in his part of the camp and they tended to stick together. Oliver from near Chirk became a good friend and they walked along the seashore together or joined others in the *Ty Coch* or *The Sun* in Abergele. The owners couldn't believe their luck that the camp had brought them so much trade even though they had to hold their noses at the hordes of unwashed squaddies drinking themselves stupid every night.

Oliver was older and engaged to a girl called Ada from Ruthin. He carried her picture in his wallet and talked of the life he hoped to have when they married. Ada's father owned a little shop in the town and mended boots and shoes. Ada had no brothers and Oliver was sure that it would be his one day. To Iant, it sounded like the kind of life he would settle for.

Before he had joined up, Iant had worked for a time at

Ffestiniog in the quarries and he had little appetite to go back. He had started an apprenticeship and supposed he could return after the war, but he hoped he might get a job that involved less hardship and which took him back to the countryside and villages that he was used to. In the digs he had in Ffestiniog he felt lonely and surrounded by men whose harsh lives had made them difficult company.

He and Oliver were walking back from *The Sun* one evening when he needed to piss. Oliver walked on as he found a gap in the bushes at the side of the road. As he unzipped his fly, he heard noises a little further into the undergrowth. He pressed on a little and he saw through a gap in the next hedge an enormous sergeant's arse moving up and down. The noise he heard was the man's grunting. Faintly disgusted he began to move away when he caught a glimpse of the girl's face in the moonlight. It was the one he had noticed a few weeks ago, standing apart from the rest at the gate.

Their stares met so briefly that he felt he could easily have imagined it, but in his heart he sensed her disgust and contempt. Not just for the mass of grunting flesh that had her pinned to the hard, dry ground but for him for being there at all. He made a noise by treading on a stick that finally penetrated the man's preoccupation and he shouted loudly for him to 'Fuck off out of it, you little shit!' It was dark and Iant was certain that the man would not know who he was because he was hardly in a position to turn around and face him. Nevertheless, he turned and moved away as quickly as the undergrowth would allow. His bladder was bursting, but he needed to be away from there now more than he needed to piss.

A week or so passed before he once again allowed himself to sneak down again to the vantage point from where he could see the transactions at the camp gates. There was no doubt that what he had seen haunted him a little. His inexperience made him despise himself, but he was also drawn to this woman in ways that confused him and played tricks with the memory of what he had seen that night. He wanted to think of himself as the hero, throwing the sergeant aside, kicking him in his fat, ugly face, wrapping the woman up in his coat and carrying her away. He also knew that his seventeen-year-old body wanted to do things to her he was only just beginning to understand.

As he once again caught sight of her, Iant indulged himself in thinking how he might approach her and treat her better than anyone else. He wanted to take care of her, look after her and then, after that, well, it would be ok because she would want him too. A tall gangly soldier smoking a cheap cigarette approached her and they walked away, wordless. Iant saw his own foolishness and sprinted away back to his hut and the loneliness of another night of waiting and wondering what would eventually happen to him.

Oliver had heard of a dance in Rhyl the following Friday. It was only in a church hall, but it would be a break from what had become a grinding routine. They joined with a group that set off to walk the four or five miles to get there. It was a beautiful evening and as they crested the small hill between them and their destination the sun was reflecting off the sea in the distance. The normally muddy-looking stretch of the coast suddenly looked inviting and the rest of the walk towards the dance was full of optimistic banter. They'd known that the Methodist church hall wouldn't have a bar and most of the men had bottles of various kinds.

As they reached the hall Iant's heart sank at the tinny sound of the piano inside playing sedate music. He had rarely danced and the scene glimpsed through the doors looked both dull and intimidating. He said he was staying outside for a smoke and he walked on past the entrance door with the wide-eyed girls collecting the entrance fee in an old tin and leant on the side wall of the wooden hut. He tried not to look too self-conscious as desultory groups of young men and girls drifted down the lane towards the dance, but after a while, it was more effort than actually going inside.

As his eyes adjusted to the dim light he briefly spotted Oliver dancing with a girl with flaming red hair. So much for

7

Ada, he thought, uncharitably. He found a friend of Oliver's, who had a bottle of rum and they both took swigs as discreetly as they could in a corner of the room. The room was getting full and the scene that had filled Iant with anxiety was improving with the aid of the rum.

Nobody had much experience of dancing but there developed a general feeling of goodwill and bonhomie. Feet were bruised and tunes were murdered but everyone knew it was important to live just a little. Iant still found it difficult to join in, but his sense of obligation made him try and he eventually relaxed. After a while, almost wordlessly, he found himself dancing with a rather severe looking young woman who seemed as worried as him. As they moved stiffly around the little dance floor he smiled to himself at the picture they made, of almost rigid anxiety.

It was so long since he had touched anyone other than during some training exercise that Iant began to feel glad of even the briefest pressure from the hand of the young woman whose name, he eventually discovered, was Mary. He tried Welsh, but she seemed more comfortable in English and the exchange of pleasantries got easier. Her brother was about to go to France and, once she had told him that, there was at least some connection between them.

Iant asked Mary if she would like a cigarette which seemed to surprise her, but it seemed a good way to end the dance without awkwardness and they made their way to the exit. He caught sight of Oliver smirking and winking at him and he hoped that Mary hadn't noticed. Once outside they felt awkward again. There seemed always to be something expected of them. They were glad of the ritual of lighting a cigarette in the gentle breeze. The touch of her small hand as he struggled to keep the match alight was so delicate. He suddenly felt responsible for making her so nervous.

'Are you cold?' he said rather tamely.

'A little' she said and looked away.

He slipped off his jacket which suddenly looked its age and

put it around her shoulders in a gesture which he knew was as old as time, but nevertheless, it made him feel stronger.

'Where are you from?' she suddenly said.

'Near Corwen. Out in the country a bit.'

'I don't know where that is' she replied, perhaps a bit dismissively he felt.

'There's not much there. It's home though.'

'Do you know when you'll be leaving here?'

'No. They said twelve weeks when we arrived, but they seem to be speeding things up all the time.'

'Are you frightened?'

He didn't like thinking about this question. You would have to be a fool to say no but saying it and facing it was another thing.

'I suppose everyone is. Some don't admit it.'

'Michael wouldn't. My brother.'

'Not to you perhaps.'

'Not to anyone. He always plays the big man.'

'There are a lot of those in the camp.'

'Not you though?'

'You don't think so?' he laughed, teasing her a little.

She fell silent now not knowing whether she had offended him or not. He wasn't sure either.

'Would you like to dance again?' he said.

They walked back inside and drifted around the hall with all the others for a while. Their grip on each other was a little less tentative this time.

After a while, Mary led him outside and into the darkness at the back of the hall. Her back was against the rough brick wall and her kiss surprised him with its strength. As her tongue explored the inside of his mouth, he initially became embarrassed by his involuntary physical reaction. Soon though his hand explored her breast and his own kissing became more urgent. He realised that he was thinking about the girl at the camp gates and pulled away.

'Am I a good kisser' Mary asked.

'Yes, you are.'

9

Her mouth reached for his again and this time he tried to respond more gently. Before long the area around the back of the hall began to become crowded.

As Iant's hand began to explore further he felt Mary stiffen and pull away.

'It's getting cold. Can we go inside?'

'Yes, if you want to.'

Iant knew that the night was still warm but followed her back inside. Mary excused herself and went in the direction of the toilet. As Iant looked around the room he saw the desperate gropings of his comrades. Without quite understanding why he slipped out of the hall and walked quickly off into the night.

Chapter 2

There were rumours that they were not going to France. At first, there was great relief that they were to escape the trenches, but this quickly gave way to a realisation that the fighting in the east had been very fierce and the heat was supposed to be terrible.

Just the names sounded impossibly distant – Cairo, The Dardanelles, Greece, Macedonia, Salonika. Like most of them, Iant had only the dimmest idea of where they all were and how they related to each other. France was exotic enough, but these were places from children's stories and glimpses in newspapers. He could no more imagine what the land would be like than he could imagine the moon. The idea of such temperatures filled him with dread, but only because he knew what it was like to be doing manual labour in the full heat of a Welsh summer and he knew it would be a lot hotter than that.

Rumours began to circulate, not only about where they were going, but what had happened to some of those who had already been to that part of the war. Most people had heard about Gallipoli. Thousands and thousands had died on the beaches, but still, it was not the mud and trench foot in France or Belgium.

Iant had not been outside Wales before unless you counted a trip to Chester with his auntie when he was a child. Part of him could not help looking forward to travelling somewhere different, whatever the reason and he tried to focus on that as much as he could.

The training was stepped up. The fitness and weapons courses had already been completed, at least to a basic level. Now they were given instruction in a wider variety of things. Gas attacks were something everyone dreaded and the preparation involved small amounts of real gas that burned your eyes and lungs. The idea was that a 'taste' of it would improve the incentive to complete the drills as fast and efficiently as possible. In Iant it tended to induce panic which was heightened by his need to wear glasses and the effect that this had on the clumsy

11

process of getting into a gas mask at high speed.

They had to learn tactics too. It wasn't very advanced but consisted of using different formations across types of terrain and when and where to fix and use bayonets. Charging at stuffed sacks and ripping out the sawdust 'guts' struck Iant as a mixture of the ridiculous and slightly disgusting. Some of the lads liked the outlet of this and used bayonet practice to take out the frustrations of waiting around.

Discipline was harsh and became worse now that they were close to being moved out. Some of the NCOs meted out violent punishments whenever they could, both officially and unofficially. The worst crime was being too 'fucking clever' and if anyone got close to humiliating one of the sergeants or corporals they would often end up on the wrong end of a fearful beating somewhere quiet and after dark.

One incident started so comically but ended with a young man from Wallasey hospitalised with a broken nose and arm. They were on the open range shooting with live ammunition and the sergeant in charge was parading up and down watching them fire at targets on the hillside. Two along in the row from Iant was this man, Tim. A bit dopey but nice enough Iant had thought. As the sergeant passed him, he called out that his rifle was jammed. As the sergeant approached Tim swung his gun round so that it was practically pointing at the sergeant's head. Apparently calm, the sergeant said, 'Just point the gun down the range son and then lay it down so I can look at it'. Seconds later he was all over the young soldier, screaming in his face, dragging him to his feet, kicking and punching him.

'You stupid little cunt. The fucking thing could have gone off any fucking minute and blown my fuckin brains out! I should stick the fucking thing up your miserable arse and see if you fancy inspecting it from there!.'

The funny side to it disappeared as the man's face became bloody and he cried out in pain from the blow to his arm from the sergeant's boot. No-one lifted a finger or uttered a word in protest and Iant felt disgusted with himself. He hadn't seen it but

12

people had been court-martialled and shot for defying the authority of an officer or an NCO and this one seemed out of control and capable of practically anything.

They didn't see Tim for some days and when he re-appeared his arm was in a sling and it was obvious that wherever they were going Tim would not be joining them. The mindless brutality of the sergeant had just succeeded in putting another able-bodied young man out of the front line.

Iant didn't enjoy the camp, but he instinctively understood how to survive and find a place for himself in the complex little hierarchy that governed army life. He stayed out of the way of the natural bullies and kept to himself and the small number of friends, such as Oliver, that he felt safe with.

Boredom was the worst of it. Endless hours of repetitive jobs followed by periods of time passing so slowly that it made your body ache. Iant and Oliver thought that boredom was part of preparing you to go and fight. When the order came you would be so glad to be finally doing something that you would forget any danger.

Letters from home were a relief. They rarely said anything of note, but they broke the monotony and reminded Iant that there were people to go back to. Despite it being a life that had little material comfort he had grown up in a place that wrapped itself around those who lived there. So long as you lived a life of god-fearing conformity, as Iant had done, so far at least, there were people who would look after you.

His sisters were the ones who wrote most. Their lives had expanded because of the war and they wrote about the jobs that they now had for the first time. Beneath their complaints about the hard work, Iant could hear that Gwennie and Dorothy were seeing more of life than they would have done without the war. Gwennie joked about the boys in her factory in Wrexham and the old battle-axe of a landlady where she boarded during the week. The poor food and the hard lumpy bed was the worst of it. His younger sister, Dorothy, had stayed at home but was working in the fields and learning to look after the animals. His mother too wrote occasionally. Iant could see that her world was changing all around her too. Many of the boys received long sentimental letters from their mothers begging them to keep safe and out of danger. His mother's contained no such endearments and tended to be formal with numerous references to duty and God. She had little to say that was much comfort. His father never wrote though Iant was sure that he had seen him writing at home.

Gwennie's letters began to mention a young man, Berwyn, alongside strict instructions not to say anything to their mother and father. Berwyn had a reserved occupation, something to do with manufacturing and lived in Wrexham. They visited the little picture house and took walks together by the river in the evening. The landlady had a strict curfew, which they kept to for fear she would contact Gwennie's parents.

Iant felt some protective feelings towards Gwennie but knew she could look after herself. Nonetheless, he would like to have met this Berwyn and reassure himself that he was honest and respectful towards his sister. Gwennie and he had often fought as children, but he would have fought for her if necessary.

She never wrote about the physical side of her relationship, if indeed there was one. This didn't stop Iant thinking about it and wondering whether his sister had allowed herself to be kissed and fondled by this man that he had never met. It also made him think more and more about how he would like to spend more time in the company of girls before he was sent away. He wondered if he would see Mary again at another dance.

Later in the week, he was lying on his bunk wondering how to get through the time before it got properly dark and they could sleep. Oliver and some of the others had gone again to The Sun. He had nearly gone himself but decided at the last minute that he didn't want to spend any more of his money on the watered-down beer that they seemed to have decided was good enough for soldiers.

He decided to walk down to the perimeter of the camp and felt himself inevitably drawn to the place near the main entrance

14

where he knew the girls gathered. He quickened his step until the main entrance was nearly in sight and then slowed down, walking close to the trees that grew at the side of the track. At first, he couldn't see anyone there, but moving a little closer he finally saw her, leaning on a tree the other side of the road. Even from this distance, anyone could see her reluctance to be standing in such a place.

He edged along the line of trees and eventually he could make out three other girls spaced out along the road. They called out to men as they came and went from the main camp gate, but the girl he had recognised almost hid in the undergrowth when anyone approached. Iant circled back around and approached the place where the girl was standing as quietly as he could.

She was, he could see now, very slight. She wore a small black hat and her dark hair stretched beneath it all the way down her back. It was clean and shiny in the rays of the evening sun that reached through the trees. Iant could feel how soft it would feel from thirty yards away. Even though the evening was still quite warm she had the same coat as when he last saw her wrapped tightly around herself.

He didn't want to startle her too much so eventually he picked up the courage to call out. '*Noswaith dda'* he said as softly as he could. She turned sharply. Evidently, he had alarmed her despite his best efforts.

'You scared me!' she said.

'*Siarad Cymraeg?*'

'*Tipyn bach.* I prefer to speak English.'

Iant noticed that she was quite well-spoken, with no trace of the local accent.

'That's fine. I can manage that' he said.

'What are you doing, creeping through the trees like that?'

'I was just out for a walk.'

'Don't you do enough walking every day with all that marching they make you do?'

'I like to walk a little at my own pace without someone shouting in my ear I suppose.'

15

'Did you want something?'

Iant had hoped that it wouldn't come to a head quite so quickly. He was almost enjoying talking to her or at least listening to the softness of her voice.

'I, er....'

'Well? Because I haven't got all night' she said, not completely convincingly.

'I'm sorry. I didn't mean to waste your time' Iant said and half turned away.

'Wait a minute' the girl said. He could hear her move gradually through the trees towards him.

'You're shy'.

Iant turned and saw the girl just a few yards away. The light wasn't good but he could make out her face now. It was thin and quite drawn and he could see her nervous eyes trying to make him out. He didn't know whether they were beautiful eyes, but they made his heart beat a lot faster and he felt short of breath.

'Yes I am' he found himself saying.

'Do you have money?'

He was taken aback by the directness and found himself rummaging through his pockets.

'Well?'

'How much do you need?' Iant found himself saying.

'How much do I need? What do you think I am? A beggar?'

'I mean how much do you…charge?'

'What do you want?'

Iant felt a rising wave of panic and started to turn away when he felt the girl's hand on his shoulder.

'It's all right. Don't go. I'm sorry I snapped at you.'

'I…I don't know anything.'

'Have you got a pound?'

'Yes.'

She held out her hand and he gave her a one pound note. She took his hand and led him along a rough path through the trees. They were soon out of sight of the camp though he could still hear voices through the trees. Eventually, they came to a

16

clearing and there was room to lie down. She took off her coat and spread it on the ground. Iant noticed that she was wearing only a thin nightdress.

'Lie down' she said.

Iant did as she said and she lay beside him. Almost immediately she reached over and began undoing the buttons on the front of his trousers. Instinctively he half turned away.

'What's the matter?'

'Nothing' Iant said.

'You have paid me now. Don't you want your money's worth?'

'What's your name?'

'What does it matter?'

'I just want to know your name.'

'It's Clara.'

'Is it really that?'

'You don't believe me?

'I don't know.'

'Why are you doing this?'

The woman sighed and sat up. Iant could see that she was impatient with his questions, but he was desperate to know more about her. He realised that what he really wanted was to be alone with a woman.

'Don't people usually want to talk to you?' Iant said after an awkward silence.

'Sometimes.'

'Don't you like it?'

'Like it? What is there to like about doing this?'

'Why do you do it then?'

'Are you really this stupid?'

'Perhaps I am. I know you do it for money, but....'

'That's all you need to know. That's all you are entitled to know. For a pound.'

'Yes that's fair I suppose.'

Iant turned away. He felt utterly ridiculous. After what felt like a long time, he felt Clara's hand on his shoulder.

17

'Come on. You may as well have your money's worth. If you don't word will get around.'

'I won't say anything.'

'Is it your first time? You look quite young.'

'Yes.'

'I can help you.'

She undid his belt. After that, the mechanics of it all happened very quickly. Too quickly of course, as he had heard it would.

Afterwards, Clara got up and began to arrange her clothing. Iant lay still, feeling relieved that it had happened at all before he was sent away.

'I need my coat.'

'Oh, yes. I'm sorry.'

Iant fastened his trousers and stood up. He picked up the coat and began brushing off the dried leaves and debris that had stuck to it. He went to put the coat around Clara's shoulders but she took it from him and wrapped it around her. The evening had been warm but now there was a chill in the air and the ground had started to become damp.

'Leave a few minutes before you go back to the road' she said.

'Alright.'

She had already turned and was starting to make her way out through the trees.

'Goodbye' Iant said, quietly.

'And thank you....'

He thought he heard a laugh come from the darkness, but couldn't be sure. He sat until he started to feel very cold and quietly picked his way out of the wood and back to the main track.

Chapter 3

They had been in camp for three months when they were allowed a short leave. This usually meant that they were close to being shipped out. Not all the men went home. For some, it was too far to make it worth it. For others, there was not much to go back for.

For Iant, it was easy enough to get back and he looked forward to seeing his home again, though his mother was never one for making a fuss. Iant doubted that she would make an exception this time, even when faced with the prospect of not seeing him again for several years. Dad would be stoical, but he hoped he might feel just a little proud when he turned up in his uniform. He could expect a few tears from his sisters of course.

The train up the Dee valley to Glyndyfrdwy felt especially slow. He only had two days and he felt impatient to be home. The wet spring had turned the mountains especially green and the river itself looked inviting even though he knew it would still be freezing cold.

As he got out at the little station he wished he had been able to let his sisters know when he was coming. He would have liked to have been met on the platform. Instead he got off and was alone. He noticed the silence of the little place in a way he had never done before.

He began the long walk up the village and then out along the track, hoping that Gwennie and Doy would be home when he arrived. The track was steep and rough and he was tired from the journey. He longed for something to soften the inevitable disappointment of his mother's greeting. Dad would be up the fields somewhere. In the backyard, the old dog was still tied up on his length of rope. Ugly old bugger, thought Iant as Bob snarled and barked at him like he had never seen him before.

'What's the matter with you Bob?' Iant said coaxingly and eventually, the snarling became a more friendly whine and he lay on his back for his stomach to be scratched. He was full of fleas

19

and his differently coloured eyes made him an unnerving sight, but he had been around for as long as Iant remembered and there was a kind of comfort in seeing him again.

His mother appeared in the doorway.

'You're back then?'

'Hello mam.'

'Have you had anything to eat?'

'I'm always ready to eat.'

'There's some pease pudding. And half a loaf. Do you want tea?'

'Thanks Mam.'

His mother went inside and to Iant's relief Gwennie rushed out and embraced him.

'How long are you back for?' she said.

'Two days.'

'Only two days. That's not enough.'

'It's all I've got Gwennie. They'll shoot me if I'm not back on Sunday night.'

Gwennie stood back from him and looked him up and down, smiling approvingly.

'They are filling you out a bit.'

'Aye, maybe.'

'Too much beer!.'

'Chance would be a fine thing!.'

'I see Mam hasn't changed much.'

'Except we get it all now. We need you back to take your share.'

'Thank you. I'm glad to have been missed for something!.'

'Is Doy at home.'

'She's up the field. Helping Dad to mend a fence. She gets to be the honorary boy more than me.'

When he had finished eating Iant said that he would take a walk and find the others. Gwennie asked to go with him knowing that she would incur her mother's displeasure but felt it a price worth paying. Sure enough, as she followed Iant out of the door she heard her mother remark that she wished *she* had time to gad

20

about in the middle of a fine day.

As they walked up the lane that led to the crest of the ridge Iant offered Gwennie a Woodbine, not thinking she would take it. He had only started smoking himself to fend off the boredom. Gwennie took one but it was too strong for her and it was soon abandoned on the track.

Iant looked back down the valley and for the first time realised that it could be a long time before he saw this place again, if ever. Optimistic by nature Iant had nevertheless been around the camp long enough to absorb the odds of surviving the war. It would have been different he thought if he had been allowed to join up earlier. At the start of the war, no-one thought about death, except for the idea of slaughtering the enemy. Now there was no disguising the heavy losses and tales of whole villages with hardly a man surviving.

Gwennie sensed his pre-occupation and tried to distract him with gossip. She even resorted to a mention of her Berwyn or 'Ben' as she liked to call him. Iant could see how much she was changing now she was living away from home for part of the time.

She told him about their working together at Powell Brothers. Ben had been apprenticed there, making ploughs and harrows, when war broke out. He had been part of the group of men that had adapted the factory to make mortar bombs. He wanted to join up when he was old enough in 1915, but his job had been made a protected occupation.

Iant found himself resenting this young man. He knew about these protected jobs and understood why they had to exist. Part of him, though, thought they were sought out by those that didn't want to fight.

As if reading his mind Gwennie elaborated, telling him how much Ben would have loved to have joined up and how strict they were about keeping people in the factory. She said that it was dangerous and they had asked for volunteers to work in the 'danger zone'. She had thought about doing this herself but had been talked out of it by Ben. In any case, most of the women in

21

the danger zone were older, often widows with, it was thought, not so much to lose.

Gwennie described the frequent checks and searches that were carried out in the factory. Mostly they were looking for matches and cigarettes, anything that might cause an explosion in that highly volatile environment. Some of the searches she said were just an excuse for some of the men to put their hands all over the younger women.

She told him Ben had risen up quickly to become a kind of foreman in one part of the factory. He was responsible for checking the quality of the finished shells and doing spot checks on whether they were effective. They had to test and fire a small quantity each day. It was the closest he could come to being at the front Ben had said.

Gwennie related an incident in which she and Ben had been walking together in Wrexham when a woman came up and presented Ben with a feather. He didn't react very much but Gwennie lost her temper and ended up ripping off the women's hat and pulling her hair. She would have gone further if Ben had not pulled her away. He had pretended that she was making a fuss over nothing, but she could see he had been affected.

Part of Iant enjoyed the stories and seeing his sister growing into an adult, but it also brought home to him that he was away from the people he loved and that the world here would go on changing without him. As though if he never came back it would hardly matter.

By now they had reached the field where his father and younger sister were working and Doy ran over to greet him. His father put down his saw for a moment and shook his hand.

'How are you keeping?' his father asked.

'I'm well thank you, Dad.'

'It's not all over and they've sent you back then?'

'Not yet Dad.'

'Well what are you all playing at then?'

'They are just waiting for me to get stuck in.'

'You are off then?'

'Next week probably.'

'Do you know where?'

'Not really Dad, they don't tell you. It might not be France though.'

'Do you think it'll be somewhere cushy?'

'I don't know Dad.'

'Some places they say all the soldiers do is lie around in the sun and drink beer.'

'Well, that would be nice.'

'Aye, better than this then. Have you come to give us a hand?'

'What needs doing?'

'Well, you can hammer in a few of those posts. It takes Doy half an hour to do each one!.'

'There's gratitude for you' Doy said but smiled at her brother.

Their father could be gruff and severe but you could usually win him over with a bit of good humour. For the next couple of hours, Iant helped his father and sister with the new fence, the sun was out and he was happy to be there, exchanging a few words every now and again. Gwennie had returned down the hill to their mother. Eventually, he felt that he should do the same.

That evening he walked over the fields to *The Grouse* at Carrog. He hoped to see some of the boys from the surrounding farms and especially to show off a little to Frances if she was behind the bar. It was a longish walk there and back, but he made it while it was still light and there was a full moon by which to get back.

As Iant entered the tiny bar, there was a bit of a cheer and someone bought him a pint. He caught Frances's eye, but the pub was crowded and she was rushed off her feet. They barely knew each other he realised. He had probably only ever exchanged a handful of words with her. This might be the last chance he would get though.

As the evening wore on and the beer took effect Iant became a little maudlin. It was not so much his impending

23

posting, but the pointlessness of the conversation around him and particularly the idea of talking to Frances. His evening with Clara had stayed with him of course. It made him wary of talking to women. He was almost superstitious that they would know somehow about his 'experience'. It was ridiculous, but it had an effect on him, even when talking to his sisters. He only felt a little of the kind of conscience that his chapel-going had instilled, but there was something else, perhaps knowledge of his own frailty, that haunted him and stopped him talking about it even to Oliver or any of the boys back at the camp.

By closing time he had, in truth, been ready to start the long walk back for some time. He said his goodbyes and started off up the village, glad of the moon to help him up to the ridge. He had gone a few yards when he heard Frances call out very quietly.

'Iant?'

'Hello.'

'Are you going without a goodbye?'

'I'm sorry. It was busy in there.'

'Yes.'

'You must be tired.'

'I am.'

'Do you work tomorrow?'

'On a Sunday?' she laughed.

'I've lost track of the days' Iant replied.

'How long are you home?'

'I am going back tomorrow.'

'That's quick.'

Iant hoped he could hear a bit of disappointment in her voice.

'It is. That's all they let us have.'

'Well…I just wanted to say hello and goodbye.'

'Yes. Thank you.'

She reached out and pulled him close to her to give him a peck on the cheek. In his drunken state, he held her face tight and forced his tongue into her mouth. After just a moment he ran quickly up the steep slope, not pausing to look back. After a few hundred yards he stopped, exhausted and threw up most of the beer he had drunk leaning against a tree to stay upright. At least, he thought, the walk home would be easier.

Chapter 4

The next day Gwennie and Doy walked with him down to Glyndyfrdwy station. They chattered pleasantly enough, full of grumbles about Mam and her domestic tyranny. Doy was envious of Gwennie's freedom and couldn't wait until she was old enough to get away to the munitions factory. There was no talk of Iant's posting until they got to the platform and they could hear the train coming down the valley.

'Keep yourself safe you stupid boy' said Gwennie

'What do you think I'm going to do?'

'Fall over in the middle of a charge' said Doy

'What do you mean 'a charge'? Do you think I'm in the bloody cavalry Doy bach?'

'I mean when they run at the enemy. You're so clumsy.'

'Thank you!.'

'Well, you are. Always dropping things!.'

The train was now close to pulling into the station and Doy flung her arms around him and squeezed so tight he thought she might break a rib.

'I was only joking! You will be the brave hero I know it!' Doy said before giving way so that Gwennie could say her goodbyes.

'I hope you will not play the hero!' said Gwennie, 'Just come home safe. And write to us.'

'I will. Write to me too. Send things.'

'What would you like most? Not one of those old scarves they are knitting I bet!' said Gwennie.

'No! Food. Send food. As much as you can.'

By now he was half on the train and the two sisters stood back as the guard blew his whistle.

'Remember. Food!' said Iant.

'Alright, alright' they shouted in unison.

Doy by now had tears running down her face and Iant longed for the train to move. At last it did, though he stayed leaning out of the window until his sisters disappeared as it rounded the sharp bend. He found a seat and closed his eyes, a slight headache starting up again as the sunshine combined with last night's beer.

As soon as Iant returned to the camp he was informed that he would be part of the next group moving out. They were still not told exactly where they were going, but the first part of the journey would take them to France in any case. From there they would find out if they were going to the Western Front or to somewhere even less familiar.

The main reaction from the men was a kind of euphoria. Life at the camp had become repetitive and dull. They would be glad to be at least doing something different. The preparations to move Iant's battalion had already begun and the days seemed shorter now that they were busy. The training was stepped up and they had additional duties loading stores and equipment.

They were never told the precise day, but Iant knew that he didn't have long and on the third night back he once again took his circuitous route to the main entrance. It was now much easier to move around unnoticed as the camp was so busy and, in any case, it had grown to the size of a small town.

As he approached the gates along the line of trees his heart sank. There were dozens of men and women milling around. There was little attempt now to disguise the fact that couples were disappearing every few minutes into the surrounding woodland. It would be impossible to find her here.

Iant wandered aimlessly past the gatehouse itself, intending to take the long way back to where he had started. He felt intensely lonely and disappointed, though his memories of his first encounter with Clara were not completely happy. More than anything he thought he wanted to feel the warmth of her, lose himself in it for a few minutes. The sex itself was a relief but if he could have that few minutes after the sex again, that was what he remembered most. She hadn't lingered long of course, but it was enough for his memory to hold on to. Warmth from the body of another human being had opened up something in Iant

27

and he felt compelled to look for it again before he was moved out.

He had walked up and down twice before finally he noticed her half-hidden in the shadows and leaning against a tree. Most of the women he had walked past had called out to him, but Clara didn't move. As he moved to approach her another soldier came from nowhere and was quickly next to her. They turned and moved to walk deeper into the woods before he could do anything. Instinctively he called out.

'Clara!.'

As she and the man turned he moved through the trees to stand close by Iant.

'What's the matter, mate? Can't you wait your turn?' said the soldier.

Iant ignored him and spoke to Clara directly.

'Can I speak to you?'

'Did you hear me?' said the soldier.

'Clara, can I speak to you?' said Iant.

'Clara? That's a posh name for a tart.'

'Perhaps you could go and look back down by the gatehouse. There's plenty of girls there.' Iant told him.

'Perhaps you can just fuck off mate,' the man said.

Iant wanted to turn and smash the man's head against the nearest tree but it dawned on him how stupid he must look. He turned and began to walk in the other direction. The soldier roughly took Clara's arm and practically marched her further into the woods. The light coming through the trees was weak, but as Iant turned he thought he saw Clara take just the briefest of backward glances.

The next day saw the preparations speeding up. Great unidentifiable mountains of stores created valleys and ravines in the centre of the camp while Iant and his battalion took part in more and more frequent drills. The morning run was stepped up and the shouting of the NCOs got louder and more aggressive.

Most of the men took to writing home, even those that had little appetite for such things. The army advised everyone to do this, though no-one actually told them that it was 'in case you don't make it back'. In truth, Iant struggled to find things to say but thought he must make the effort. It would have been unfair on his sisters especially not to receive something from him when it might be a long while before he got another chance.

> *Dear Dad, Mam, Gwennie and Doy*
> *I hope this letter still finds you well. If the weather is the same with you as it is here then it hasn't been too bad has it?*
> *As I thought when I came to see you we are being shipped out at the end of the week for certain now. They are busy here preparing all we need to take with us. There are many men leaving at once and we all eat anything we can lay our hands on so there is a lot to pack up. There are some beautiful horses Dad, mules as well.*
> *I am asking that you don't worry too much about me. I am not allowed to say where we are going but perhaps you can guess. As it happens we don't really know yet, but there are rumours. It will be a relief to move and do something as life here gets quite boring at times.*
> *Oliver and I are in the same company so will be moving together. He is the one I told you about that is engaged to the girl from Ruthin. You wouldn't know he was engaged to see him when there is a dance, but mum's the word eh?!*
> *I will miss you all of course but hope to see you again as soon as possible.*
> *With great affection*
> *Iant*

Iant hoped that this struck the right note. The greeting at the end was what some of the other blokes had picked up from somewhere and he thought that his sisters would like it. He put the note in the envelope leaving it unsealed for the censor and handed it to the sergeant. He felt somehow better that he had done his duty by his family and could think of them without conscience.

He decided that evening to go once more to the gate house. They had not been told that they were to move out tomorrow, but it was obvious from their orders to prepare that a big change was imminent. The amount of personal possessions was to be reduced to a minimum. This was not much of a problem for Iant, but some of the men had accumulated all kinds of things in an attempt to make their lives more comfortable. There therefore developed a healthy trade with those remaining in camp. Stone hot water bottles traded well as did non-standard issue blankets and sheets. Books, paints, bulkier food all got traded for tobacco, rum or extra rations that could be secreted away.

Iant's preoccupation with seeing Clara again had the advantage of diverting him away from many of the petty squabbles that arose out of the imminent departure. He thought of little else until it was time to follow his familiar circuitous path through the edge of the woods.

This time he saw her quickly. She still hung back in comparison to some of the others, but he still spotted her and practically dashed to the place where she was half-hidden.

'Are you alone?' he said.

'What does it look like?' Clara replied.

'I should watch that one love he looks a bit bloody eager!.'

'What's up, mate? There's plenty to go round!.'

Iant turned to see a group of men he didn't know, watching and laughing. They had seen him break into a run and stood staring at him.

'Can we go?' Iant said, feeling the men's eyes on the back of his head.

'Have you got the money?'

Iant handed her a pound.

'It's gone up. It's another ten bob.'

Iant felt in his pocket and produced the note.

'Sorry. Supply and demand I think they call it.'

She moved quickly into the woods and began to take off her coat.

'Can we go further?' Iant asked.

'Alright. No-one can see us here though.'

'Just a bit further.'

They moved on in silence until Iant saw a place with a lot of dry leaves.

'Maybe here?'

Clara stopped and lay down her coat.

'We are leaving tomorrow' Iant said. 'There's a lot moving out I'm told.'

Iant was pleased that she had replied. It had been so hard to talk to her before.

'Yes. We're not sure where. Just rumours.'

'I envy you.'

'What? Going to get shot at?'

'Just going. Anywhere.'

Now his delight that she was talking to him overwhelmed him and he couldn't think of the right thing to say.

'Do you live here' he said eventually.

'Yes.'

He had a thousand questions suddenly, but he knew if he asked almost any of them there would be silence.

'I'm from near Corwen' he blurted out.

'Farm boy aren't you?'

'Sort of. I've been in the quarries too.'

It was better than last time, but he sensed her being conscious of time and sure enough, she gestured for him to sit down beside her on the coat.

As she reached for his belt he held her wrist for a moment.

'Could you hold me?' he said.

She sighed. Iant knew that this was not the first time she had been asked, though she seemed more tolerant than before.

'I know. I have only paid for my time. I'm not stupid. But just a moment.'

As he lay with his face close to hers Iant felt that this might be the best he could expect. In a week, two weeks, he might no longer exist and this might be all he had to warm him if he died alone.

'Why do you have to do this?'

He knew he had made a mistake as she sprang away from him.

'I'm sorry. That was a stupid thing to say.'
'Yes.'
'Please lie down.'
'I don't want you wasting my time.'
'Look. Here's more money. Surely that's enough?'
'What is it you want? I only do straight sex.'
'I want to know you.'
'You can't know me.'
'Where do you live.'
'Abergele.'
'Your voice and your clothes....'
'I don't sound like a tart?'
'No.'
She laughed quietly and Iant lay back down.
'Will you still be here if I came back?'
'And do you know when that will be soldier-boy?'
'No.'
'So how can I answer you?'
'I've got a pen. Will you write down where I can find you?'
'I think you are trying to be kind, but this is stupid.'
'What harm can it do?'
Clara sighed but took the pen and paper.
'There. Satisfied?'
'Yes. Thank you.'
'Remember what I am. Who I am.'
This time it took longer and Iant was grateful for that. She dressed quickly afterwards and began to walk away back towards the camp.
'Take care of yourself' Iant called to her.
'It's me that should be saying that soldier boy.'
'I'll write to you when we're away.'
'If it makes you feel better.'
'I will see you again.'
Then she was gone and Iant got to his feet. Even though it was hard to find a way he was determined to avoid the main entrance to the camp. Eventually, he stumbled out on to the lane

and stumbled towards his last night in this place. He had something to take with him he felt.

When he was back in his bunk he looked at the scrappy piece of paper. Clara Johnson, 15 Penrefail Street, Rhyl. She could have written anything he thought, but it felt good to be taking this with him. He put it away safely with the letter he had written to his family and tried to catch some sleep.

Chapter 5

The embarkation point at Folkestone was heaving with bodies. Everywhere soldiers were flooding off trains down to the quay side with little direction or idea of which ship they were headed for. The only possible way to find the right place to go was to stick firmly to those you were with and hope that someone had some sense of where to go.

Those returning from France were supposed to be kept apart from those leaving so as not to risk any damage to morale, but this system quickly broke down and the damaged men hoping to crawl back to some sort of normality became entangled with the wide-eyed thousands going the other way. Iant lost Oliver in the chaos and, faced with what was in front of him, his eyes desperately searched for someone or something familiar. A hairy arm grabbed him around the neck from behind.

'C'mon boy, what did you expect, a bloody picnic?'

It was Gethin Williams from Wrexham. He had met him a few times in camp but hadn't liked him too much. At this moment he felt like a long-lost brother.

'What do you mean?'

'You look like you've seen a bloody ghost.'

'Well, good as.'

'Aye, poor bastards.'

'Where do you think we're going Geth?'

'Someone said Macedonia.'

'Where the 'ell is that?'

'How do I do know?'

NCOs with megaphones were striding around shouting, ordering people into never-ending queues. Some of them had sticks and were poking the men as if they were stray pigs. Some scuffles broke out as people jostled and pushed their way towards the departure point.

'Christ I hope it's better organised when we have to actually try and kill a few Germans.'

Iant and Gethin found themselves near the back of a line of men that stretched along the quay side and then doubled back on itself towards one of the waiting ships. As they shuffled forward Iant could make out the name, *Llandovery Castle*. The Welsh connection made him feel momentarily comforted, though he knew it was foolish.

The smell was terrible, mostly because of the hundreds of horses being transported, but the men were not a great deal better after hours on packed trains. Several soldiers fainted but were given little sympathy.

Eventually, they reached the gangplank and as they moved along it the real extent of the crowded conditions hit them both. Even Gethin's gallows humour began to fail him as they could see that even precious space lying down on the open deck was already taken.

Swept along by the force of the men behind them they eventually came to a natural halt jammed up against those in front of them. The idea of seeing the last of your country as the ship pulled away became a bad joke. It was better not to even think about whether they would be fed. Iant tried to forget his sudden urgent need to piss.

'Hey, Sarge, we aren't goin' all the way to fucking Macedonia like this surely?' Iant couldn't tell where the voice was coming from.

'Who said anything about Mac-a-fuckin-donia you stupid little twat. This old thing might get you to bloody Boulogne if you're very lucky.'

'Thanks, Sarge. Very fuckin' comforting,' said the disembodied voice and a kind of nervous laughter broke out.

By some miracle, the crush shifted and Iant found himself in a sitting position, though moving was impossible. He managed to fumble in a pocket and found his Woodbines and matches.

'Want one Geth?'

'Aye, go on, ta.'

The weather was dry at least and as they both inhaled deeply they felt the ship move for the first time.

'Did the earth move for you my darlins?' someone shouted and the communal laughter eased the tension a bit more.

'Home by fuckin Christmas' said Gethin.

'You reckon?'

'Course not you daft bugger. You all a bit twp or what up in the Berwyns?'

'What do you mean?'

'It's what they've told every miserable bastard that's crossed the Channel since the war started.'

'Oh. I see what you're on about.'

'If we're home by Christmas, it'll likely be in a pine box.'

Soon the ship picked up speed and the wind and spray were in their faces. At first, Iant enjoyed it and the freshness of the air helped to counteract the smell. After a while, though it grew cold and damp and the chances of finding enough space to dig in his pack for something to cover himself seemed remote.

As the wind got up a bit and the ship moved more, some began to vomit. Iant found he could tolerate the ship's movement himself but worried instead about those around him and being covered in the contents of their stomachs.

'You all right Geth?'

'I've been better. Got any rum?'

'That won't do you any good if you feel sick..'

'Never know.'

Iant felt in his pocket for the little flask and passed it to Gethin. He didn't get it to his lips before he vomited over both of them. Worse still the flask dropped from his hand and the rum went everywhere. The combination of the two smells was overpowering and Iant's stomach started to feel less strong.

The crossing felt like days but in reality, it was just a few hours. They landed in Cherbourg in the dark and were ordered to begin a long slow march to a camp some miles outside the town. Despite mutinous grumbling everyone fell into line eventually and found themselves in pitch black, walking, half-asleep along lanes with hedges so high that it was impossible to have any sense of the countryside. The only blessing was that it was flat.

As dawn broke they saw that they were approaching a sea of tents and were ordered to join another queue. Eventually, they were given rations and told to find somewhere to eat quickly as they could be moving again any time.

By now Iant and Gethin's exhaustion overrode any sense of anger and they ate in silence sitting close to the small paraffin stove that they had been given to heat soup. That and the stale bread was the first meal they had eaten in a day.

To Iant's amazement, just as they had finished their meal they were joined by Oliver.

'Thought you could shake me off eh?'

'Christ mun, what happened to you?'

'Came over first class didn't I?'

'Did that mean you had space to sit instead of stand all the way?'

'Aye, something like that?'

'Got fags?'

Iant got out the Woodbines and they all lit up – the sun was up now and it had got just a little warmer. Iant closed his eyes and imagined he was on a break from the sheep on the hillside above Carrog.

'C'mon you lazy fuckin' Taff bastards – what do you think this is? A bloody week by the seaside?'

He couldn't remember sleeping but the sun was higher now and the staff sergeant's piercing cockney cut right through his splitting headache. The three men got to their feet and, after gathering their belongings, began to move in the direction where they could see a lot of other soldiers gathering and forming yet another queue.

'Not that way you dozy twats. Gather near that red flag.'

In the distance, they could see a makeshift flag run up a pole. Soldiers drifted towards from all parts of the camp.

'Where we going Sarge?'

'You'll find out soon enough. Just get a bloody move on.'

As they joined the larger group Iant began to recognise

37

some faces from Abergele, but there were also hundreds more. Corporals moved among them sorting them into some kind of order.

There was a long wait and Iant began to take in where they were. It was a vast field bordering others on a wide flat plain and, in the distance, the sea. From the little he knew about the geography of France he didn't think that they were close to where most of the fighting was taking place. He realised how little the names had meant to him until now – The Somme, Mons, Ypres, Verdun – all places that he, Gwennie, Doy and most of the village would know, but which might have been on the moon for all that they knew about them. Apart from the huge encampment, this place looked just like good farming land.

By now he, Oliver and Gethin were in one of hundreds of rows that had been formed and the order came to move out.

'For God's sake, we're going back the way we just bloody came' said Oliver.

'You sure?'

'Course I'm sure – see that church further down the lane. We came past it last night.'

'We're off back home boys. Reckon they can do without us' shouted a voice from somewhere behind Iant and there was a wave of laughter.

They walked for about a mile until they reached a station on the outskirts of the town. The sign on the station told them they were back in Cherbourg. As they got closer they saw that several enormous trains were queuing at the station and the first wave of men were being loaded onto them.

They shuffled forward a few feet at a time for what seemed like hours. There was little talking by now. Even Gethin's bolshy good humour had vanished as everyone became pre-occupied with what lay in store for them.

All kinds of rumours circulated. They were going across France to reinforce the Western Front because the Germans had broken through. They were going to Africa. They were going to Turkey.

Finally, they reached the train which seemed to stretch for miles back along the track. The noise of the engines and countless whistles and orders was deafening. There was little choice but to allow yourself to be squeezed through the narrow carriage doors.

Once inside the conditions were better than the train down through England. Most men could find somewhere to lie down, even if only a lucky few found space on a seat. After a long wait, there was a lot of shouting in French and English, more whistling and the train slowly moved. Every now and again a basic food ration came round. It was dry and tasteless though everyone ate it with little comment. The journey seemed interminable and the basic toilets gave way to a complete lack of sanitation.

Iant could not help admitting that, despite his first impressions, Gethin was the most resilient of the three of them. The journey was taking its toll on them all, but Gethin managed better than most, trying to keep his own spirits up with outbursts of dark humour and insults. Before joining up he had worked at the Wrexham Lager company. The company had originally been set up by, as he put it, 'fuckin Gerries'.

'They knew a thing or two about beer though mind.'

'The Gerries still there or what Geth?' asked Oliver.

'God no. They'd mostly gone before the war. Wrexham boys run the place now.'

'What's lager when it's at home?'

'Just beer. Only paler.'

'I heard it tastes like piss.'

'That's just what the other brewers want you to think. It's lovely. Got to drink it cold mind. Gets you pissed quick. Could do with a pint now mind! Nineteen bloody breweries in Wrexham there are – world capital of getting drunk man!.'

'It's not a real Welsh place mind' said Oliver.

'What you on about?'

'More English there than Welsh.'

'Is there fuck man.'

Iant had heard this kind of sparring before. His father

39

occasionally went to watch Wrexham play football. He used to boast that it was one of the oldest clubs in the world. It seemed unlikely, but his father always insisted. Iant hoped it was true. There wasn't much about their corner of the world that made anyone take notice.

'What do you think Iant?' said Oliver

'What's that?'

'Wrexham. It's an English shit hole, isn't it?'

'I dunno. My Mam likes it.'

They all burst out laughing and he felt stupid.

'My sister works there,' He said quickly, hoping they would move on.

'Oh ay. Where's that then?' said Gethin.

'Munitions place.'

'Is she a looker?'

Iant felt angry but didn't want to show it.

'I suppose.'

'You don't fancy her yourself, do you? Only I've heard about some of you farm boys.'

'Fuck off Geth.'

'What's her name?'

Iant didn't feel like mentioning Gwennie's name.

'C'mon on man. I might know her.'

'That's why he won't tell you her name.' Oliver said.

'She only started after we were all called up.'

'You want to watch her. Wrexham lads are notorious. Tell me her name and I'll have one of my mates watch out for her.'

'Of course you will.'

'I will.'

'She's got a boyfriend. She'll be ok.'

'That's what you think!.'

Iant knew it was good-natured enough, but he was tired of the conversation. It made him homesick and anxious though he knew he couldn't show it. To his surprise, Gethin threw an arm round his shoulder.

'It's all right Iant, we're only messing.'

Someone produced a pack of cards and they played for matches for what seemed like hours. The boredom became intense, almost physical until finally, they stopped somewhere in the pitch dark. NCOs walked up and down the platform shouting:

'One night's stop. Stay on the train or get out and stretch your legs. Some locals will appear selling food, drink and God knows what. If you buy it you takes your chance alright?'

No-one stayed on the train of course. Military police were all over the place so you couldn't go far, but it was such a relief to get up and move around that the mood lightened at once. Oliver, Iant and Gethin bought sausage and bread and a bottle of wine. It was the first time any of them had drunk wine. They found it disgusting at first, but it grew on them. They found some shelter in a shed inside the station perimeter and with the aid of the wine slept for a couple of hours until before dawn when they heard voices ordering everyone back on to the train.

It took nearly three days for the train to reach Marseille. By then most of the men were half-mad with boredom and fatigue. Conditions on the train had spread gastroenteritis through many of them and the rest had eaten too much unfamiliar food.

None of this though stopped them being awe struck by their first glimpse of the Mediterranean in springtime. After days of travel and being cramped up against other snoring men who smelt like cattle, the port of Marseille looked and felt like heaven. The colour of the sea was unlike anything Iant had ever seen and the warmth of the sun put life back into all of them. The port was lined with stalls and cafes that seemed to be unaffected by the war. You could smell coffee, spices and food cooking on open fires. The noise of men shouting at them as they came down the gangplank was deafening. They seemed to mostly be offering food, souvenirs and especially the women who stood nearby.

After one more enforced march to a camp on the edge of the old city, the men were given two days leave. For virtually all of them, it was their first time in any kind of foreign city. If they felt nervous most were determined not to show it and, as Iant joined Gethin and Oliver at the back of a long line of men, his mood was better than it had been for some time.

Chapter 6

Even on army pay, Marseille seemed to Iant a cheap place to enjoy yourself. Food and drink were plentiful, especially if you were happy to try new things. Iant found that he was. He had never seen rice before and now it was being put in front of him covered in seafood and meat. In all the cafes people played music and sang. Most of the locals welcomed anyone in a British uniform. There were a few fights, but nothing serious.

They lost Gethin early on the first night. He could do nothing until he had been in the arms of a mademoiselle he said. Iant and Oliver fell in with a crowd more interested in getting drunk. After the last days in Abergele, Iant had been left with more anxieties about women than he wanted to admit and Oliver was mildly obsessed with diseases and their impact on his long-term future in boots and shoes.

Iant was no big drinker, but the warm air and the relief of not being cooped up on train meant that he enjoyed the cheap wine and brandy more then he thought possible. In the early hours of the morning, he sat with Oliver on a stone wall overlooking the harbour and realised that for the first time in a good while he was relatively happy. He felt, after a night in old Marseille, like a man of the world, someone who knows life beyond the narrow confines of where they were born. The cheap wine and brandy swilling around in his stomach made him temporarily forget why they were all here.

Two days later Iant's company was given orders to pack up their equipment and prepare to move out. This time they were issued with a lot more kit and equipment and told to expect a sea voyage. Iant wasn't sure what to expect, but it was certainly not the sight that confronted them all when they got back to the port.

HMT Transylvania was a liner requisitioned from the Cunard company when war broke out. It still looked, at least from the shore, like a something built for pleasure. As they boarded the ship it was clear that this was not a cruise liner anymore, but it still offered the men a better standard of accommodation than any have them had previously experienced. There was hot water and most had a bed to themselves. The decks were wide and offered the chance to walk and get fresh air.

Iant, Oliver and Gethin shared a two bunk cabin with each taking turns to take a night on the floor. It was luxury.

Once they were underway it was confirmed that they were heading for Salonika. No-one really knew where that was, but despite that, they were glad to put a name to where they were going. Some of the men had heard that Salonika was a 'soft' posting. Some even feared that they would be seen as inferior when they returned home. A holiday posting someone called it.

As they cruised through the Mediterranean, stopping briefly at Malta to take on supplies, the comparative ease of the interlude was broken only by periodic warnings of U-boats. For many of the men, it was their first encounter with even the idea of a submarine and it only dawned on them slowly that, without warning, their ship could be struck by something they would never see.

Iant found that the life on the ship was more than enough to counteract the fear of submarines. He enjoyed the time without hard physical labour and the chance to stroll around the deck, smoke, engage in idle chatter with his mates. He wondered if it might be the only time in his life when he could do these things without fear of being told off.

After Malta, the atmosphere on board changed and the number of lifeboat drills and evacuation rehearsals intensified. The troop ship was accompanied by two Japanese escort ships whose job it was to protect the *Transylvania* against the threat of U-boats or other enemy vessels. The escort ships were always at such a distance that you could never make out the sailors manning them. Iant could not help but wonder at the idea of men from a place so remote in his imagination having the job of protecting him and his comrades.

At a certain point, the threat from patrolling U-boats caused the convoy to divert and anchor up a river delta on the north coast of Africa. Here the heat had become intense and a lot of energy was spent finding shade and getting enough water. After three days it was judged safe to make their way out across the Mediterranean. A few hours on and suddenly the air was alive with panic. The dreaded torpedo bubble had been sighted heading for one of the destroyers.

On the *Transylvania,* all the men were ordered on deck and into the formations that would be used to evacuate the ship. Officers shouted for calm, but their voices betrayed the panic that they were obviously feeling. A sense of terror spread quickly through the crowds of men. In what seemed like seconds the first torpedo hit the Japanese destroyer causing an enormous explosion that caused a tremor to run through even a boat as huge as the *Transylvania.* The life jackets soon ran out and most just clung irrationally to anything that felt like it was immovable.

At a distance, the screams of men on the destroyer could be heard and these sounds mixed with the terrified noises coming from the stalls that held the horses on the ship. Within moments the destroyer was on fire and this was followed, very quickly, by a huge explosion as the fire reached the boilers in the engine room. In very little time at all Iant and his comrades could only watch in horror as the vessel disappeared beneath the calm waters.

To Iant's dismay, the *Transylvania* had changed direction as rapidly as such a large boat was able and was steaming away from the devastation. Through the smoke, it was possible to see survivors bobbing near the surface. Why were they not going to help them?

Oliver came alongside Iant at the rail.

'Poor bastards. Can you hear them?'

'Why are we leaving them?'

'We don't have a choice. It's us they are really after. We need to get away before they have us in range.'

'So we just leave them in the water?'

'There are some life rafts. There will be rescue boats eventually I suppose.'

45

There was another huge explosion and a column of water rose in the air.

'Depth charge' someone nearby said.

The other Japanese destroyer had changed course and released first one and then a second depth charge, but the waves it produced also had the effect of rocking and capsizing some of the life rafts. The chaos of orders and counter orders mingled with the fading cries for help as the *Transylvania* moved as fast as its lumbering shape would allow.

The silence on board had become eerie. This was the men's first genuine encounter with the war. It had come too at a time when most were least prepared. The passage though the Mediterranean had been such a welcome relief that Iant and his comrades had become almost relaxed. Yet of course they were lucky, they had just been spectators. It would take many nights though before the sounds of the men and the horses that had echoed across the sea would fade from Iant's imagination as he drifted towards sleep.

The second Japanese destroyer caught up with them and was their sole escort for the rest of the journey. Word spread that some survivors had been taken on board, but there was no detail as to how many.

The tiny islands that appeared on the horizon as the Mediterranean became the Aegean would have looked magical in other circumstances. Iant was not alone in sleeping badly and he often found himself with strangers on the ship's deck at dawn, staring across the water at another tiny island bordered by impossibly tall cliffs and tiny beaches. The colours of the water and the skies were intensely beautiful and the sunsets impossibly vivid.

However, the pall left by the destroyed ship was impossible to shake off. For Iant, it was not so much the danger, though he would have readily admitted to being terrified. And the impotence. To watch across a calm stretch of water as men and animals struggled to survive ate away at him and on-board ship, he had little outlet for his guilt. He suspected that Gethin and

Oliver harboured similar feelings but it was hard for any of them to talk about it.

The officers stepped up physical exercise in the last week. Even on a large ship like the *Transylvania,* there wasn't room for much more than limited stretching and jumping. Some tried to organise make-shift games, but they tended to be somewhat half-hearted.

Inoculations were another diversion. They were painful and made you feel ill for days afterwards but it meant some brief contact with the very small number of women on board. Mostly the women remained virtually invisible, confined to their own quarters. They were nurses and officer's servants for the most part.

Gethin claimed to have made an arrangement with one woman and was full of improbable stories of how they met at night and what they got up to. Iant thought most of it was fantasy. It was hard to find enjoyment in the brief touch and brusque manner that was adopted to deal with the endless queue for the malaria or typhus injection. For Iant, it was better to concentrate on closing down that side of himself even though it had so recently been opened up.

He could, though, not entirely stop his mind wandering back to Clara. He was, he decided, a romantic. Not for him the crude fantasies of Gethin or the pragmatism of Oliver and the married life he had mapped out for himself already. Iant dealt with his feelings by seeing women as mysterious. Without a doubt, his experiences with Clara had left him with a potent mix of guilt and yearning.

As dawn broke on what promised to be another endless day, Iant smoked on the deck, once again turning over the memories of the last months. He saw on the horizon what at first looked like yet another island, but as the ship grew close it became obvious that it was a much larger land mass. He had seen the Greek mainland for the first time and quite quickly the outline of what looked like a fantasy version of an eastern city.

As the light grew stronger the landscape appeared more

clearly and Iant found himself staring up at a mountain that reminded him of home. It was on a grander scale for sure, but the covering of snow on the peak made it, from where he was standing, look like Snowdon.

'Home of the Gods.'

Iant looked round and a young officer had come out on deck behind him.

'Sorry, sir?'

'Mount Olympus, Private. Home of the Greek gods. You know, Zeus, Apollo, Aphrodite, all that jazz.'

'I see sir.'

The names were familiar to him, but he found it hard to make sense of what the officer was talking about.

'Magnificent sight isn't it?'

'Yes sir.'

'Don't suppose we'll have much time to think about that though.'

'No sir.'

'The war has taken us all to places we would never have gone eh Private?'

'Yes sir.'

'Where are you from Private?'

'Near Corwen sir. North Wales.'

'Bit hotter here isn't it.'

'Yes sir.'

'Only a few more hours and we'll be off this wretched boat.'

'I'll be glad of that sir.'

'Yes, Private we all will. No telling what we'll find when we get off I suppose.'

'Where are we going sir?'

'God man, hasn't anyone told you?'

'I don't think many of us know sir. The name Salonika is mentioned a lot, but that's just the port isn't it? There are rumours but nothing definite.'

'Well if it's a secret it's a bit bloody late now eh? This is Salonika yes and we're off to fight Johnny Bulgar eventually.'

'Johnny Bulgar sir?'

'The Bulgarians. Fearsome fighters apparently. God knows what they are doing in this war in the first place.'

'No sir.'

'Well, at least we got to see this while we had a chance Private.'

'Yes sir.'

The officer moved off towards his quarters. Iant remained staring at the overwhelming sight of Olympus changing and shifting as the sun rose. The officer's tone had been light-hearted but he could not help thinking about what he might know and what it meant for all of them.

After what seemed like hours the city of Salonika came clearly into view. Olympus was behind them and now more and more men were on deck.

'Thank bloody God. It looks like we'll soon be off boys.'

It was Gethin whose spirits had risen at the sight of a place that looked as though it had things to offer him.

'You missed Mount Olympus Geth.'

'What's that then?'

'Home of the Gods mate.'

'Oh aye? You been on this bloody boat too long. Time to get off, have a few drinks and see how friendly the locals are. You know what I mean boys?'

By now the giant ship was close enough to see the details of the town. It stretched in an endless tangle of tiny roads and lanes up steep hills on all sides. Minarets poked into the sky above painted buildings. Buildings crowded the slopes of the town and narrow lanes led off into the maze of markets. What seemed like thousands of people and animals covered the quayside and even from a distance the sounds and smells of the place drifted out on the hot air. A mixture of spices, scents and animal shit. Already the number of flies in the air had increased dramatically. If Salonika had looked romantic before, its reality began to hit Iant even before they had arrived. It dawned on him with some force how far from home he really was.

49

Chapter 7

Iant could see The White Tower from where he sat outside his tent. Someone told him it had sat guarding the entrance to the old port for centuries. After three weeks in the heat of the camp, he would cheerfully have seen it blown to hell. The days were punctuated by doses of quinine to try and prevent the dreaded malaria, but the medicine caused stomach cramps and sometimes vomiting. To much hilarity, they were also warned that it might cause something officially known as 'erectile dysfunction'. Iant smiled to himself as he remembered Gethin's response, 'Chance would be a fine thing sir!'

So far the war had been with no human enemy as far as the men were concerned. Countless hours were spent on draining ditches, clearing scrubland and diverting streams. All in pursuit of the tiny mosquito. Hundreds contracted malaria every day they said and many had to be sent back to Britain. Some even contemplated getting it as a 'Blighty', but it was a dangerous course of action. Bullet wounds healed, but you could get malaria for life they said and ghoulish stories of turning yellow and shrivelling from the inside circulated to discourage anyone who was tempted.

There was a general atmosphere of discontent. A few of the thousands now camped on the hillside had already been on the Western Front. They knew that if you served there you could get leave back home. Or, at the very least in some cosy French town with good food, drinking and a chance of a visit to the thousands of brothels that had sprung all over northern France.

Here, not only could you not go home but, at first, only officers were allowed into Salonika at all. Rumours circulated of golf courses and tennis courts being built for the high command while the men dug in on the hillside with little to do but count the mosquitos. After a month of feelings running high, the orders were changed to allow restricted leave to the city. Sports and other activities were also stepped up. Though the heat and the flies remained unbearable there was at least the prospect of a change of scene to look forward to.

The prospect of being involved in any fighting seemed remote. The training went on in a slightly aimless way, but despite the official line of being constantly prepared the feeling was that of having landed in a backwater of the war with poor hygiene and food.

Being in one place for a good while did mean that some mail caught up with them and Iant was glad to receive a letter that had been written by Gwennie sometime before.

Our dearest Iant

To think we don't know where you are reading this is very strange. We imagine you in all sorts of places. Perhaps soon you will be able to tell us where you have been. I think it must not be France because Berwyn's cousin from Gobowen has had leave and come home. We would have seen you by now if you were there perhaps.

Life here is as exciting as ever! Dad and Mam work hard to keep everything going and Doy longs to get away and join me, never mind the dangers and the long journeys on the bus! I think she will be able to next year, though perhaps by then we will have no need of shells.

I am still fond of Berwyn. He asks to be called Ben. I like Berwyn but he insists! We still go to the pictures and go on walks on a Sunday. I hope you will like him when you get to know him. I think you will Iant.

Doy says that she will never meet a boy stuck out here and so many away at the war. Also, Mam and Dad would put off anyone. I tell her she is too young to worry, but I feel sorry for her. Perhaps you could say in a letter that they should be more lenient with her?

Dad gets a lot of rabbits and that keeps us going. I hope you are getting enough to eat. We hear a lot how soldiers get a bit fed up with the 'bully beef'.

If there is a way to write to us I know we would all be so grateful to know how you are.

With much love from all your family

Gwennie

Iant knew he should write back straight away, but it was hard to think of what to say. In any case, the truth of where he was would not reach them and to write it would only get him into trouble. He would think it over and try the following day.

He went back to the tent, thinking to share his scant news with Oliver and to see if he had any in return. To Iant's surprise, Oliver lay on the ground covered in a blanket. As he approached him he could see the sweat beads on his forehead.

'What is it?'

'Probably just the bloody quinine.'

'Have you had any food?'

'No. I'm not hungry.'

Iant knew this to be a bad sign. Most of them were hungry most of the time despite the heat. Food here had to come from much further afield and was less plentiful.

'Have you seen the doctor?'

'I'll be ok. Just let me get a bit of kip.'

Oliver turned away again and Iant left him alone. He thought Oliver was unwell, but illness was a fact of life in the camps. He would check on him later and get a medic if necessary. He hoped that he would recover by the time they had their precious leave. Iant did not want to be let loose on Salonika with just Gethin for company.

That evening Iant sat down to write back to Gwennie and his family. He found himself instead fumbling in his belongings for a scrap of paper. He amazed himself by his sense of panic when he thought he had lost it. It had been some weeks since he had actually seen it though he had thought of it quite frequently. Finally there it was Clara Johnson, 15 Penrefail Street, Rhyl.

He wasn't quite sure what impelled him first to look at her address and then to write to her. He was sure that he was not in love with her, still less obliged to her. He shuddered at the thought of the tortuous expressions of love and duty that Oliver seemed to feel the need to send Ada, but he felt even worse when he thought of Clara standing outside the camp night after night. The sickening image of the sergeant's huge white arse came back to him much more vividly than he would have liked.

He had guiltily come upon one of Oliver's letters once, on

board the ship. Fragments of it came back to him as he wondered what he would say to Clara.

My dearest sweetheart

I hope that you and your family are well…I think fondly of you each night as I am about to sleep…the kiss we had on my last visit to Ruthin has stayed with me…I hope the shop does well and that your father is happy in his work…

Iant had known Clara long enough to be intrigued by her. He had no idea whether such a person would be enjoyable to live with but for now, she remained someone that he would like to know more. He thought of her often and in ways that would not have got his letter past the censor, but the idea of ever having contact with her again seemed very remote.

Dear Clara

It sounded quite formal, but he could hardly make it more fulsome under the circumstances.

I expect you barely remember me

He could not help starting with low expectations.

You were kind enough to give me your address the last time we met. I have meant to write to you to find out how you are keeping. I have now found an opportunity so there we are.

You will know I am sure that I cannot say precisely where I am. It is perhaps enough to say that it is a long way from the sands at Rhyl, though there are donkeys here too!

Compared to many I am sure, the war has not (so far at least!) led me into too much danger. For this I am glad of course, though myself and my comrades are also itching to do our bit. We spend long hours on quite humble tasks which are very necessary but leave us feeling a bit frustrated.

We do not starve but also do not eat quite like princes. That is to be expected of course.

I wonder if you have a sweetheart yet? I cannot help but also wonder if you are still compelled to work at the camp. I am sorry if this is a presumptuous question, but I never felt that this was the place that you should be. I was also surprised that someone as pretty as you would not already have been snapped up.

If the answer to my first question is 'no' I wonder if you would be kind enough to send me a picture if you have one to spare? I remember your face very well, but it had an angry expression some of the time so I would love to see a picture with a smile as I know it would suit you!

I think I will close now as I can feel myself getting into trouble!

With very good wishes

Iant

He put it into the envelope and walked along to the post tent to put it in with the mountain that the censor had still to read. As he returned to the tent the smell hit him straight away. Oliver's vomit was all over his bedding and the ground below, but he seemed oblivious.

'Oliver!.'

When there was no response Iant felt his rising panic.

'Oliver! Wake up man, you've been sick everywhere.'

He shook him then and was relieved to hear a slight groan. However, his face was very pale and when Oliver touched his head it was fiercely hot despite the cool evening.

Iant fetched water and some rags and tried to clean up as best he could. It was all he could do to stop himself retching. Oliver was not aware of anything happening to him and Iant decided he needed to do something quickly.

The Red Cross station was some way across the camp and dark was falling. Iant picked his way as best he could through the crowded encampment. He should have got a lamp, but in his anxiety, he had decided that he had to get help as fast as possible. He blundered around wildly, at one point tripping over ropes and kicking a pot of some kind.

'For god's sake what's the bloody hurry?' someone called.

The Red Cross tent was, luckily, exceptionally quiet. The endless quinine dispensing was going on and in the hospital tent there were rows of malaria patients in various states of recovery.

'Can't he get here himself?' was the first response.

'I don't think so. I couldn't really wake him.'

'Are you sure he isn't drunk?'

54

Iant stared at the nurse as if she was insane.

'I'm afraid it happens a lot. Homemade usually.'

'No. I am sure he isn't drunk.'

'Alright. If you wait a moment I'll come with you.'

It seemed like a long wait until the nurse emerged with a small bag. He was relieved she had a lamp and he hoped he could find the way without too much difficulty. When they reached their tent Oliver had vomited again and looked, if anything, worse.

'Get some water can you?' the nurse asked Iant.

As he did so he could see her feeling Oliver's pulse and trying to get a thermometer to stay in his sagging mouth. She used the water and some antiseptic from a bottle to clean Oliver again.

'How long has he been like this?' she asked.

'Just today.'

'He has gone down quickly.'

'What do you mean.'

'The malaria has taken hold fast. Has he been using the quinine?'

'As far as I know yes. It gave him the runs mind.'

'He might have stopped taking it because of that. Stupid man.'

'What can you do?'

'We need to get him to the field hospital. Will you stay with him while I get some stretcher bearers down?'

'Of course I will.'

The nurse quickly packed away her things and moved to the tent opening.

'If he vomits again try to keep his head up. He's quite weak and could easily choke.'

'Ok. I will.'

When she was gone Iant felt very alone. He wasn't used to looking after anyone and the smell of Oliver's vomit was still in his nostrils from before. He prayed he wouldn't be sick himself. Oliver's colour had almost gone. He thought he should talk to him perhaps. Try and keep him awake.

'Heh Oliver, c'mon man. This is no time to get like this. They are going to let us out next week. We'll be living it up down in the city.'

He was fairly sure he couldn't hear him, but Iant felt he should keep trying. He hadn't ever imagined how difficult it was to talk to someone who didn't respond at all.

'What would your Ada think if she saw you like this eh? You'd have to smarten yourself up or she wouldn't recognise you.'

He thought perhaps mention of Ada would stir something in him.

'She's a pretty girl mind, Oliver. Not sure what she sees in an ugly bugger like you. Good mind to tell her about you chasing women at the dances in Rhyl. See what she thinks of that.'

Oliver let out an involuntary groan but Iant thought it best to keep going.

'I was only joking mate. I wouldn't do that honest. Her dad would bloody kill you mind wouldn't he? He'd be after you. There'd be no cosy shop for you then. Just think of it Oliver – it'll be like paradise compared to here. Get your feet under the table and you'll be made for life. People will always need shoes won't they?'

Iant got up and went to the door hoping to see the stretcher bearers. He was anxious for Oliver's sake, but he also wanted to stop having to talk. He had never felt so inadequate.

'You'll be having children in no time I bet. That'll be good eh Oliver? Being a dad. You'll have some stories by then eh? How many do you think you'll have Oliver? Three or four I reckon. Living at the back of the shop, coming in and bothering their dad.'

At last, the stretcher bearers arrived. They were just blokes like him. He wanted to ask how they thought he looked, but he could see there wasn't much point.

'What's his name mate?'

'Oliver. Oliver Edwards.'

56

'He a Taff as well?'

'Yes.'

'Oliver mate. We're going to lift you now, alright?'

'I don't think he can hear you' said Iant

'You'll be surprised. Docs say you can still hear even when you look half dead.'

'Right, that's got you on board. Better tie you down. Don't want you escaping do we?'

The two men fastened straps across Oliver lying on the stretcher. He never moved a muscle and they lifted him carefully and disappeared out into the night.

For a long time, Iant just sat on his bed and thought about what had happened. It seemed like days since he spoke to Oliver earlier in the evening. Perhaps he should have told someone then?

Outside the sounds of a Greek night were in full swing. At first, the cicadas had kept him awake. Even now it was the strangest thing to think of all the thousands of creatures making that noise. Mating someone said.

He hadn't known Oliver very long, but they had stuck together on the strange journey they had made and he found himself frightened that anything would happen to him. Iant couldn't face being on his own and went looking for company. Gethin had found a group of Welsh boys from Cardiff and the Valleys and was playing cards and drinking rum with them. Iant joined them on the edge of the light.

'Ianto. Come and join us.'

'Not another Gog' said one, laughing.

'Take no notice mate. We'll take anyone's money!' said another.

Iant joined the circle and was dealt into the next hand. Soon the rum and cigarettes had done their job. Iant sat under the enormous moon. They had all come to take this startling sight for granted in such a short time. He found himself joining in and losing himself in the endless chatter of his companions. After what seemed like hours he crawled into a nearby tent, found a space on the ground and drifted, exhausted, into sleep.

Chapter 8

Oliver remained in the hospital for the next three days. There was never any possibility that the doctor would allow him out for the long-anticipated leave. Iant contemplated staying with him but eventually thought better of it. His friend slept a great deal and was too groggy to enjoy company. He was wary of Gethin's idea of a good time in a strange city but felt desperate for something other than the monotony of the camp.

There was transport to take them into Salonika and they could stay a night if they chose to. It was a long arduous drive and Iant decided in the end to stay overnight. They had to catch transport back for the return journey at 5 pm on the second day.

Even though they had been in the country for some weeks none of the men had much sense of what it was really like. For those like Iant who had spent little time in any large town or city area, let alone one in the Levant, the shock was overwhelming. The sheer number of people was hard to comprehend and the constant irritation of the flies wore at his patience.

As they got off the truck on the quayside they could barely move for the crowds. They were immediately under siege from men and children selling things or wanting to shine their boots. The harbour was full of boats and ships of every kind. Some were military but a lot were very old fishing vessels that looked like they came from another century.

Despite the crowds, a slight breeze blew from the sea and it was a relief to be off the truck. Gethin's optimism carried them along and Iant fell in with him and what Gethin called the Rhondda boys, despite only one of them coming from the Rhondda valley.

They could find nothing that could have been reasonably called a pub or a bar. To their amazement, they were directed to what people called a tea house. It did sell beer, though at prices that made them gasp.

It seemed as though every language in the world was being

spoken all around them. Iant and the others had only heard English and Welsh, though they knew that the French and the Russians had huge encampments outside Salonika too. Then there were those that actually lived here. In theory, this was a Greek city, but in a place so close to so many borders there were Turks, Serbs, Jews, Bulgars. Some of them were, theoretically at least, the enemy, but who could tell them apart.

They eventually found what was a huge makeshift music hall. Some of the Rhondda boys had been to one before and everyone followed them in. It was so crowded that at first, they couldn't get inside. Some gave up and turned away, but Iant managed to squeeze into the standing area with Dan, one of the boys from Tylorstown.

They didn't have a very good view of the stage and the singing from most of the acts was terrible, but it was a welcome change from sitting around waiting to catch malaria. Iant realised half-way through one act that the singer in women's clothing was actually a man. He and Dan had a good laugh about it.

As the crush became more intense they decided to leave and wandered up through lanes to a part of the city high on the hillsides. It was easy to lose your way as all the lanes looked the same and they seemed at times to double back on themselves. Every building seemed to be a shop of some kind though often they contained very little that anyone would want to buy.

Eventually, they stopped at a tiny café that had a view over the city. No-one here spoke English and they were just brought very small cups of bitter coffee. With a cigarette and a lot of sugar, Iant found that it grew on him. They were tired now and happy to take in the view as it grew dark and the lights in the city came on below them.

They wandered back down narrow lanes finding it impossible to trace their steps. The city was taking on a different personality as night fell. Out of some of the windows, girls called 'Johnny, Johnny' as they passed. Dan and Iant exchanged glances but at this moment their taste for novelty had been satisfied by the city itself.

Dan was married already even though he was only the same age as Iant.

'Had to do the right thing like' he said.

Dan had only seen his son for a few weeks and then once more during a brief leave before they were shipped out. He showed Iant a picture, not a very clear one, of a young woman holding his son, Bryn. To Iant, all babies looked the same, but of course he was too polite to say this.

'You got a girl back home Iant?'

'Not really.'

'What do you mean?'

'There's a girl I've written to once or twice.'

'Don't rush into it mun. You'll have your pick when you get home.'

'If we ever get home.'

'Don't say that mun. Anyway, not much sign of anything going on here. Most likely die of boredom!.'

By now they were back down near the quayside and spotted some of the rest of Dan's mates from the Rhondda crowd. Gethin wasn't with them and Iant imagined him tucked up with a 'Johnny, Johnny' girl.

They bought some food from one of the street hawkers selling spicy meat in some kind of bread. It was hot and delicious after the monotony of camp rations. They washed it down with cheap beer and then took to drinking some kind of local spirit because it was cheaper.

At one point, someone said they had been told of a place they could sleep for a few pennies. Locals opened up anywhere with a bit of space and Iant and the others found themselves quite comfortable on piles of dusty rugs in a tin shed at the far end of the harbour. They slept soundly until almost dawn when they were woken by what sounded like an enormous explosion.

'Shit boys we're under attack' shouted Dan.

Scrambling to their feet and pulling on boots they all made for the rusty makeshift door. As one of them got it open they could see a thick cloud of black smoke climbing up over the city.

There was a series of small explosions and the sound of flames crackling in the distance.

'Come on we need to get up higher' someone shouted.

Iant found himself running up hill on one of the twisting lanes. Even though it was barely light the streets were suddenly full of people. They were all carrying things. Sewing machines, large pots of oil, beds mattresses and even impossibly large wardrobes. The sound of screaming babies and children was deafening and it was joined by the barking of hundreds of dogs.

As they got higher they could see that the biggest source of the smoke was further off, in the Jewish quarter, as they later found out. It was, thought Iant, close to where he and Dan had sat and enjoyed some peace the evening before. There was no time to stop and look. One man shouted that there was shelling from the harbour and that they needed to run for their lives.

A child fell in front of him and Iant stopped and put him on his feet. He was nearly knocked to the ground himself. The child's father thought Iant was trying to carry the child off and began to berate him furiously. There was no time to stop and argue though as the stampede carried him up the hill.

The smell by now was vile as the dense black smoke crept upwards and the heat of the sun began to grow. Iant felt he would faint but always he managed to keep just ahead of the worst of the cloud.

All the time he was thinking about being fired on. After the constant training and drills, he had no weapon or means of defending himself. He could easily meet his end here on the street shot down like a criminal on the run.

By now the buildings became more spaced out and patches of scrubland appeared. It seemed safe to pause to look, even if only to decide where to run next. To his relief, he saw Dan and at least one of the others close by.

'Is there still firing?' asked Iant.

'It might be shooting. Someone said it's a fire.'

'It must be a huge one.'

'Half the city is burning it looks like.'

'It's still dangerous. We shouldn't wait around.'

'Does anyone have an idea of how we can make our way back?'

'See that bloody big mountain? Well aim for that and run like fuck!.'

The laughter broke the tension a bit and Iant could feel his own sense of panic subside a little.

'We should try and stick together boys' he found himself saying.

Eventually, they reached what passed for a major road. It had been made good by one or other of the armies that had descended on Salonika. Gratefully groups of men were trudging along in the direction of what they hoped was safety.

Every now and again Iant paused to look back. Even from such a distance, the devastation looked terrifying. Smoke, flames and small explosions erupted all over the city. The view of the sea beyond was almost completely obscured.

'It's like the bloody smog all over again' said one passing soldier.

After they had walked for hours in the morning heat they were met by a small fleet of trucks. Two of them stopped and there were shouted orders to climb on board. There wasn't room for everyone and those left on the road shouted obscenities.

'There'll be more coming. Orders came to evacuate the city and its all hands on deck' shouted the driver.

'What the whole bleedin' city?' asked one of the men jammed in next to Iant.

'No, you dummy. Just the army lads stuck down there.'

'Is it shelling mate?'

'Nah. Came through on the wireless that the city's on fire.'

'Yeh, but a shell wouldn't do that.'

'Some old dear left the chip fat they reckon.'

'Very funny mate.'

'God's honest truth.'

No-one knew who to believe now. As the truck load of men fell silent Iant remembered the terror on people's faces as they

63

ran like rats up the hill. Lots of them would have lost their houses. That little kiddy he picked up, he hoped he was alright.

Gethin. What had happened to Gethin? What if the big daft man had burnt alive in some tart's bed? What would they tell his Mam and Dad? Somehow he felt that Gethin would have got out ok, but he wanted to know nevertheless.

As the winding road made another twist the view of the city once more became clear through the open back of the truck. It had been several hours since they had been woken so suddenly and if anything, the fires looked even worse. They had spread right across the city now and the whole horizon was covered in smoke. The flames must have been huge because you could make some out even from this distance.

The pathetic sight of people struggling with huge and useless objects came back to Iant. He supposed they were things that would help them survive afterwards. Food in the camp would be in even shorter supply now he thought selfishly.

After what had seemed like an endless journey squashed into the back of the bouncing truck they were finally back at the camp. More and more trucks were disgorging men in various states of exhaustion. None seemed badly hurt though there were some that looked as though they had been close to the smoke.

Iant made his way in the general direction of his billet. He hadn't eaten since the day before nor had much to drink. He thought he would try and scrounge some food and water before finding out if anybody had heard about Gethin. As he approached his tent he was surprised and relieved to see him about fifty yards away down the row. He was in conversation with a group that Iant knew, but as he approached Gethin broke away and walked towards him.

'Blimey. How did you make it back so quick? Thought you'd still be tucked up with a Greek goddess Geth? Get a bit hot for you did it?'

'You haven't heard yet have you?'

'Heard what?'

'Iant.'

'What, what is it?'
Before Gethin could open his mouth he knew.

Chapter 9

There was a military cemetery at a place called Lembet Road. It had been started when there had been fighting earlier in the war. Since then most of those buried there had died from disease or accidents. There were French and Italian sections, a smaller Russian and Serbian one and the largest was British.

Iant, Gethin and four others formed the small burial party. There were two NCOs and a handful of men from the company.

Oliver's condition had deteriorated badly on the morning of the visit to Salonika. The doctors had done all they could for him and were considering transferring him to one of the general hospitals in Salonika the next morning when the fire broke out. When Iant asked the doctors said that it probably wouldn't have made much difference. He was too far gone.

Iant asked if he could see him but by then he had been put into the simple coffin and he was told that it wouldn't do him good to dwell on his friend's death. Gethin had seen him. He said he looked peaceful which is what most people seemed to say when someone had died.

Iant thought that to die from disease in war time was doubly hard. You are still a long way from home and your family would find it difficult to ever see your grave. But on top of that, you are denied the little bit of glory that comes from dying fighting for your country. It's small comfort, but Iant thought that his own family would have preferred to hear that he had been killed in action rather than some disease carried by tiny insects.

There were a lot of stories about relatives being told that someone had died fighting when really it had been a stupid accident or someone's incompetence. In Salonika, this would have been difficult because there had not been any fighting for so long, since well before Oliver had arrived there. His family would just hear that he had died from disease. With any luck, the person who wrote the letter might add something about bravery and endurance to the official sounding statement.

As they lowered Oliver into the ground Iant realised that it was the first funeral that he had ever attended. When his grandfather had died he had been too young to be allowed to go. He remembered looking out of the window and seeing the little procession go up through the village, his grandfather's coffin on a cart pulled by a horse and everyone walking behind it.

Here the sun was quite low in the sky. They had left the burial until late in the day so no-one had to stand around in the heat. The army chaplain looked like a kind man who was doing his best, but he had no idea who Oliver was and the short service was a formality. As the little burial party moved away and some hired helpers began to fill in the grave Iant and Gethin stayed behind a moment remembering their friend.

'Long way from home he is' said Gethin.

'I wonder how long word takes to get to his family.'

'I dunno. I heard its quite quick. That might be France though. God knows how long from this bloody place.'

'I thought I might write to his girlfriend. You know, Ada.'

'I wouldn't know what to say.'

'No. I might try though. Do you think she would like it Geth?'

'Probably. I don't know.'

'I heard of people doing that.'

'Aye. Well, if you think you can like.'

They moved away slowly and Iant tried to memorise the spot. Already the cemetery was large and he thought he might try and visit the grave sometime. They hadn't been friends for long really but the long journey from home had made them each glad of someone that knew the places with which they were both familiar. Iant knew they had been lucky so far. Compared to some they hadn't had to face losing friends all the time. In a way, it made Oliver's death harder of course.

He asked the adjutant if he could have Ada's address which would have been in Oliver's things. He gave it easily enough. It seemed to be a normal thing to do so he decided to write to her that evening before he changed his mind.

Dear Miss Lloyd

I know that you will have heard by now the tragic news of your fiancée Oliver. Please would you accept my very sincere condolences.

Oliver and I had become friends in the training camp after we joined up. We travelled here together as well. He talked of you very often and very fondly. He also spoke affectionately about your family.

Oliver was very unlucky. Many soldiers get this disease, but most recover. The Doctor said he just had it worse. The Doctor also said that Oliver did not have much pain or suffering. We can at least be glad of that.

His little funeral was very dignified and his friends paid their respects.

I would be grateful if you would pass on my condolences to Oliver's family and of course to your own.

With kind regards

Private Iant Evans

Iant was not a scholar, but he had diligently learnt what he needed to at the village school. He looked over the letter and thought it was the best he could do. He took it to the post office tent and imagined it arriving in the respectable market town of Ruthin and the little boot and shoe shop that had once been Oliver's destiny.

The day after Oliver's funeral the daily routine began to change. Rumours spread that some kind of movement was imminent though they were often contradictory.

When they arrived they had all been issued with gas masks but they had mostly lain dormant apart from one chaotic exercise. Now suddenly there were daily drills and soon they were told these would involve small quantities of actual gas.

They were also made to dig trenches. Iant, like everyone else, had heard about the trenches in France and Belgium. Here on the rocky slopes above Salonika nothing like that was possible. The grave that they had lain Oliver in yesterday was barely deep enough to contain the wooden box and the trenches that they practised making here were the same. 'Slits' they called them.

In small groups, they were sent out on to the stony ground

above the camp and made to dig these slits while being yelled at by officers and NCOs. The idea was to simulate the pressure of battle. However loud and obscene the obnoxious sergeant made his voice it was hardly a substitute for a machine gun.

Unexpectedly Iant found that his experience with the slate became useful. He understood some things about the ways to split rock efficiently and he began organising others in his group. The work was tedious, but it replaced the endless waiting around and most of the men welcomed it. The time was passing more quickly.

The aftermath of the Salonika fire went on for weeks. The fire itself burned in pockets for a long time after the main inferno had died down. The Balkan News, a newspaper churned out for the troops and usually relentlessly cheerful, carried some graphic accounts of the damage to the city. In the descriptions, Iant recognised the cafes they had visited and realised that it had been for the first and last time.

It was now established that the fire had really been started by a woman in her kitchen. It had spread easily because of the crowded design of the city and the flimsy construction of the makeshift buildings. All over the world soldiers were trying their hardest to obliterate everything in their path and here an ancient city had been all but destroyed by cooking fat. Amazingly, the direct causalities of the fire were very few, but thousands were homeless and without any way of making a living. Collections were made around the camp, usually by the chaplains, to buy food and shelter for those left without anything.

The army's own supplies were interrupted and Iant felt himself to be continually hungry. This was made worse as the weeks passed and the weather began to shift from one extreme to the other, almost overnight. A freezing wind, the 'Vardar' it was called, blew much of the time and they were told it would be like this until spring.

If conditions were poor for those in camp, then the stories about those made homeless by the fire were horrifying. Disease and cold were claiming countless lives, especially children. Iant was sent one day as part of a party delegated to build some flimsy shelters on the northern edge of what remained of Salonika. He saw countless children begging amongst the broken buildings and fire-damaged streets. The soldiers shared fragments of chocolate with them, realising as they did so the futility of their gesture.

Before winter took a grip, some British troops had been involved in skirmishes with the Bulgarian army higher up the narrow valley north of the camp, but the snow and freezing temperatures meant that there was little to be done but dig in and hope to survive until the weather improved. Iant was issued with clothing that was meant to protect from the cold, but it was a losing battle.

One day, to his surprise, Iant learnt that he was to be promoted. He was made a Lance-Corporal and given charge of a detail that, when the weather allowed, took part in the building of what became known as The Birdcage. It was an enormous length of barbed wire fencing that stretched in an arc across the land north of their camp. It took months to complete and everyone joked that it worked to keep them in as much as the enemy out. No-one as far as Iant knew ever tried to cross the wire from the enemy side.

He wrote home telling them of his promotion.

Dearest Mam, Dad, Gwennie and Doy

I am writing to tell you the surprising news that I am now to be a Lance Corporal. I am to get a small (very small!) rise in my pay and a stripe to wear. You also have to be the butt of your fellow soldiers' jokes, but that is quite bearable.

I think my promotion is on account of my quarrying experiences. This is quite funny as I sincerely hope not to see Ffestiniog again when I return home!

If I can get a picture with my stripe I will send it to you.

Thank you for managing to send a parcel. All the things were useful. Razor blades and cigarettes that can actually be smoked without choking are very precious. Also anything to help keep warm now.

70

We still miss Oliver but it does not do to dwell on such things so far from home. Though of course I must say that I miss you all too.

I hope that winter will be kind to the animals and of course to all of you.

Your loving son and brother

Iant

Once the Birdcage was complete most activities ceased altogether. There were patrols but little or no action. Gethin joked that they were all budgerigars now except budgies got fed and watered more regularly.

As Christmas approached the sense of frustration in the camp grew greater. There were pointless route marches ordered to combat boredom and keep the men fit. As a Lance Corporal Iant found himself supervising some marches and felt some embarrassment. He felt the futility of every step but could not show it. His friendship with Gethin had survived his promotion, but there was certainly some tension between them.

On one very long march, Gethin was part of the platoon. Iant caught his eye a few times, but Gethin looked away. As they reached the high point of a pass on a road built by the British some months earlier it began to snow very heavily. Some of the men near the back began to grumble quite vociferously and the effect of the near-blizzard was to make their comments more and more barbed.

'Eh, corp. Are you lost?'

'We'll be alright. A Taff on a bloody mountain's quite at home.'

'No sheep to shag though.'

All this was quite normal of course and Iant ignored it, but when it was clear they were intending to press on the talk became more mutinous.

'Taff, are we headed back or what?'

'Yeh, for fuck's sake turn us round Taff before we die of frostbite.'

Still Iant ignored the comments and carried on leading from

71

the front. Eventually, three or four of the loudest at the back stopped moving.

'That's it. I'm not going no further.'

'Yeh, enough's enough.'

Iant decided on persuasion though inside he was both angry and embarrassed that they felt they could treat him like this.

'Come on boys, only another mile or so before we turn round. There's another path that crosses back over to that other valley.'

'Another fuckin mile? You must be joking. We can't see a thing here and half of us have got frostbite.'

''Cmon I'm turning back. We can say he got us lost. Anyone coming?'

There were murmurs of assent and several rows of men began turning round and heading back off down the pass. Iant felt a rising panic. He would look very stupid indeed if he couldn't stop a few men that had got cold from disobeying him. To his surprise, he heard a voice from behind him.

'You stupid bunch of cunts! Do you want to get a couple of you shot?'

It was Gethin.

'It's not the bloody playground. They won't give you a smack on the hand and keep you in after school.'

'What the fuck you on about?'

'It's another Taff.'

'In case you hadn't noticed they don't think too hard about court martialling a couple of squaddies every now and again.'

'His word against ours innit.'

'Think about it. Brass are sitting round freezing their bollocks off just like us. They know everyone's sick of it all. They could do with an example being made to shut people up for a bit.'

'Bollocks.'

'Do you want to try it? I know what I saw up here if it goes further.'

'Stick together don't they' someone said near the back.

72

'Maybe we do' said Gethin 'That's the idea isn't it? Aren't we all supposed to do that?'

Iant felt both grateful and humiliated. It should have been Gethin, not him, trying to lead a bunch of bolshy squaddies. That was how the army worked though. Gethin was too mouthy to be trusted they thought. Iant decided that he needed to save a bit of face.

'You lot at the back, fall back in and we'll say no more about it.'

After more barely audible grumbles they all formed back into the lines. As he walked back to the front he caught Gethin's eye and wanted to mouth 'thank you' to him, but he knew there were a lot of eyes on him. He would try and catch him later, join him for a smoke and give him some extra rum. Gethin though looked intent on staring ahead as rigidly as possible. It had cost him to do what he did and he wasn't in any frame of mind for any old pals act.

As Christmas approached someone in high command had the bright idea of producing a Christmas card that the men could buy and send home. Not many were in the mood, but everyone was hoping for some parcels that would brighten up the dreariness of daily life. Maybe the cards would tug a few heart strings at home.

The one they chose would set a few tongues wagging back in Corwen thought Iant. It was a picture of a group of soldiers in the traditional pose, one line kneeling in front of another line standing. Each soldier was a different nationality in a different uniform and the caption read 'Historic Group of Allied Comrades in Arms' and above the photo 'Merry Christmas 1916 from the Salonica Army'. There were Indians, Chinese, Russians, Japanese, French and god knows what. It made it look like the men all mingled happily in harmony. Iant had hardly exchanged a word with anyone who wasn't British. Still, harmless enough he thought and eventually he sent one to his family.

Just when most of the men were beginning to despair about getting anything, a delayed post arrived on Christmas Eve. It

73

contained a pile of patronising official cards from the likes of 'The Princess Mary', but also blessed parcels from home. Tobacco and chocolate, little Christmas puddings, gloves and socks, bulls eyes. Some got 'Tommy Cookers' and canned food to heat up. Iant and Gethin compared Bara Briths over a Christmas armistice all of their own.

On Christmas night they toasted Oliver with the last of the rum and got sentimental together for the first time in months. Despite his faults, Iant told Gethin he was a true friend and Gethin replied that Iant wasn't bad for an arse licking corporal.

The respite that Christmas brought didn't last long. Soon the deadening routine reasserted itself and 1917 started with more blizzards and winds that blew down all the way from Siberia. As January ended Iant felt that the men were at breaking point from cold and boredom. Just at the point when he thought that real mutiny might be in the air, news began to circulate of a real mobilisation.

There wasn't any plan to actually make these men so desperate to escape the boredom and cold that they would have done anything, but that was the way it was going to work thought Iant. They had come to feel like a part of the war that had been forgotten by everyone, including the enemy. For good or ill that was about to change. Most of the men had reached the point when they would welcome the idea of the fighting that was to come, but it might be different when it actually began.

Chapter 10

As winter ended more supplies got through. Food was better if still in short supply. The trucks brought more and more ammunition, especially shells for the big guns. They were to become part of a major push.

Iant's platoon was involved in numerous 'rehearsals'. They mainly had to attack a piece of higher ground that was defended by another group of men. The exercises were mainly futile because the attackers were in plain sight of men well-positioned and dug in. They could just be picked off.

Gas was clearly going to play a large part in what was to come. The drills were endless and consisted both of defending against gas and using it in attack. Most of the men 'tasted' small quantities of their own gas. Sometimes accidents happened and men were ill for days with the after-effects of gas making contact with their eyes or throats. Iant was lucky. He had suffered only smarting eyes. It hadn't felt much worse than when they were burning the stubble back home.

His responsibilities as Lance Corporal became easier. Men who could see that they were about to do something were more willing to take part in drills and to carry out the endless maintenance of weapons and equipment.

The Greek spring was now fully underway. Though it felt like a hot summer in the Berwyns, it was pleasant to be free of the cold and endless wind. Wild flowers sprang up in places that looked barren and the insects and snakes began to wake up. Strangest of all were the tortoises that ran around wild. Some men took up racing them for money; once, a crowd of a hundred men gathered round a makeshift 'track' screaming abuse at a shell marked with a number. There were amateur bookies and race stewards. Iant was unsurprised to see Gethin making good money out of taking bets.

Finally, at the start of April, they were to move. The route was straight up the Struma Valley which was discouragingly already nicknamed 'the valley of death'. This was because of all the past fighting that had taken place between Balkan countries. Human remains still littered the ground in many places and most of the villages were deserted.

The terrain was difficult and the advance was very slow. Iant tried to set an example to the small troop that he led, but his feet were sore and swollen each night and inwardly he shared the complaints at the lack of water as they walked. Each night, when they made camp, the food was cold and identical to the previous day's. Morale flagged but was partly sustained by the prospect of a fight at last.

However, even those with the most bravado became daunted when they first had proper sight of where they were to attack. In front of them was the fantastic sight of Lake Doiran made bright blue by the blinding sunlight. Behind the lake was the towering half-circle of mountain range on which the Bulgarian troops had been sitting waiting for them for nearly a year. It seemed to Iant that they were being led straight into the most obvious of death traps.

Among the many names that the various hills were given, one stuck out. Pip Ridge sounded like somewhere you might head out for a Sunday walk. In fact, it was a series of impregnable peaks on top of which sat, as they were soon to find out, enormous battery ranges with good supply lines behind them.

They were still far enough back to pitch camp safely, but it would probably be the last night. Tomorrow they had been told they would advance and dig in. He would be quarrying again after all thought Iant as he settled down to try and sleep.

That night was interrupted by the sound of distant guns. They were far too far away to threaten them, but it was a taste of what was to come. One of the officers told Iant that there were French and Russian troops approaching from a different direction and the firing meant that they had begun to get into position.

'They'll take most of the flak as we take them by surprise' he said.

To Iant the idea of surprising anyone sat on top of a bloody mountain while you tried to creep up on them from below was laughable, but he kept his mouth shut.

The following day they rose at dawn and made much of the march to the new positions before the sun was too high. The ground here was even more unrelenting than where they had trained near the camp and they had to start work immediately to try and dig in.

Though Iant and his troop worked fast the bombardment had begun before they had dug anything big enough to shelter a dog. Luckily, the Bulgarian guns took a while to find any kind of range and, though the sounds were unnerving, Iant's troop were not in immediate danger. The fire was now being answered by their own field guns and the result was a kind of deafening stalemate. Like two old drunks slugging it out after the pub someone said.

Their position was not ideal, but it was the best that they could manage on the terrain. Iant felt that they had done a good job, but could not see where they would go from here. It was not his job to think that far ahead he supposed, but like everyone else, his eyes were continually drawn upwards to the black mountains and the flashes of flame that signalled another shell.

The next day came the startling news that they were to be part of the attack on what they came to know as the Petit Couronne. This was a very steep slope forming part of the western end of the series of ridges. It was particularly important because it commanded one of the ravines that was vital to the Bulgarian supply line. Iant could see why the high command might be desperate to capture this place. He was less sure that they had really thought through whether it was a realistic thing to attempt.

The attack was to be later that week, though they had not been told exactly when. They wouldn't know until it was imminent. Until then their job was to hold this new position and make themselves ready for the important job that awaited them.

Though they had not yet been realistically threatened Iant

could see a small change in the way that the men conducted themselves. There was still a lot of outward bravado and talk of sorting out the 'murdering fucking Johnny Bulgars' but there was also a lot of nervousness and tension in their voices. The guns were a constant backdrop and at night the sky was often lit up. The Bulgars had searchlights that roamed across the ground a mile or so in front of them. They were out of range at the moment, but any advance would bring them within the scope of the lights. They would be lit up like Christmas one of the men said.

Is this when you should write to your family thought Iant. Something that could be given to them if you ended up as one of the corpses on the side of the mountain. In the end, he decided against writing. He felt that it would be inviting fate to come and do its worst. It had enough encouragement as it was.

Many of the men did write letters, he noticed. He wasn't sure what they did with them or what they said, but he hoped they gave the writers some small comfort.

They were told to be ready to advance under the cover of darkness that night. Everyone knew that the idea of darkness was really a lie. Even if the searchlights could not reach them then the sky was lit up by the guns. Their own guns were supposed to bombard the Bulgarian defences and give them a chance to break through. There would then be a position on the mountain from which to make another advance.

From the beginning, it seemed as though no-one really believed in the operation. He could tell from the faces of the officers that even the optimistic ones could not see them taking a mountain where the Bulgars had dug in for months. The Bulgars understood their territory in a way that any potential invader could not.

It was probably months of inactivity that made so many of the men champ at the bit, even for such a dangerous and, probably, stupid attack. There were nerves, but in the hours leading up to the offensive, there was also a keenness to get on with it.

The Allied guns started a relentless barrage that made hearing orders almost impossible. When this was answered by the Bulgars it was deafening. Iant felt disorientated but tried to keep a clear head. His responsibilities were small, but he still felt them. He was to lead a small section close to the left-hand end of the advance. The line stretched much further than could be seen so it was hard to tell whether you were out of line. It was Iant's job to make sure that his men were not.

Somehow or other, by a miracle, he received the order to advance. He had heard people speak of 'going over the top' in France. This did not feel anything like that. It was more of an undignified scramble out of the slits. As if there were not enough noise from the heavy artillery the air was now thick with whistles and then the dreaded sound of automatic fire.

For the first several hundred yards it was all open ground. The officers gambled on them only just being in range of the guns. They therefore ordered a rapid advance on the run, then to take cover in a line of boulders and rocks that marked the very beginning of the foothills.

Iant's section sprinted across the ground, many of the men making unearthly noises. To Iant's relief, they made it all together and reached cover without being too strung out. With some effort, he could call out names and all were present.

Those in the centre of the advance were less lucky. They came just in range of the Bulgars' automatic fire and from a distance, Iant saw men leap into the air and then fall. There was shouting from all directions and terrible cries for help and stretcher bearers. For most of them, it was the first taste of being under fire and then seeing comrades fall by your side. Nothing could prepare any man for that and Iant and his section could see clearly what happened.

No-one knew how long they would have to hold their positions. There was no possibility of excavating even a simple slit, but many of the men dug in as best they could. There were isolated trees and dips in the hillside as well as craggy boulders the size of a house. Iant and his section were safe enough from the guns at present, but it was a very precarious position.

As he lay obscured by a rock Iant tried to keep his mind on what he had to do to keep himself and his section safe and alert. He had no idea how orders would reach him. How long would it be before he had to decide on their next move, he wondered? His mind kept returning to the men that had run straight into the machine guns. The way the men quickly became like children's toys thrown in the air, involuntarily jerking and twitching as each round hit them. That could easily have been him. They had just been lucky not to have been at the centre of the advance.

The guns had been quiet for some time and Iant felt it was likely that the night's attack was over. They would have to try and make their position safer when it got lighter. Suddenly, what seemed like more shelling began, only to stop quite abruptly. Again, no shells landed close by and this time there were no bursts of machine gun fire.

After a moment of eerie quiet, Iant heard the first of many cries, almost pathetic in their inadequacy: 'Gas! Gas!.'

They had all been drilled of course, but the drills were not in the dark and dug into the side of a rocky mountain under enemy fire. Most of the men instinctively tried to get further under cover. They all knew that gas sank once it was discharged, but all logic was abandoned in the moment of panic.

The side of the mountain was alive with horrible screams. At first, these were not from physical pain, this was still to come. The fear of what they had been told about the gas was what initially took hold. There had been little suggestion that gas would be used by the Bulgars. The shock and terror spread quickly across the mountainside as what had happened sunk in.

Iant was as terrified as any though tried to remain calm, shouting to his section to get gas masks on as fast as they could. He knew that getting down low was wrong, but if they stood he feared that they would be cut to pieces by the guns. He struggled with his own mask, though he eventually got it on.

It was after a few moments that he realised that he had been just slightly too late. The first sensation of burning around his face and eyes came on slowly. He wanted to rip of the mask and allow the air to get to his skin, but his mind was still clear enough to know that this would expose him further to the gas. All around him, muffled now, he could hear the shouts of others that were also feeling the first effects. He felt utterly helpless. He struggled hard against it but slowly he lost consciousness, his head propped at a painful angle as he attempted to lift it off the ground where the concentration of gas was at its worst.

Chapter 11

The smell of antiseptic was overpowering and Iant felt sick most of the time. If he needed to vomit he had been told that you should raise your arm as well as call out. There was usually a nurse passing and willing to help.

From what he could hear many of the nurses were Greek, though they were supervised by British and Canadian women. After his time out on the mountain, it should have felt good to have just sat back and enjoyed the sheets and the regular food, but Iant could not stop thinking about what was going on around him. The first doctor that had spoken to him had suggested that he would regain most, if not all of his sight, but he could not promise anything. The effect of mustard gas was not fully understood yet he said.

As the acute anxiety began to subside, boredom took over. Without the distraction of watching the comings and goings on the busy ward, Iant found that the days seemed interminable. He even wondered if he would not rather still be out with his section laying barbed wire across the hillside.

Some of the nurses that helped him eat were friendly and chatted as much as they could. They were busy and needed to move on, but one or two tried to spare the time. He liked the Canadian accent and he was able to talk about some of the boys from the village that had gone to Canada before the war. He jokingly asked one nurse if she had come across his old friend Lloyd Bowen from Corwen back home. She thought that he was simple and explained that Canada was several thousand miles across and she had never even met anyone from Toronto.

Iant was quickly encouraged to try and feed himself. He didn't mind this as it was humiliating to be fed like a baby. One evening he was struggling badly with some kind of meat stew. Half of it was spilt down some pyjamas that he had only just been given and he had more or less given up, despite being hungry.

'Would you like help?'

The nurse spoke with a heavy Greek accent, though she seemed to speak English confidently.

'If you aren't busy.'

'We are always busy, but you need to eat so we can get rid of you quicker!.'

She had a lovely gentle laugh Iant thought, and he tried to imagine what she looked like.

'If you didn't feed us you could get rid of us even faster.'

'That's true, I will suggest it to the sister!.'

There was a silence as the nurse patiently fed Iant the rest of his food, but Iant wanted to prolong this break from the boredom for just a little longer.

'Are you from Salonika?' he asked.

'Not far. My family live in a small village just south of the city.'

'What is it called?'

'You would not know it. The fighting has all been to the north, thank god.'

'What is it called anyway?'

'Plagiari. It's a few houses and a lot of goats!.'

'Sounds like where I am from except that we have sheep instead of goats.'

The food was almost gone, but he wanted just a moment or two more of this friendly voice.

'Can I ask what your name is?'

There was a second or two of silence and Iant thought that perhaps she had moved away, though he thought he could still sense someone close by.

'Sara.'

'Is that Greek?'

'I don't know. There are others called Sara. I think it's a name for everywhere.'

'It's a nice name.'

'So. You have eaten properly?'

'Yes. I have eaten properly. Thank you.'

'Good. I want to see you stronger each day.'

'Then you can get rid of me.'

'That's it. We can get rid of you. But not before tomorrow, I think!.'

'No, perhaps a little longer than that.'

'Good evening then.'

'Good evening. And thank you again.'

Iant heard her footsteps move down the ward and she exchanged casual greetings with some of his fellow patients. Ridiculously, he felt jealous.

As he began to feel better in himself Iant's boredom led his mind to places that he didn't really want to go. The mountain and what had happened to his section of course, but also home. He thought of how strange his encounters with Clara had been and realised that she had never sent a picture. One night he dreamt that Oliver had been with them on the mountain and that he needed to go and find him.

Iant had asked about what course the battle had taken after he was stretchered down, but received only vague answers. Clearly, there was not to be good news, or they would have told him. He hoped that the men around him had been more adept with a gas mask than him.

The men in beds either side of him changed frequently. Sometimes they spoke no English as the hospital seemed to contain men of all the nationalities fighting on the same side. Eventually, he was joined by an Englishman who was a bit more talkative and this helped some of the days to pass more quickly.

At first the Englishman, Johnny, seemed obsessed about getting him to talk about rugby. 'All you Taffs love a game of rugby don't yer?' he kept saying. Iant tried to convince him that up north it wasn't the same, but he remained stubbornly determined. Despite this Johnny was cheerful company who, apart from anything else, was able to reassure him about the state of his injuries.

'Yeh. You aren't gonna be anymore ugly than you were before mate' he said, 'Soon as they got your eyes sorted out you'll be out on the razzle good as new!.'

Johnny had been part of the offensive, but at a completely different point some miles away, so he couldn't give Iant much information except to say that the attack had been repelled by the Bulgars and that it looked like there had been heavy losses. Johnny had a nasty leg wound, but the surgeons had managed to save it and he was hoping, he said, to get shipped home when he was well enough to travel. His family had a greengrocer's shop in Bexley in Kent and he hoped eventually to take it over from his father.

Johnny's outlook on life was cheerful and positive and it rubbed off on Iant. As Johnny imagined a life after the war full of girls, beer and, eventually a few cheeky kids to look after him in his old age so Iant began to look forward. He made an effort to think less about his experiences on the freezing slopes and the dreaded Bulgars pouring down all kinds of hell on them from above.

Compared to Johnny's world, Iant felt that his own home life had been somewhat narrow and confined. Johnny hadn't lived with luxury, but he seemed to come from a home that embraced what the world had to offer. He began to think that if he made it home in one piece he would look for a life with more possibility then the one that he had previously mapped out for himself.

Despite these thoughts, Iant wrote home diligently, reassuring his family that, although wounded he was well and recovering. He never once mentioned that he was, for the moment, blind.

'So you have been practising?'

Her voice was quite distinctive and Iant was surprised to feel his heart race a little and what felt like a blush run across his face.

'Yes, I have. I only miss my mouth one in five times now!.'

'Well done. Very good boy.'

'We haven't seen you for a few days. I mean....'

'I have been visiting my family. I had a few days leave.'

'Did you enjoy the visit?'

'Well, my father complains all the time. The war, the

85

shortages, the Bulgarians, the British.'

'He sounds like my mother!.'

Sara laughed and Iant desperately tried to think of another joke so that he could hear her again.

'How do you say your name? I-ant, like the insect is it?'

'No, it's Yant.'

'Aaah, like Yannis.'

'Yes, I suppose so.'

'Is it a strange name?'

'Not where I come from.'

'Where is that?'

'Wales. North Wales.'

'So you are not British?'

'Yes, well, sort of. Not English though, that's important!.'

'Why important?'

'It's complicated. We speak another language.'

'You speak English.'

'To you I do – at home, I speak Welsh.'

'Well I don't really understand, but is there anything I can help you with Mr Welshman?'

Iant tried to think quickly but found himself saying that he was fine.

'Ok. Well, then I must get on as you all say.'

'Could you come back tomorrow' Iant blurted out, unable to think of another way to detain her.

'Maybe. Will you need something then?'

'I don't know.'

'I am just teasing. I will call by tomorrow and check that you are still finding your mouth. Ok?'

She was gone and Iant was woken out of his daydream by Johnny.

'Hey Taff, who's your little friend then?'

'Sara. She's just one of the nurses.'

'One of the bleedin' nurses! You've got your tongue hangin' out so far you could lick your own bollocks!.'

Iant couldn't help laughing, though he hated Johnny just for a moment.

'I could tell you she looks like the back end of a bus and you wouldn't know any different would yer?'

'What does she look like?'

'Like the back end of a bus!.'

'Does she?'

'Naw, just kidding. She looks very…Greek. She's a titch and all.'

Iant's head was full of pictures – of a small dark-haired woman with enormous eyes and a huge smile. With a start, he realised that the image was partly of a Clara who smiled and laughed and didn't have the cares of the whole world on her shoulders.

'Put it this way mate, I wouldn't mind a bed bath if it was on offer if you know what I mean.'

'She wouldn't want to catch something, Johnny!'

'Cheeky bastard! Anyway, better hurry up and get them bandages off so you can see what you been missing eh?'

The rest of the day felt interminable. Iant's eyes had ceased to be so painful but had begun to itch. One of the doctors had told him that this was a good sign, it meant that they were healing, though it felt hard to believe that. He developed games in his head where he imagined himself in places he knew and walked around them, trying to remember as much detail as possible but he couldn't stay interested for long.

Sometimes one of the nurses would spare the time to help the blind patients walk around. It helped to stop their muscles becoming wasted, but it was time-consuming and was therefore a rare diversion that could not be relied upon. Iant longed for these short and very limited excursions and wondered if Sara would have time if he asked her.

Despite himself, Iant began to drift into a shallow sleep. Now that his body was getting stronger he tried not to doze too much in the daytime as it meant that the nights seemed longer. Despite his loss of sight, Iant could still detect the coming of darkness and the hours when there were fewer nursing staff were filled with men shouting for help or groaning in their sleep.

He thought of home and his head was full of images that were partly dream and partly his imagination trying to fill the long hours. When he was fully awake he couldn't distinguish between them. Sometimes he felt as if he had not slept at all only for Johnny to tell him that there was food on the way, even though he could swear that they had just been fed.

He wondered yet whether they would have had the news of him at home. It seemed miraculous to Iant that a message could reach his home from where he was. Like all the men he longed for a letter back, better still a small parcel, but it had been some weeks now and everyone blamed some blockade or other out in the Mediterranean.

It was the best time of year now at home, thought Iant. Some chance of dry weather, even in one of the wettest places on earth. Some of the early vegetables would be coming up in the little garden, everything green would look even greener in the occasional sunlight. Here there was plenty of sun but the green of the olive trees was muted in the fierce heat.

'Fag?'

Johnny could reach out far enough to put a cigarette in Iant's mouth and light it. After that, he could manage. Johnny was a generous man by nature, but he couldn't help having some fun with Iant's situation. Sometimes this involved sticking the cigarette in his ear or up one of his nostrils. This time he did neither and Iant leant back enjoying the smoke. Apart from occasionally misjudging how far it had burned down, the blindness enhanced the pleasure Iant thought.

There was a strange stillness around the hospital and the town. After the series of setbacks on the mountain everyone said that the generals had settled for a waiting game. This meant that the hospital saw very few comings and goings. Iant had been brought here in some chaos, but since then it had got quieter and quieter. Guiltily, Iant realised that he had fleetingly thought that this enhanced the boredom of his condition.

After a restless night and a breakfast that he didn't really feel

88

like eating Iant lay back on his pillows and steeled himself for another long day. The heat gradually increased and by noon his bandages itched to the point where he thought he would have to tear them from his head.

'How are we today?'

Even though he had thought of it often Iant was alarmed at the effect that her voice had on him. He felt sure that he betrayed signs of what he felt and tried to answer as casually as he could.

'Oh, fine. Just fine thank you nurse.'

'I am very pleased to hear it.'

He thought he sensed her moving away and his alarm made him almost cry out.

'Nurse!.'

'What is it?'

'It's just that I was wondering if I would be able to get up. Perhaps take a walk outside?'

'I don't think you would be able to manage. It's very crowded in the corridors.'

'Yes, I know. I wondered if…somebody might help me. I need to start moving again.'

'I might have a little time later. I'll have to see what is needed from me.'

'Yes. Of course. I know it's asking a lot and you are very busy.'

'I'll see what can be done after the food is served.'

'Thank you. That's very kind.

It was enough to sustain Iant for the next few hours, though he tried not to get his hopes too high. Much as he wanted to move and feel some air on his face it was the idea of her touching his arm and guiding him that was so wonderful that he could hardly bear to think about it.

He worried that Johnny had overheard their conversation. Perhaps he would say something tasteless and put her off? All afternoon, every time Johnny opened his mouth Iant wanted to scream at him to shut up, but he said nothing except the usual bursts of chatter that he seemed to be able to keep up for hours, days, on end. Usually, this helped the time to pass, but not today.

Lunch came and went. Another nurse helped him eat, though it was all food that he could manage with his hands. At least another hour passed after the clatter of plates and cutlery had finally ceased. Iant had given up and was sinking into as black a mood as he could remember since he was brought in.

He must have drifted off, exhausted by nervous tension and the poor sleep of the previous night. He was woken by the very faintest of touches on his arm.

'You are too tired perhaps?'

Instantly he was wide awake.

'No, no, really. I was just dozing. It's very warm in here now.'

She helped him swing his legs over the side of the bed. The flesh wound on the side of his knee had healed, but the scabs tugged when he moved. This was the most movement he had asked of his legs since he had been brought here. He instantly tried to stand, afraid that she would think him too weak to walk. It was a mistake and his legs buckled under him. Fortunately, he was still close to the bed and he only sat down sharply and without dignity.

Sara was very patient and encouraging and, after standing still for a few moments, she took Iant's arm. Soon he was putting one foot in front of the other as she steered him gently around objects and out of the ward. Before long Iant was moving relatively quickly down what she told him was a long corridor with equipment at either side. Her touch on his arm was, thought Iant, one of the greatest pleasures of his life so far.

As they finally reached an open doorway the heat was shocking. The old building in which the hospital had been created was, by comparison, naturally cool, though Iant hadn't realised it until now.

'Would you like to sit a moment in the sun? Or is it too hot?'

'Yes, yes I would like to sit.'

She steered him slowly to a bench and he instinctively lifted his face to the sun. He could feel that he was not in direct sunlight and thought that perhaps it was coming through a tree. Until he got a little too hot it was glorious. Sara fetched water from somewhere in a metal cup and he sat sipping it not wanting to be anywhere else.

Chapter 12

According to Johnny, they had been in the hospital for six weeks. Iant had grown a beard and the length of it gave him a sense that Johnny was about right. There had been no more major offensives so the days and nights remained quiet. There seemed little to do but sit it out.

Eventually, a letter arrived from home. Despite what he had told them the letter was full of anxiety from his sisters. What kind of wound did he have? Was he being properly treated? Why couldn't he be sent back to convalesce? Iant thought of writing back and telling them about his sight just so that they would stop fussing, but he decided that it would be unnecessarily cruel. He kept being assured by the doctors that he would see again and so he decided to leave it as a heroic story that he could tell on his return.

Iant didn't want to admit it to himself but his need for his sight had intensified now. Sometimes, when he heard her voice, he could hardly bear it that he couldn't put a face to it. He daydreamed about asking if he could run his hands over her face so that he could have a sense of what it was like. Fortunately, his keen sense of what was polite prevented him.

Sara's presence, even the prospect of it, was what kept Iant sane. There was now no denying it and an unhealthy portion of each day was spent straining for the sound of her voice. This was followed by the disappointment of realising that it was not her that he had heard after all. Naturally, this was not something that he shared with Johnny. He had learned to affect a nonchalant outward appearance when Sara was actually close by. At least he hoped that was the impression that he gave to anyone watching.

Iant had become much more at ease when moving slowly about the room and even down the corridor to the toilets. He was returning from one of his short expeditions one morning when he heard the unmistakable sound of Sara's voice coming from the area that he was heading back to. She and Johnny were chatting amiably and he heard the sound of Sara's laughter. He realised once again that he was quite irrationally jealous.

'Ah, Iannis' she said. For a moment, he felt as if he could actually be a Iannis, growing vines and peppers or maybe owning a small boat for fishing.

'Hello'. He hadn't meant to sound quite so downbeat. It was simply that he hated the idea of Sara having a conversation or sharing a joke with anyone else.

'Oh dear, are you feeling worse today?'

'No...no.'

'You don't sound full of good spirits.'

'Tell him he's a miserable little Welshman nurse.'

Iant was glad of Johnny's usual hearty good humour. He didn't know how to snap out of his low-key petulance but he also didn't want to waste the precious time.

'I had come to see if you would like to take another small walk, but perhaps you are not feeling like it?'

Though he felt foolish Iant could not help the fact that his heart leapt and that he wanted to reach out and embrace Sara and not let her go for some while. Instead, he tried to stay calm and polite.

'No...no, I'm fine. I would love to...get some fresh air. If you are not too busy that is.'

'Good. Can I come back in an hour? I have some jobs first, but by then I will also like some air.'

'Thank you.'

'Well. I will see you in about one hour.'

Iant manoeuvred himself into a sitting position on the bed and sat in silence. His mood had changed completely and he had no idea whether he had successfully hidden the fact from Johnny. He quickly realised that he hadn't.

'Blimey Taff. You got it bad or what?'

'What are you talking about?' Iant knew he had been rumbled but tried to keep up a front as best he could.

'It's you that's blind mate, not me. You looked like you was gagging for it!'.

93

'Shut up you filthy little cockney.'

'Nothing wrong with it mate, just saying that's all.'

Iant didn't want to talk about it. In fact, what he wanted to do was lie back on his pillows and think a lot about the walk he was going to take and the few precious minutes that he would get to listen to Sara's voice and feel her presence close by, but Johnny didn't want to let it go.

'Worrying thing is I reckon she fancies you an' all. She must have left her own white stick back at home. Shame. Lovely girl like that with fading eyesight!.'

Despite Johnny's relentless bantering tone, Iant couldn't contain his feelings. Even this joking suggestion that Sara shared what he felt was enough for him.

'What do you mean?' he found himself asking, trying hard to keep any hint of eagerness, or even interest, out of his voice.

'Well, do you see her offering to walk any of the other poor buggers?'

'I don't know, doesn't she?'

'Course she don't. And I seen her looking at you.'

'I'm not talking about this anymore' said Iant, though he wanted to talk about it more than anything else.

'Suit yourself mate, but I'm telling you. You lucky bastard.'

Iant lay back on his pillows and made himself slow his breathing. He wanted to feel calm again. He wanted to be in control of himself and to act like a sensible human being when Sara came to take him on the walk. In his mind, he took himself up to the top of the hill that gave the best view down the Dee Valley and waited there, as if he were to meet Sara off the train from Llangollen.

After what felt like a very long time he heard footsteps and guessed correctly that they were hers. Johnny had been wheeled off somewhere so he was spared the jokes that he had been fearing. He eased himself into a standing position and with Sara holding his arm they moved off down the passageway. Iant felt the warmth on his face from the outside door at the end of the corridor.

Sara talked comfortably about the banal comings and goings in the hospital and the way that the weather had been behaving. They talked about Johnny and they talked about missing their families. Iant thought he had rarely felt happier, yet he was blind and stuck in a hospital in the middle of a war in a foreign country.

'Here is a cooler place to sit perhaps'

Sara steered him towards a stone seat in a spot that felt as though it were under trees. As Iant's eyes healed he was beginning to make out more and more patterns of light and he felt the fierce sun disappear off his face.

'Can you tell me what you can see?'

'There is not much. This was a nice garden but it isn't getting tended enough.'

'What do you mean?'

'There are plants growing into each other. There are bright flowers, but they have become tangled and they are struggling to find enough light.'

'Is there anything else?'

'Can you hear water?'

'Yes.'

'It's a small fountain. I am surprised that it is still working. It is a small trickle but there is water and a little pool. There are plants in the pool.'

He could feel that she was close beside him on the seat. It was all he could do to prevent himself from reaching out for her hand. He wondered what she might say and whether he could pass it off as a mistake if she took offence. To his great surprise, he felt her hand brush his cheek and he instinctively reached for it and held it.

'I thought I saw a fly on your cheek.'

'Did you?'

He had not let go of her hand and neither was she pulling it away.

'I didn't feel anything.'

'Perhaps it was just a speck of dirt.'

Iant released Sara's hand and she moved it slowly away.

They sat in silence now, not uncomfortably, but Iant wished he could say something clever or funny. He wanted to prolong a moment that he knew would end soon.

'What else can you see?'

'We are quite near the walls of the hospital. They are old and crumbling in places. Like a lot of this city, they are needing repair.'

'Were you in the city when the fire broke out?'

'No. I was at home. Some of my family, my cousins, lost a lot. Some of them have no home now.'

'I saw some of it. People were very frightened.'

'Yes. Everyone thought it was the war but in the end just stupidity. It would be funny if it hadn't been so terrible. It happened like so many things in my country I think.'

'What do you mean?'

'Mistakes. We are always making stupid mistakes.'

'Not just your country.'

'Perhaps not.'

Iant and Sara talked for some time. Iant started to lose the worst of his anxiety, but he still felt as if he were always on the point of drying up. Sometimes he saw himself looking into space for the next thing to say. They exchanged stories of their families and discovered how alike and unalike they were. They both came from people who never starved, but who also had to constantly think hard about making a living. For Sara, the war had given her a chance to do something outside the confining world of her small village. Iant understood that, for all its difficulties, the same was true for him and for most of the young men with whom he had travelled all this way.

After some time Iant heard another woman's voice calling in Greek and Sara shouted a reply. Sara explained that her friend was warning her that the ward sister was looking for her and that they needed to go. Iant hoped that he heard some regret in her voice but he could not be sure. As Sara led Iant back down the corridor he felt something had shifted slightly between them.

That night Iant's dreams were full of Sara. During the day,

he tried to focus on the daily chit-chat coming from Johnny and others. He had become a little more adept at a range of practical tasks and he threw himself into improving as best he could. He was beginning to feel stronger and there was now something to look forward to each day. Iant was slowly thinking less about the misery of the last few months and more about what might be to come.

It was two days before he heard Sara's voice again. He made himself stay calm and sound as relaxed as he could. He had been trying to make himself think of almost anything else except Sara since their last time together. He had tried to piece together even the misery of the time up on the ridge and the details of the battle. Even Oliver's death and the simple funeral that had followed. He wanted to stop himself thinking too hard about what it felt like to feel the brush of her hand on his face.

'How are you both today?'

'He needs a bit of cheering up nurse.'

Iant braced himself for what Johnny might say. Something crude that might ruin the moment for him. Instead, for once, he was unusually restrained and Iant felt a warmth towards him out of all proportion to his actions.

'Perhaps you would like to take a little walk Iannis?'

Understandably she still stumbled over the oddity of his name, but it felt to Iant like something to treasure. He added it to the list of things he sometimes thought about in the long hours when he was awake.

'Yes, yes I would if you can spare the time.'

'I can spare the time. It's been quiet today.'

She suggested that they get a little more adventurous and go outside the hospital grounds. Iant still walked with a pronounced limp, but Sara said that it would do him good to move further. The hospital was on the northern edge of Salonika, but there was a small collection of shops and cafes just a short walk down the hill towards the main city.

As they left the hospital grounds and moved out of the shade of the trees, Iant felt the heat and the light penetrate

97

sharply through the bandages. Instinctively he lifted his free hand to shield his eyes and Sara steered him onto the shadier side of the road.

Mostly they walked slowly and in silence. The heat was strong but quite bearable in the shade. It was enough for Iant to feel the gentle pressure of Sara's hand on his arm. Occasionally she murmured a warning of an obstacle or a kerbstone. As they neared the café where there they had agreed to sit for a while Iant could smell the Greek coffee and something else which he realised was honey.

He had a little Greek money that he had been careful to bring with him. As they sat he insisted that he buy her coffee and something to eat. Iant had drunk the small cups of Greek coffee before and had not cared very much for it, but the prospect of sipping it now was very different. The café owner brought small pastries flavoured with the honey he had smelt and Sara encouraged him to try one.

The pastry was delicious though Iant was self-conscious about eating in front of her. He took the smallest bites and wiped his mouth carefully each time. There was a small glass of water alongside the coffee and Iant took sips to wash down the bitterness. He felt a fingertip brush his cheek and before he could think his hand was on hers and bringing it to his mouth where he kissed it very gently before letting go. He was relieved that she had not snatched her hand away but was still very embarrassed at what he had instinctively done.

'I'm sorry I....'

'It's alright.'

'You didn't mind?'

'It's hard for me to say.'

'What do you mean?'

'I didn't mind.'

Iant felt her hand reach for his under the table. He took it gently in his and didn't dare move or breathe for what seemed like a long while. He was afraid that she just pitied him and saw this as an extension of her duties. He desperately wanted his sight back now. He wanted to see her face, but also what she was thinking. He forced himself to speak.

'Have you been feeling….'

'Yes.'

He laughed instinctively.

'I haven't said anything.'

'I have been feeling…what else is there?'

'Yes. I am so glad.'

'Your coffee will go cold.'

He withdrew his hand slowly and he sipped the coffee. She asked if he liked the baklava and he took another bite. It felt as though they were playing a fantastic game when she once again brushed away a crumb and he was able to kiss her hand, less hurried now. He reached towards her face with his other hand and she guided him towards her cheek. After letting it rest a moment she moved his hand back to the table.

'I am sorry, but I am in uniform and maybe….'

'It's alright, I understand.'

And he did understand. There was nothing that would spoil this he thought.

'I want to see you so much.'

'But if you did you might not like what you saw' The tone of her voice was light though.

'Johnny teases me and says how beautiful you are and that I am missing so much.'

'Johnny is a bad man.'

'He is a bad man.'

They laughed together at the thought of Johnny and what he would say if he saw them like this. They ordered more coffee and sat with one hand in each other's beneath the table cloth and forgot the time. Or, if they remembered, they chose to ignore it. Eventually, Sara's sense of the consequences if she did not return came back to her and they began the slow return to the hospital. This time Iant could feel the pressure on his arm without anxiety, knowing that it was intended.

It was late afternoon now and the heat was just beginning

to fade. As they neared the door of the hospital both of them resisted going inside for as long as possible. Eventually, Sara steered Iant down the corridor and back to the ward. As she helped him to sit on the bed her hand once more squeezed his elbow just a little tighter. Then she was gone.

Chapter 13

Iant had no idea whether what was happening was either permissible or sensible. All he knew was that he longed to spend time with Sara. He also wanted his sight to return more than ever, but he was partly afraid of that happening. He had fallen for someone that he had never seen and part of him was fearful of what happened when that changed.

Though the loss of his sight was the main reason for his remaining in hospital Iant had also suffered some damage to his lower back during the battle. For some weeks his lack of movement had meant that the extent of this was hidden. Now that he walked further with Sara the injury became more apparent and he began to need a stick to walk. At times the pain was quite acute, but the last thing he wanted to do was stop walking.

Two more weeks had passed when Iant woke one morning with strong light coming through his bandages. He had experienced flickers the whole time, especially when he was outside. He felt they were becoming stronger, but hadn't dared to hope too much. This time he felt sure that something had really changed. It was just after dawn and the ward was quiet, so he decided to remove his bandage himself. It was only held on by a safety pin but Iant's anxiety made him struggle and he wanted to rip and tear at the material. As he unwound the long strip of bandage he tried to stop himself thinking about seeing Sara's face.

The light hurt his eyes and the shapes and colours in front of him were very unclear, but the nurse who eventually came to him said that this would improve gradually. He must keep his eyes covered for some of the time and allow them to adjust gradually to the light. On no account must he expose them to direct sunlight, perhaps for some weeks. Iant barely heard the warnings and cautions. All he could think of was that this was the beginning of the end of his blindness and he was overcome

101

with a mixture of happiness and fear.

When he looked across at Johnny in the next bed he could just see an outline and some movement. He could tell that his hair was dark and that the nightshirt he had on was a lighter colour. He tried to force himself to keep his eyes closed but the need to see if there was improvement, even minute by minute, was overwhelming.

A doctor came to see him and appeared pleased at what had happened. He repeated the warnings not to rush things and to avoid direct sunlight but was otherwise certain that this was the start of Iant's sight returning. The doctor said that he would arrange for a pair of glasses with darkened lenses to be prescribed and left to continue his rounds.

As he opened his eyes to watch the doctor retreating down the ward Iant found it difficult to contain his excitement. Sara had not been sure when her next shift was to be when they last spoke. It might be today and Iant was overwhelmed by the idea that he might see her. If there was a chance that he might not like what he saw, then for the moment that idea didn't enter his head. He could only think and imagine that this would complete the picture that he had of the woman who had brightened his days and filled his imagination ever since he had first heard her voice.

Johnny was not how he had imagined. Iant had thought of him as thick-set and pugnacious-looking. In fact, he looked quite slight and had the air of someone much more mild-mannered. He had an engaging smile, the kind you saw on the face of somebody who was always looking for the next bit of mischief.

Johnny wasted little time in finding new ways to taunt Iant now that his sight was returning. He teased him that he would realise that all the nurses were beautiful and that his 'little bit of Greek skirt' was nothing special. He could leave her to him he said. Iant knew better than to take the bait and just retorted that Johnny was even uglier than he could have imagined.

As the day wore on Iant gradually allowed himself to open his eyes for a bit longer each time. He ate now with pleasure, even though being able to see the food put in front of him was not without its drawbacks.

When evening came and Sara was not among the nurses that appeared to relieve those that had worked all day, Iant found it difficult to contain his disappointment. Johnny had passed him a yellowing copy of a newspaper that had been around for some while and he tried to read to take his mind off Sara. His eyes were not really ready and the combination of the physical difficulty and his wandering attention meant he had little patience, even though he had longed to be able to read again.

The next day Iant made mental lists of what he would be able to do again now that his sight was returning: write a proper letter home; walk to the toilet without his arm stretched in front of him; lose money at cards to Johnny; take walks in the fresh air; get sent back to the front; go to a bar and drink a beer without dripping it down his chin; shave properly. Even the thought of being sent back to the front could not detract from the pleasure of being able to see again. After one more check that he could make out the fading shapes in the darkness, Iant drifted into a restless sleep.

He heard her voice first and it became incorporated into his dream. They were arguing about putting his bandages back on and giving his eyes some rest from the light. As his eyes flickered open there was a face close to his and weak light was just beginning to infiltrate the ward. At first, he could only see an outline and the white of her uniform with its red cross on the front. He struggled to move himself upright and she stepped back. He rubbed the sleep from his eyes and tried to take in as much as his still-bleary sight would allow him.

Her hair was mainly hidden by the cap and headdress that all the nurses wore, but wisps of it escaped around her face and it was the blackest hair he had ever seen. In this light too her eyes also seemed black. She smiled nervously and he laughed involuntarily out loud. It was partly his nerves but also the ridiculousness of seeing someone for the first time when you feel you have already known them for so long.

103

'They told me....'

'Yes. I began to see yesterday. It's getting better all the time.'

'You mustn't look at the light for too long.'

'Not you as well. That's all anyone tells me.'

'I am sorry. I just don't want you to lose your sight again.'

Perhaps for the first time in his life, Iant felt the meaning of the word 'overwhelmed'. He thought she was so beautiful that he could hardly bear it. He felt guilty at his relief. What did it matter what she looked like if he already felt so close to her? All these thoughts were running around his head in what felt like an instant.

'If I got dressed would you have time to take a walk with me?'

She looked around to check who was watching before nodding her assent and he climbed slowly out of bed. As they walked out of the ward and down the corridor Iant realised that she no longer needed to take his arm, but she did so anyway.

They didn't speak at all until they reached the sunlight at the open door and she once again cautioned him to shield his eyes. Iant struggled to think of what to say. The awkwardness between them was palpable and he felt an overwhelming sense of disappointment.

They left the hospital grounds and walked silently for some way with Sara carefully steering him into the shade as much as was possible in the fierce heat. Eventually, Iant felt he couldn't walk any further and suggested that they sat on a stone wall down a side track off the road. There was a large patch of shade under some olive trees and a dog was stretched out asleep. Iant bent down and patted the dog's back and it stirred but was too content to move.

'You like dogs?'

'I suppose so. On the farm, they just worked really. They were not pets.'

He found himself sounding harsher than he meant and was struggling to understand why he felt as he did. His sight was returning and he could see for the first time this beautiful woman sat beside him. Why then did he feel so awkward and ill-tempered?

They sat in silence for what felt like some time and the small distance between them on the wall felt enormous after the small intimacies of their last meeting. When Iant could barely stand the silence anymore he heard Sara as if in the distance.

'I am sorry that it is disappointing for you.'

'What do you mean?'

'To have your sight return.'

'It isn't disappointing. I am just getting used to it.'

'But what you see is disappointing.'

He was overcome with the idea that he was making her unhappy. Instinctively, he reached for her hand and then that felt very inadequate. He looked up and, for the first time, he was able to meet her stare for just a second. He tentatively moved his head and touched her lips with his own. Her hand moved to his face and with great tenderness, they kissed.

'You were so quiet' Sara whispered.

'Please don't say anything.'

Iant and Sara stayed on the wall at the side of the dusty track for what felt like hours. They spoke little, there was an understanding between them. At last, Sara spoke:

'You must be thirsty. It is very hot.'

'Yes.'

'And, I am sorry, but you must rest your eyes.'

He laughed, without any hint of reproach, and she helped him to his feet.

Sara led Iant further down the track and into a twisting maze of side streets. He kept his eyes shaded, but enjoyed the colours and shapes of the unfamiliar buildings until in the end they turned onto a little square with a stone fountain at the centre and a café to one side. Some tables were arranged under a tree. They sat and ordered water and tea that turned out to be made from mint. After initially pulling a face Iant began to enjoy it.

There was more silence, but this time it felt less tense. Iant and Sara caught each other's eyes and smiled, though neither

105

could be sure of what would happen next.

'Would you take me and show me where you live?' he said suddenly.

'Do you mean now?'

'No, not now. But could we arrange it?'

'It is not a very interesting place.'

'I would still like to see it. Now that I can.'

'Perhaps. If you would like. It is a long walk though.'

'If you can manage it then so can I.'

'I should get back. I am only supposed to be helping a patient become more mobile!.'

'And you are.'

'I'm not sure this should include sitting drinking tea in the shade.'

'Or holding his hand? Or this?'

At this Iant leant towards Sara and kissed her. There was no one else sitting in the square and the kiss was more prolonged than perhaps either of them had intended.

'You are very beautiful. I knew before but now I can see.'

'I really have to go now.'

'I had to tell you. I should have said as soon as I saw you.'

As they walked slowly back to the hospital Iant could feel that the heat was just going out of the sun and he felt the sheer pleasure of being in the air. He enjoyed being able to see even the mundane surroundings through which they were passing. He felt strongly alive for the first time in months.

At the door to the corridor that led back to the ward Iant hesitated.

'Could we meet? I mean away from here?'

'You have only just started being out of bed on your own.'

'Yes. But in a few days. The doctors will want me to start being more up and about.'

'Perhaps.'

'But you do want us to meet?'

'Yes, yes of course.'

'Do you know anywhere, maybe a bit further away?'

'Let me think about it?'

Iant was disappointed at the idea of waiting, but he did not show it. He was impatient for his life to begin to move again, but he tried to understand her caution. They barely knew each other and she had to be careful of her position in the hospital.

'Alright. Will you tell me tomorrow?'

'I'll try.'

He said he would go on in by himself, trying to show some understanding of what she was feeling. He looked around to check no one was watching, kissed her lightly on the cheek and walked alone down the dark corridor.

Chapter 14

As his eyes grew accustomed to their recovery Iant became more and more mobile. He tried to go for a short walk at least twice a day, but he was always worried in case he missed Sara. He found himself obsessively looking out for her and then, when she was there, staring at her much more than he should. He wanted to pursue the idea of them meeting elsewhere but there seemed to be so many difficulties. He had not yet been cleared by the doctors to leave the hospital on his own and Sara seemed always to be too busy to catch for even a moment.

Now that his sight was returned Iant was subject to an assessment by a doctor. He assumed that it was simply to test his sight but the doctor asked him to walk back and forth across the room and appeared to be looking at his feet.

'How long have you been limping Lance Corporal?'

'Limping sir?'

'Yes, you are dragging your left foot.'

'Am I sir? Perhaps it's because I have been in bed so long sir?'

'I doubt it Lance Corporal. What were your other injuries when they brought you in?'

'I think they said there were the burn marks down my side, but they've healed now sir. I had a bad back and I think my ankle was sprained, but I didn't get out of bed very much at first.'

'I think it was more than a sprain Evans. Have you tried running?'

'No sir. Because of my sight, I have only been able to walk on my own for a few days.'

'Do you get any pain from your ankle?'

When Iant thought about it, his ankle did hurt after he had walked any distance. He had only really walked with Sara and he realised that he had probably not been paying much attention.

The doctor asked him to lie down and he manipulated his foot in different directions, taking notes occasionally as he did so. Finally he asked him to get off the bed and sit opposite him.

'I think I have good news for you, Evans?'

'What is that sir?'

'We'll need to get you back home.'

For a moment Iant could barely think. For most of the last two years, the idea of going home would have overwhelmed him with pleasure. Getting away from the endless routines, the boredom, the smells and the noises seemed something he could only fantasise about. Now it felt like somebody had punched him. A feeling of panic began to rise in his throat.

'Why, sir?'

'Well we don't have x-ray machines here like they do in France, but I am quite sure that you sustained a fracture to your foot when you fell. It has probably healed badly but it needs proper assessment and in all likelihood a small operation.'

'Can't this be done here sir?'

'What's the matter with you man? I thought you would be jumping for joy. Even with a broken ankle.'

'Oh, I am sir. I just thought....'

'This isn't a place for heroics Evans. Everybody knows we are engaged in a sideshow here. Get yourself home and properly fixed up. Otherwise, you'll be a cripple for life. You're no good to anyone here anyway. Getting back up to that bloody ridge needs both legs at the very least.'

'When would it be sir?'

'Oh, I don't know Lance Corporal. Not my department. I just sign the orders. There always seems to be some bloody great hospital ship setting off, though I suspect it could be several weeks before they get you on one. My advice is to take the time to enjoy whatever is left of this godforsaken place while you can. It's not as though any of us will be coming back is it?'

'No, sir.'

Moments later Iant was walking back down the corridor with a chit in his hand. He was to move out of the hospital bed and into an area where the less seriously wounded convalesced in tents. In due course he would be given orders to prepare

109

himself for the long trip home.

Iant tried hard to stay calm. He was the luckiest man alive surely. His sight was getting better by the day and he had one of those injuries that so many dreamed of. Everyone had heard of the poor bastards that had injured themselves deliberately and ended up in front of a firing squad. He wouldn't have to worry about any of that. And even the pessimists thought the war wouldn't last another year.

Soon he would be back home, being fussed over by his sisters and scolded by his mother for malingering. He would feel cold rain on his face and the smell of grass in his nostrils. Chasing sheep in a howling gale would seem like paradise. All the endless heat and filthy red dust of Salonika would feel like a bad dream.

But he could appreciate none of this. The feeling of panic that he had managed to contain in front of the officer began again and he badly needed air. He moved as fast as he could down corridors to a place he had discovered near the back of the hospital. No-one went there because it was too close to the stench of the incinerators nearby, but for now, he had to be on his own. He realised how small his world had become in the past weeks and he headed for one of the few places he knew where he was sure of being uninterrupted.

Iant felt the heat burn his throat and he drank deeply from the bottle he carried before emptying the rest over his head. He rubbed furiously at his face. He had to calm himself before even thinking of seeing Sara again. What was he to her anyway? He thought she enjoyed his company, but they had known each other such a short time and exchanged only faltering words. For all this, the idea of telling her that he was soon to return home filled him with fear. Despite all that had happened to him in the last year, he felt more desperate than at any time. The feeling was physical and he felt sure that he was going to vomit. In the end, he pulled himself together and walked slowly back towards his bed.

Iant knew that Sara was not on the ward that day so he decided to collect his few belongings and start the process of

110

moving to his new billet. It would involve mistakes, form filling, impatient NCOs and he thought he may as well face it while he was already in such a miserable state of mind. Nothing could make it worse.

As he approached the ward he realised too that he would miss Johnny. In the hardest times of his blindness, Johnny had bludgeoned him out of himself and helped him recover. He would be furious if Iant betrayed even a hint that he was not delighted by his good fortune. Johnny had talked constantly about finding a way to get sent home and longed for it more than anything else.

'What's up with you Taff? Are they gonna chop it off or what?'

'Aye. Something like that. Won't have to put up with you anymore. That's something I suppose.'

Johnny's face fell, though he carried on in his usual way.

'They sending you back already? With your bloody eyesight, you'll end up killing half the battalion.'

'Yeh, moving out Johnny. Can't stand another night of your bloody snoring.'

'What now? You're moving now?'

'Looks like it?'

'Blimey. Don't mess about do they? Where do we find you if someone comes looking for their money?'

'Transit mate. At least I think that's what he called it.'

'That's where they put people getting shipped home....'

Iant's face told Johnny all he needed to know.

'You jammy little bastard. And you let me think you were off up the Ridge again. Here, your little Greek nurse won't be happy.'

This was too much for Iant. He felt, ridiculously, that if he didn't get out of the room he would burst into tears and make a complete fool of himself. He turned away and began stuffing oddments of clothing into a kit bag.

'She'll have to turn to someone with a broad shoulder to cry on, eh?'

'Just fuck off Johnny will you?'

'Touched a sore spot, eh?'

Iant turned now, not able to fully control himself. He moved close to Johnny and shouted into his face.

'I said fuck off. Didn't you hear me?'

For the first time since they had lain beside each other, all those weeks ago, Iant saw Johnny fall silent. He regretted his outburst, but he didn't know what to say. Instead, he turned away again and slowly finished packing his belongings. When he was ready to leave he wanted to rush from the room and not face Johnny again, but there was something he had to say. Half turned away he said, barely audibly:

'If you see her, you won't say anything will you?'

'Why shouldn't I?'

'Because I need to tell her myself.'

Johnny heard the crack in Iant's voice.

'Fuck me, mate. You're in a bit of bother here aren't you?'

'Yes. I am.'

'Jesus Christ. You get a cushy passage home and you come on all love struck. You stupid sod.'

'I know.'

'Tell you what, tell 'em to send me instead. You can stay here and look up at the stars with your little Greek friend. How's that?'

'Alright, Johnny. I'll give it a try!.'

They both laughed, the tension between them dissipating and Iant felt a rush of warmth towards Johnny.

'I won't say nothing. Promise.'

'Thanks.'

'Few days out in the Med on that boat. You'll forget all about her.'

'You think so?'

'Definitely mate. Especially with all the squaddies throwing up all around you. Dampen your bloody ardour that will.'

Again the laughter between them was real enough, though Iant knew, and he suspected that Johnny did too, that he would

112

not forget Sara so easily. His mind raced with thoughts of just what to do about it.

'So I'll see you on Battersea Rise one Saturday then?'

'Or on the High Street in Corwen.'

'Nah. Not getting among the sheep shaggers.'

Iant went to punch him playfully on the shoulder, but Johnny grabbed his hand and held it fiercely.

'Grab the chance when you get back home, son.'

'The chance of what?'

'Of being alive you stupid bugger.'

'I will, Johnny. I promise.'

'Now fuck off and leave me in peace will you?'

Iant turned and picked up his kit bag. As he reached the door he glanced back but Johnny was very intently rolling his next fag.

Chapter 15

Iant trusted Johnny not to speak to Sara, but when she saw that he had been moved out of the ward it would surely soon be explained to her where he had gone. He had to try and contact her before then. He knew she was working the following night but had no idea of when she would arrive.

The name of her village came to him from somewhere and, in the state in which he found himself, it suddenly made some sense to try and find her and speak to her before anyone else did.

'Plagiari' Iant repeated to himself a few times before it slipped away again. His memory had not been as sharp since he was injured, a consequence of the pain medication and the lethargy of lying about in the hospital. But the place could surely not be too difficult to find if Sara could walk to the hospital each day.

He tried repeating the word several times to some of the Greek men that worked around the camp as orderlies, but they all looked at him as if he were mad. It was either his pronunciation or that this village was so tiny that they had never heard of it. Salonika was a sizable city and many of its inhabitants might have hardly ventured outside its walls.

He began to panic and considered waiting all day outside the hospital until she came before he realised how many entrances there were. He became desperate and could think of nothing but the single idea that he must talk to Sara before she spoke to anyone else.

Finally, after what seemed like hours of wandering the hospital camp asking, he was directed to a particular officer. He had been part of the group responsible for mapping the city's defences when the Allies had taken control of Salonika and the surrounding area. At first, the name of the village meant nothing to him, but with some reluctance, the officer produced a well-worn map and together they located Plagiari. Iant had little experience of using maps, but he estimated that it was about an hour's walk from the camp. With some effort he tried to commit a route to memory as there seemed little question of the officer loaning out his precious map.

Iant waited until late afternoon when the sun had begun to cool and set off. He had little plan beyond finding the village and then asking in the first house he saw whether they knew a woman called Sara. He walked further and further into the maze of streets that he first had to cross before getting on to an open road. As he did so, the absurdity of his idea crept upon him. He had no idea if Sara was the most common name in Greece or not. They might look at him as if he was a lunatic.

There was also the question of how he would be received. British soldiers were currently discouraged from venturing outside the camp and the main area of the city. The long occupation had not been popular with some factions in the Greek government. Greece had changed sides at least twice during the campaign and some of this had managed to trickle down to local populations. Iant was only vaguely aware of the significance of any of this, but it added to his anxiety as he walked.

The foot injury which had set him on this miserable quest was now as if in spite, making itself felt with a vengeance. Iant had not walked far at all in weeks and the pain in his ankle was getting more and more acute. His eyes also were not used to so much sunlight and he began to need moments to rest in the shade.

After some time, he felt as though he were reaching the southern outskirts of the city and the countryside seemed to be opening up in front of him. He wasn't sure whether the road, little more than a track, was the one he half-remembered from the map, but as he caught glimpses of the sea in front of him he knew he was heading in the right direction. Just when he began to doubt his memory there was a sign ahead of him suggesting a right turn for what looked like Plagiari. This wasn't what he thought the map had said, but equally, he could easily have strayed in the wrong direction so decided to take the narrow turning. The road was pitted with large rocks that made his painful ankle twist and turn.

Eventually, he reached a small wooden sign on which the name of a village had been painted by hand. It looked like Plagiari but was very indistinct. A small dog ran from a doorway and feebly barked at him as Iant wandered towards the house. He had learned, without confidence two words, 'Yassas' and 'Kalispera' and he called them out now.

Eventually, an elderly woman emerged followed by a small girl half hiding behind the older woman's skirt.

'Kalispera.'

'British?'

Iant was startled that, out here, this woman could speak even a smattering of English. He felt foolish, but all he could think of doing was repeat Sara's name. At first, the old woman just shook her head until Iant realised that she thought he was asking if that was her name. He gestured towards the wider village, repeating 'Sara'.

The old woman looked confused but eventually counted to three on her fingers and indicated up the same side of the road. She was counting the houses he realised.

They were still on the edge of the village so it was several hundred yards until Iant reached the third house. It was small but beautifully kept with flowers growing in pots around the dusty yard. As he approached he again tentatively called Sara's name. Instead, another young woman, of a similar age to Sara appeared from around the side of the house.

'Are you looking for someone?'

'Yes, yes I am. The lady down the road sent me.'

'She knows I speak English, that's all.'

For a moment Iant's heart sank. Against all likelihood, he had begun to hope that the older woman had sent him straight to Sara.

'Do you know someone called Sara who lives in the village?'

The woman smiled knowingly.

'There is more than one Sara, but I think I can guess who

116

you mean.'

'So you know her?'

'She is my friend.'

'Can you tell me where she lives?'

'Well, I should find out who you are.'

'My name is Iant, she is...a friend of mine. Sort of a friend. She was a nurse at the hospital where I was treated.'

'Were you wounded?'

'Yes, I lost my sight.'

'She has spoken about you.'

Iant felt his cheeks redden. His delight in hearing this also reminded him of the difficult conversation with Sara that was to come.

'Does she live far away?'

'You can see her family's house from here. Does she know you are coming?'

'No...I have only recently been discharged from the hospital. It's a...surprise.'

'You will need to speak to her father first, of course.'

'Yes...of course.'

'Well then...it is the last house that you can see from here. On the left. Its door is painted blue.'

'Thank you, thank you very much.'

'Good luck...Iannis.'

Iant smiled at the memory of how Sara had translated his name and headed for the house with the blue door.

In those few hundred yards, Iant struggled to get his thoughts into order. He could hardly contain his pleasure that Sara had spoken of him to her friend, but that made the idea of telling her that he was being sent home even worse. He had no experience to prepare him for this kind of moment. Fleetingly, he even thought of turning around and just disappearing back into the sea of armed men that would soon leave Sara's country behind. That was beyond him though. He could not stand the thought of not seeing her again.

As he approached the house a grey-haired man was watering

tomatoes outside. He stood and watched Iant approach the house.

'Kalispera.'

'English?'

'Yes.'

'I speak a little.'

'My name is Iant.'

'Hello.'

'I am a British soldier.'

'I see that.'

'Yes. Sorry.'

'I wondered if I could speak with your daughter?'

At this moment a woman appeared at the door and spoke in Greek to the man.

'My wife. She asks who you are.'

'Is your daughter at home?'

'I am Andreas.'

The man held out his hand and Iant shook it. He was relieved that his greeting was not hostile at least.

'This is my wife Maria. She does not speak much English.'

Iant offered his hand and the woman smiled slightly and took it.

'You look for Sara?'

'Yes.'

'Does she know you are here?'

'No...no...I don't think so.'

'You look tired. Will you have something to drink?'

Andreas motioned towards some chairs in front of the house. The sun's strength was much less now but they were still positioned in the shade. Andreas spoke to his wife and she went into the house.

'You know my daughter at the hospital?'

'Yes, yes I do.'

'She is your nurse?'

'She was. I have recovered now.'

'What was wrong with you.'

118

'I was blinded. By the gas.'

Andreas winced and looked up at the sky.

'It is barbarism. That is the right word no?'

'Yes, it is.'

'But now you can see yes?'

'Yes. My eyes are still recovering, but I can see.'

Maria emerged carrying a tray with water and a cloudy liquid in two glasses. There was also some bread and some cheese. Andreas indicated that he should eat and drink and he took one of the cloudy glasses and drained it. Iant sipped the water, but it was clear what he was meant to do. Draining the glass, he congratulated himself on not spluttering though the strong spirit burnt his throat.

There was a long silence and Iant felt Andreas's eyes upon him. He desperately wanted to ask again if Sara was here but instinctively knew he must be patient. He wasn't sure whether Andreas knew enough English to ask him questions, but the silence was unbearable. In the end, he couldn't stand it any longer.

'I am very grateful to your daughter, Andreas. She was very patient with me when I couldn't see.'

'Yes. She is a nurse. She must be patient.'

'Not all of them are patient.'

'They are not nurses.'

'No.'

Behind him, he heard a noise and turning he saw Sara coming up the short path from the road. When she saw Iant the shock on her face made him smile involuntarily.

'Sara, your friend is here.'

'Iannis?'

'I'm sorry…I just needed to see you.'

Sara smiled and he realised that he had implied more than he meant.

'You will stay to eat with us.'

It was not a question but Iant nodded and thanked Andreas. He got up and went inside and Iant could hear slightly raised voices.

'I didn't want to make any trouble.'

'It's alright. My mother is just telling him off because she hasn't got special things to make dinner. She will calm down in a moment, you'll see.'

'I need to talk to you.'

'You are talking to me.'

'No, I mean I need to talk to you about something important.'

Sara looked at him with a look of alarm that went straight through him.

'Please. Don't worry. Could we just walk a little way?'

'I can say that I will show you the village. But we mustn't be long.'

Sara went to the kitchen and Iant could tell that it was not a straightforward conversation. Eventually, she returned and they began to walk down the dusty road. They quickly left the village behind, passing the white-painted church, the only building of any size. Sara pointed to houses where some of her relatives lived and Iant showed as much interest as he could.

The road meandered uphill for a few hundred yards and they reached a viewpoint. There was a view back over the city, with a glimpse of the sea in the other direction. From here Salonika looked beautiful, despite everything that had happened to it in recent times. There was a rough seat under a tree and they sat chatting aimlessly for a few minutes.

'Did you walk all this way to look at the view?'

Iant was taken aback both by Sara's directness and the note of annoyance in her voice. All the tension that they had both been feeling came to the surface. Iant knew that he could not put off saying what he had come to say any longer.

'I have something to tell you.'

'You are leaving?'

'Who told you this?'

'No-one told me.'

'Then how did you know?'

'I am not stupid Iannis. How long do you think they would have left you to lie in the hospital once you could see?'

'Yes. I suppose so.'

'Are you going back to the ridge? There is talk in the city of another offensive.'

'No. I am not going back to the ridge.'

Sara took his hand and smiled for the first time since they left the house. He couldn't help being glad that she was relieved that he wasn't being sent to the line.

'Where are you being sent?'

'Home. They are sending me home.' Iant blurted out.

There was silence between them again. In the distance, Iant noticed for the first time the sound of a hundred small bells from a herd of goats being driven across the hillside.

'That is wonderful news.'

Iant understood that Sara's natural lack of selfishness forced the words from her mouth. For a moment, the misery of what he had been feeling fell away and he held her face in his hand and kissed her. He pulled away and their eyes met properly for the first time since he arrived at her home.

'No. No, it is not.'

'You will be safe. And you will see your family. Your home.'

'But I have just begun to know you.'

Sara now turned away. The implications of what he said were too much for her. He took her hand in his and she turned back to him.

'There is nothing to be done. You are lucky to be going home. So many will envy you.'

'I know, I know, but why must it be now when I've met you.'

'When will you go?'

'I don't know. It might not be for a while. The army moves slowly. Though it would be just my luck if this time it decided to be faster.'

A wry smile passed his face and the tension between them lessened slightly. After another silence, Sara spoke.

'Then we must make the most of the time we have.'

'Yes.'

'And not waste it on being miserable.'

Though he could not quite share it yet Iant was buoyed by her positive tone.

'Now you are not in the hospital, why should we not do things together. As much as we want to.'

'Yes, you're right.'

'And my father has already seen that you are a respectable man!.'

'I'm not sure that he has decided that yet.'

'He will come round. He will like it that you came and found our house.'

'Will he?'

'Can you stay and have dinner?'

'Are you sure that they want me to do that?'

'If you don't there will be trouble!.'

'Then I better had, though I must leave time to hobble back before it is too dark or I will never find my way.'

'My father saw that you were having trouble with your leg. He will insist that you ride back on the cart. That is if you do not mind arriving in the city that way!.'

'Anything not to walk too far.'

'Right. That is settled. We should go back now.'

This time when their gaze met it was less painful and Sara leant across and kissed him, gently but with an intensity that overwhelmed Iant. Though there was no sign of anybody about, Sara was conscious suddenly that they were sitting in such a public place and after a moment pulled away. She took Iant's hand and pulled him to his feet. Despite the sadness of his news, they walked hand in hand back down the road happier than when they had walked up it, just a few moments before. They were certain now what they felt for each other.

Chapter 16

Two days after his visit to Sara's home, Iant walked towards the hospital where he had lain for so many weeks. Even though the building contained painful memories Iant found himself infuriated that his ankle would not let him walk faster. He had arranged to meet Sara when she finished her work for the day and his desire to see her again was overwhelming

As he turned the final corner he saw that she was already waiting for him in the doorway. He was both elated at seeing her but disappointed that he had not arrived first. He had found it difficult to adjust to how much his ankle slowed him down.

Most of the awkwardness between them had gone now and Sara gently pulled him into the doorway as they embraced. As it had been in the village, her kiss was open and frank and Iant felt himself responding in a way that was new to him.

'We should walk a little. People will be coming from the hospital.'

They walked arm in arm now, unconcerned that they should be seen together. Sara had brought a small picnic and they eventually came to the edge of the area around the Church of the Rotunda. Much of it had become neglected and damaged in the earthquake, but this meant that fewer people visited now and there were numerous nooks and crannies where two people could feel alone. Sara told him that some of the buildings had stood since before Christ. Though Iant tried to take an interest, all he could think of was Sara in his arms.

Deep into one of the ruins they stopped and spread the rug that Iant had carried with him. They were hidden behind a large wall and would hear anyone approaching. Sara sat down and beckoned Iant to sit beside her. She kissed him gently and Iant found himself able to respond again easily.

For what seemed like hours they lay facing each other with their lips and hands touching each other's faces. They stared at each other without embarrassment and smiled the involuntary smiles of the genuinely content. They lay in the shade with the late evening sun warming the crumbling ancient stones and Iant thought he could never imagine being happier than this.

Sara and Iant ate the fruit and cheese that she had brought and drank from a flask of still-cold water. They lay again on the blanket and looked again at each other with a kind of desperate wonder until the light had almost faded.

'You can't go home on your own, it's nearly dark already.'

'You forget, Iannis, that I did this many times while you were lying in bed!.'

'But I didn't know then.'

'Well, you must get used to it I think.'

They gathered up their belongings and got slowly to their feet. Iant's ankle stiffened badly when he did not use it and he hobbled painfully to the path where they would go in opposite directions. As they embraced again they arranged to meet in two days' time.

'Could you arrange to be free for the whole day?'

'I think I could. Now I am going to be sent home I seem to get less to do.'

'I was thinking that we might make a trip together.'

'I would like that so much, but....'

'Don't worry about your ankle, I will borrow my father's cart and the donkey. I'll tell him that I need to carry supplies for the hospital. He is so pro-British that he won't ask questions. I can be free on Saturday.'

'Shall I bring something?'

'Whatever you can find to eat and drink. I will try too. It's not so easy at the hospital at the moment though.'

They kissed one more time and Sara disappeared into the darkness.

He worried about her walking alone in the darkness and longed to be able to look after her. He also saw how capable she was. In reality, she was more likely to be taking care of him. His ankle was now giving him real pain and he set off in the direction of the camp, frustrated and lonely.

The following days were again marked by boredom and an irritation with the grind of camp life that threatened to drive Iant to the point of madness. After the euphoria of his visit to Sara's village had subsided, the realisation that they might soon never see each other again threatened to overwhelm him. Iant even began to consider telling her that he thought it best that they didn't see each other again, so painful were his feelings. He almost longed for it to end.

He simply could not face the kind of scene that would have ensued had he travelled again to her village and, besides, his ankle felt as though it wouldn't stand up to the walk. He decided to meet her at the time arranged and even mustered enough enthusiasm to scrounge bits of food. He had money too and managed to buy wine from a local shop, something he had barely tasted before, but he thought it seemed appropriate.

Iant walked less than half a mile to the junction of the main camp road with a dusty track that led towards the gentler hills to the east. As he looked to his left he could see the formidable mountains still occupied by the Bulgars and it felt incredible that less than two months had passed since he had nearly lost his life somewhere up there.

Sara was already waiting with the little cart and her easy smile was an instant antidote to Iant's obsessive gloom. She was, he understood in a moment, impossible to resist. The idea that he had contemplated not coming today, or telling her that they may as well stop seeing each other now, seemed suddenly ridiculous.

'Come on. Climb up!.'

'Where are we going?'

'It's a surprise. Have you brought food?'

'Yes. A little. And wine. Do you like wine?'

'Of course I like wine. I am a Greek girl.'

Iant struggled to get on to the cart and they both laughed at the spectacle they made as they bumped down the track. It was better than walking, but the holes seemed to get bigger, and the way ahead was difficult to see.

'How much further?'

'Not far. Are you uncomfortable?'

'No...no not really.'

'I should hope not. This is the luxury carriage all prepared for the war hero!.'

He enjoyed her poking gentle fun at him. She made him relax and stop thinking about the future so much. A little further on Sara manoeuvred the cart and the donkey off the side of the track and into a field of olive trees. She tied the donkey up and gave it water that she had brought with her.

'Now we have to walk, but not far. Do you want me to carry that?'

'No, I can manage.'

Sara walked ahead and then scrambled up a small slope at the far end of the field. As Iant reached the top he was amazed to see quite a large pool of clear blue water the other side of the slope. At the end of it was a newly built wall of rough stones.

'What is this?'

'The French soldiers built it.'

'What is it for?'

'Swimming of course!.'

Iant laughed out loud. In the middle of a war, someone had found time to make a swimming pool. It felt like something hopeful, but also ridiculous.

They found a shaded spot overlooking the pool and Sara organised the bags and the precious bottle of wine so that they would stay cool. They sat for a while in this unlikely spot, just enjoying the spectacle until Sara suddenly got to her feet.

'So, are we going to swim?'

'Really?'

'You don't think that we have come all this way just to bake in the sun?'

Iant was not confident of his ability as a swimmer. He had learned by trial and error in Bala lake along with several other boys from the village, but there had been few opportunities to practice. However, the pool didn't look very deep and Sara was very insistent.

126

He suddenly became very self-conscious as he realised that they would have to negotiate the awkward business of changing or removing their clothes in some way. Fortunately, Sara took the initiative and he understood that this was one of the many things that were drawing him closer to her by the moment.

'You go behind that tree and don't look until I tell you!.'

Silently he obeyed and then began to wonder how much of his own clothing he should remove when the time came. Life seemed suddenly fraught with all kinds of dilemmas that he had not faced before. He heard a splash and Sara called out that he could come and join her. He stripped off all his clothes except his long underwear and looked anxiously out from behind the tree. Sara was submerged up to her neck and turned away from him.

'Come on. It is so lovely and cool!.'

Iant decided that it was better to get it all over at once. He ran across the stony ground, trying to ignore the sharp stones and took a leap towards the centre of the pool as far away from Sara as he could manage. To his relief, he found he could stand and his swimming ability would not be too heavily tested. The water felt wonderful and he instinctively lay on his back and floated.

Sara swam up beside him and kissed his outstretched hand.

'See. Its lovely isn't it?'

He returned to his feet and moved towards her through the water. Their embrace in the cool water was a moment that Iant would always remember, even before he realised that Sara had removed all her clothes before entering the water. He tried not to look startled, but his face betrayed him.

'Do you think I am immodest?'

'No…no…I was just surprised for a moment.'

Their hands explored each other gently for a long time until eventually they climbed from the pool and made love on the rug beneath the tree. They were both too preoccupied to consider if anyone else might find this place or whether they had embarked on something that might one day bring them unhappiness.

127

Instead, they relaxed into the moments that were, just as they were for most people before them, far from perfect, and yet enough to make them want to stay in this spot until they grew old.

As the sun began to go down they finally ate the food and drink that they had brought. The peaches had softened in the sun and the bread and salty ham made them forget how warm the wine had become.

They started to dress, but Iant pulled Sara down next to him and wrapped his arms around her. It felt slower and gentler the second time. For a long while, they became reluctant to move, even though the warmth had begun to go out of the day. In the end, Sara reluctantly pulled herself to her feet. It was already later than the time she had promised to return with the cart.

On the short journey back, they travelled mostly in silence. Though facing away from Sara, Iant rested his head between her shoulder blades as she drove the old animal slowly back down the winding track and eventually on to the dirt road.

Before Iant got out they kissed for a long time until Sara's anxiety about her father's questions got the better of her.

Chapter 17

For the next month, they saw each other more and more frequently. Iant found it hard to be parted from Sara and every day he looked anxiously at the board near the entrance to the camp where advance warning of postings was placed.

Nearly six weeks after he had first told Sara that he was to be sent home Iant received notice that he would be leaving on the hospital ship RMS Olympic. The date was only a week away and he was overwhelmed with despair. Iant had lost grandparents and seen his close friend Oliver die out here, but that did not compare to what he felt at this moment.

Later that afternoon Iant slipped away and walked into what remained of the centre of Salonika. He needed to be by himself and to try to clear his head before he had to face Sara. He knew that she would be the sensible one, the one that would be able to stay calm and see their little tragedy for what it was. Part of him hated that. He wanted her to despair as he did.

As he walked the narrow alleys and city streets Iant turned his situation over and over in his head. He had only known Sara for such a short time, but he felt that she had changed him, and he could not see how he could go back. When he was with her he felt as though his life held out so many possibilities. He hated the idea that he would once again retreat into his more former self. Since the day they spent by the dammed river, Iant had retained the feel of Sara's skin on his fingertips, and he never wanted to lose it. As he thought of this, wandering through one of dozens of tiny bazaars, it threatened to overwhelm him and he staggered a little on his injured leg.

At first, the idea that came to him seemed foolish and he cursed himself for his stupidity, but as he walked on he felt more and more that he must do something, or he would go mad. By the time he had turned to retrace his steps, his plan had begun to take shape. Despite its implications, this new idea had already made him feel lighter and he hurried back to the camp to prepare for that evening.

As he walked towards their usual meeting place Iant's courage began to fail him, but when he saw Sara standing in the doorway his resolve returned. How could it be otherwise he asked himself? They embraced and kissed and immediately began to walk towards the outskirts of the town. Iant had a blanket in his backpack and the plan for the evening was clear to both of them without anyone saying a word.

As they spread out the groundsheet first, then the softer blanket that Iant had taken from the stores, Iant spoke.

'I have an idea.'

'I know, that is why you brought the blanket' Sara teased.

'Not that.'

'Ah. So we are to do something different?'

'No. I mean I have something to say first.'

'Iannis?'

'I have a date when I am to be sent home.'

There was a silence between them but Iant was determined to press on before the new mood could settle. He fumbled in his pocket and produced the tiny ring that he had bought in the bazaar that afternoon. It was not a ring that he would have found in Hardy's the jewellers in Corwen, but it was pretty nevertheless, and his feelings were as true as anyone who had ever saved for a diamond solitaire.

'I think we should be married.'

'What?'

'I think that you heard me. Look I have a little ring. It's nothing, but perhaps for now....'

'But when are you to leave?'

'In six days' time.'

'Six days? Iannis....'

'These things can be arranged surely. In wartime people are understanding.'

'Iannis....'

'Please tell me that you agree with me. I can't leave without this happening. You can follow me later.'

130

'It is such a short time. And my family....'

'I'll come with you to your family. I'll come tonight if you want me to.'

'Iannis they don't even know that I see you. Though I think my father suspects.'

'Well, he won't be quite so surprised then.'

She laughed, almost against her will. Iant could see that he had allowed his desperation to overwhelm him and now he was going to frighten Sara away.

'I am sorry Sara. When I saw that I was leaving, I...please don't be scared.'

'I am not scared Iannis. I promise you.'

'Then you will marry me?'

'Yes, Iannis...but we cannot marry in six days. I could not do that to my family.'

'But we only have six days.'

'Iannis we have the rest of our lives. I will take your ring and the rest will happen.'

For a few moments, Iant was crestfallen. He had relied on his plan to rescue him from the despair of being sent home and nothing else could replace this grand gesture. He had already imagined scandalising his own family by telling them that he had married a beautiful Greek girl.

Then it dawned on him that Sara had actually said yes. They would be married. This girl who had changed his life in such a short time was agreeing to be his wife and the force of this brought Iant to his senses.

Sara had her back to him now. She had wisely left him to his silence. Iant came up behind her and took her in his arms.

'You are right. I was being stupid. We do have the whole of our lives don't we?'

'Yes, Iannis.'

'Then take this ring and wear it until I can get a proper one.'

He slipped the trinket on to her finger. It didn't fit well, but Sara said that her father could easily make it smaller.

'Should I speak to him?'

'Not yet.'

'When?'

'Perhaps you should write to him when you are home.'

'Shouldn't I ask his permission while I am still here?'

'It would be too rushed. Please. Trust me.'

Iant felt unable to push any further. The speed at which events were overtaking them and his own panic had carried him this far and now he realised that he needed to just spend peaceful time with Sara.

They had only been able to make love a handful of times, but they had begun to feel at ease with each other. Each removed the other's clothes and revelled in how that felt before the full force of their passion overtook them. Afterwards, as they lay on their makeshift bed neither felt compelled to talk about what was to come, but instead, they spoke of what was around them and what they felt for each other.

One week later, inevitably, the calm was shattered as Iant faced the morning of his departure. He and Sara had spent every conceivable moment together since the evening of his proposal. They were to meet one last time just before Iant had to report to his ship. He had slept very little but he hoped that he could face what was to come that day. He very much wanted to leave Sara with the best of memories of him. He had to be strong and consider her too.

When he saw her once more, already waiting for him, he tried to stiffen his resolve. She had to work that day and so was wearing the uniform in which he had first seen her. He was glad. It was the way that he wanted to remember her in the long time ahead of them.

They planned to walk together down to the port. It was not clear what time the hospital ship would actually sail, but if possible Sara was to stand and wave as it left the harbour. Even if Iant could not see her, they had arranged a place where she would stand and he could at least imagine her there. He would wave from the ship's deck using a small scarf that she had given him.

'I have something for you Iannis.'

She gave him a small parcel of white paper which he unfolded and inside was a very simple gold band with one single green gemstone attached.

'It is not valuable. I mean it is not worth a lot of money. It belonged to my grandmother.'

'But I can't take that.'

'I am giving it to you so you know what you mean to me. Keep it safe and I will wear it when I see you again.'

'Are you sure you want me to take it?'

'Yes, but if you lose it I will kill you!.'

Iant was so grateful for her flash of humour. He parcelled up the tiny ring and put it in his breast pocket.

'Thank you.'

'Just keep it safe. And don't try to wear it, it's too small!.'

They walked, mainly in silence, the rest of the way down to the port. Eventually, they could see in the near distance a queue of variously wounded men winding its way across the quayside. The line of soldiers ended at a guard point where they were checked and counted before going on board the immense liner.

'It is a very big ship.'

'Before the war, it was built for pleasure. To take people to America.'

'You will be travelling in great luxury perhaps Iannis.'

'Yes, I expect that it will be cocktails before dinner each night.'

'Drink one for me.'

'I will. Every night.'

'Goodbye Iannis.'

They kissed and embraced and then before he could protest, Sara was gone, around a corner and out of his sight. He briefly considered following. He wasn't ready yet. But he knew that she was right. Not for the first time he was reminded who was the practical one and who would make good decisions in difficult times.

Once onboard ship Iant was bombarded with so many

133

practical necessities that he had no time to dwell on leaving Sara behind. The ship was enormous and just finding his allotted berth was a task in itself. When they set sail Iant could not even get around to the right side of the ship, let alone wave the little scarf. He wondered if Sara had found the place to stand that they had planned.

Wandering around the giant floating hospital Iant felt lucky that he was so mobile bit also angry again at the irony that he was being sent home against his will when he felt relatively well. His ankle did prevent him moving freely, but compared to some of the sad cases being carried on board he was a fit man.

Because of his state of health Iant was enlisted to help load light supplies. He carried boxes of medicines and dressings to the various wards and operating theatres below deck. For the first time in weeks, he saw men who were badly wounded and in pain. Many had already lost limbs or were in imminent danger of doing so. He found parts of the enormous vessel that many would never see, including a series of padded cells prepared for those who had been committed as insane. The terrible noises that came from this area disturbed Iant far more than the sight of other men's physical injuries.

By the time they set sail Iant was exhausted and night was falling. Those men who could move freely were fed in a large dining room and given whisky after their meal making Iant long to lie down and sleep. With difficulty, he found his way down the maze of passageways and into his tiny berth. He was asleep in seconds, fully clothed.

When he awoke some hours later it was still dark. He could feel the movement of the ship but the Aegean beneath them was relatively calm. His mind immediately returned to the sight of Sara moving away from him on the quay.

They had promised to write at every opportunity and when it was possible to travel he would return to Salonika and marry her. Beyond that, they had made very few practical plans. They had shared an unspoken wish not to break the spell of the present by talking of the difficulties of the future. Iant felt in his tunic pocket and pulling out the tiny ring with the green stone stared at it for a while, as he drifted once more into sleep. Then he slipped the ring back into his pocket for fear that he would lose it among the labyrinth of beds and equipment that covered every inch of the giant ship.

Part 2

Chapter 18

In the three months since he returned home Iant's old life had somehow reasserted itself. He could not quite account for it, but each day there were the same daily rhythms and routines. The familiar surliness of his mother, the snippets of gossip leapt on so eagerly by his sisters, the weariness of his father worn down by decades of winters on the hillsides.

Iant too felt a growing pessimism. He was not yet fit enough to return to the quarry in Ffestiniog and the army was still paying him enough to contribute to the household. The army doctor who discharged him decided that he didn't need an operation after all. It would do little to improve things. In all likelihood, he would always have a slight limp, though it would probably improve over time. Iant felt something of a fraud, but there was little he could do about it.

This made him feel even more honour-bound to help his father with the animals left on the farm. He also helped his mother with the garden and the vegetables that she bottled, pickled and eked out through the year. The hours that both his parents kept were exhausting, dictated not so much by the amount of time that was needed and more by the puritanical sense that from dawn to dusk they should be seen to work. Both Iant's sisters now had full-time jobs, which, though no-one admitted it, were necessary for them all to survive. The little smallholding had long since ceased to be enough.

With his sisters gone for most of the day, the mood around the house and its surroundings was oppressive. Iant took to walking down to Carrog station to meet them off the train just to shorten the days. This was also a time in which he could think about Sara without interruption. He wanted to imagine a future life together and to just think again about them both lying on a blanket in the sunshine. He had the night-time, but lying awake on the uncomfortable straw mattress under the eaves he could only think of difficulties. On a good day, when the sun shone especially, he could allow his mind to wander back to that harsh baked landscape. Above all, he thought of the pool built by Frenchmen in which they had swum together.

Since he had returned Iant had received only two letters from Sara. He knew that intense fighting was once again taking place in the hills above Salonika. This meant that it was unlikely that much mail could get through. That made it even worse, thinking of her in her clean white uniform attending on the handsome wounded. The soldiers of his imagination were always handsome and their wounds both slight and not visible. Iant despised himself for such thoughts, but he failed to suppress them. He thought, with a smile, of Johnny, still in the same bed laughing at him for his boyish jealousy, though of course he knew that in reality, he had probably been patched up by now and sent back to Pip Ridge, or worse was already lying near Oliver in the cemetery on Lembet Road.

From Sara's second letter he also discovered that his letters were not getting through. She had gently chided him for not writing to her, though even in print he felt her irresistible warmth.

Iant had so far told no-one at home that Sara existed, let alone that they were engaged. He wasn't sure why he kept it a secret. He knew that his parents especially would find it hard to comprehend the idea of marrying someone from so far away, but this was not the explanation. In fact, sometimes he was tempted to blurt it out just to break the mood of oppressive melancholy that pervaded the house. But he didn't because he didn't want to break the spell. While only he knew, he was able to keep the idea of a life with Sara safe and well, free from the invasion of practical objections.

Her letters were easily explained as they arrived in the anonymised military form that meant they could have come from any of the old pals that he described to his family. The idea of a Greek girl writing to him seemed such an impossible idea back here, surrounded by the wind and the rain and the Berwyns. Each day Iant could warm himself on his secret, though later in the

140

darkness it would also haunt and distress him.

Iant had few friends in the area. It was rare to meet people casually, living as they did so far outside the village. Before he joined up, he had enjoyed an odd evening in *The Grouse* so when Gwennie's young man visited one Saturday he asked if he would like to walk down the lane for a pint. Gwennie was torn between the pleasure of her brother getting to know her Ben and annoyance at him being stolen away. She knew better than to ask to go with them. Apart from the barmaids, it was rare to find a young unmarried woman in a public house, even after the war broke out.

In truth, Iant did not have much interest in Ben. He seemed likeable enough but still very young in nature even though he was only a year or so younger than Iant. As they made their way down the lane they talked mainly about football, the weather and the factory where Ben worked. The tension between those who had served overseas and those who had not prohibited talk of the war and Iant was glad of it. He was not especially pained by his experiences, but equally, he had no desire to talk with a comparative stranger about the place where Sara remained.

The Grouse was full and Iant was greeted by some acquaintances of his father and one or two of his class from the village school. He introduced Ben, though it was not a place for excessive small talk. Iant was pleased to find that Frances was still in her place behind the bar. She was not someone that he had thought of much during his long absence, but she was always friendly to him and her presence softened his mood somewhat.

'I was wondering when we might see you.'

'Oh, I've been in once or twice since I got back.'

'Not while I've been here.'

'No.'

'Hello, Ben.'

Iant was mildly taken aback by their familiarity and this must have registered on his face because Frances felt obliged to explain that she had met Ben and Gwennie in Wrexham more than once. Iant could not help notice Ben's red face.

'Are you back for good' asked Frances

'Well, for now.'

'They not sending you out again?'

'No. It'll be over before the end of the year anyway.'

'They said that last time mind.'

'That's true. Anyhow, what do we have to do get a pint?'

Frances pulled two pints and told them that the first one was on the house for the 'returning hero'. Iant felt self-conscious now and thought briefly of making an excuse to leave, but after his second pint, he relaxed and began to find Ben easier company. At least he was away from the gloom at home and Ben was happy to do most of the talking. Iant understood for the first time that Ben saw his future with Gwennie and he wanted to be on good terms with his future brother-in-law.

When Ben went outside to the lavatory Iant saw Frances notice he was on his own and she came over to his table.

'He's a nice boy isn't he?'

'Yes, I suppose he is.'

'Gwennie's happy with him.'

'You seem to know a lot about him.'

'Why do you say that, Iant. I hardly know him.'

'Just what I see.'

She smiled now

'You jealous or something?'

Iant felt himself go crimson. He took a drink to cover his embarrassment.

'I'm sorry Iant. I'm just teasing you. You are much more serious than you used to be.'

'Yes, well....'

'I'm sorry. I shouldn't have said that either. After what you've been through.'

'I haven't been through much. Not compared to some at least. I'm lucky to be home.'

'Would you like to walk with me? She said suddenly. 'After chapel tomorrow.'

Iant rarely went to chapel now, much to the disappointment

of his mother and father. He made the excuse that it was a long way to walk on his ankle, though he rarely complained about it much otherwise. He didn't know how to reply. He thought instantly of Sara of course and what she might think.

'Yes, alright. I'll meet you at the top of the village.'

Iant knew she would realise that he didn't want to be seen meeting her when everyone was coming from chapel, but he couldn't do anything about that. She could take it or leave it.

'Just after twelve?'

'Yes. Alright.'

By now Ben was back at the table and asking if he wanted another pint, but Iant wanted to leave. On the way home, Ben attempted a joke about Frances, but Iant's silence was enough to shut him up and the walk home became awkward. Iant knew that he was behaving rudely, but he could not help himself. He felt the difficulty of his life close in on him and he didn't want to speak.

Iant met Frances the next day as arranged. Somehow today he felt less anxious. What was the harm in what he was doing? After all, Sara was mixing freely with men all day, every day. In any case, he was just finding something to do that took him out of himself. Until last night he hadn't quite realised how little enjoyment there had been in his life. Surely he was entitled to walk with someone who would at least cheer him up a little.

Frances's smile as she came up the lane, very slightly late, was open and genuine. Iant felt his spirits rise as they set off over the stile and up the path towards Gwyddelwern. The climb was quite steep at first and Iant's ankle troubled him. The memory of his long walk in search of Sara's village flashed through his mind, though he quickly tried to dismiss it.

Frances talked of village gossip, much of which he had heard already from one of his sisters, but he found that he didn't mind. Frances was better at telling stories than most. He laughed out loud at her jokes and impersonations of some of the busy bodies that formed a good percentage of the population of Carrog. The job of a barmaid was not one that many of them

143

considered respectable and Frances herself was often the subject of much unfounded scrutiny.

As they reached the ridge they stopped and looked down into the valley. It was a fine day and the river Dee below them sparkled in the sunshine. They found a rocky promontory and sat for a while staring at the view. Iant had brought his army canteen full of water and they took turns drinking.

'Will you go back to the quarry?' Frances said suddenly.

'I don't know. If my ankle gets better I suppose I will.'

'It's a hard life.'

'It is.'

'Have you thought of getting away?'

Iant thought for a moment that Frances might have found out his secret, but instantly realised that this was impossible.

'Not really. This is home isn't it?'

'I would if I was a man.'

'Would you?'

'Look around you. It's pretty enough from up here. Down there they would think I was lucky if one of the ugly men that look at me in *The Grouse* took pity on me.'

'Took pity on you?'

'Had you not noticed Iant that the village is not brimming over with desirable young men?'

'I see.'

'And if it was, is that all that we are to hope for?'

Iant noticed her voice break despite herself and his heart went out to her. If Frances, who always showed such a cheerful face to the world, felt like this, the world must be full of more unhappiness than most people would admit. Before the war, Iant had wondered if he and Frances would suit each other. He admired her spirited view of the world. He was a bit in awe of it if he was honest.

'I don't know if there is more to hope for. I hope so' he replied.

'God, Iant, so do I' she said, with some bitterness.

They sat, almost in silence in the sunshine until Iant

144

suggested that they make their way back.

Chapter 19

The first signs that Iant's father was unwell were small but unmistakable. All his life Gwilym Evans had risen very early, even when there was no practical need to do so. He would shave and set water to boil so that by the time Megan had risen it would be ready for breakfast. At first, he just began to move more slowly and Megan chided him about being an old man and the water not being ready in time.

By the time the morning came, when Gwil didn't get out of bed at all, Iant could see that his mother was not completely surprised, though she was clearly shaken. She had come to his bedroom door to wake him and Iant had gone quickly to his father's bedside. He found his father alert but confused. His speech was audible but somewhat slurred. He told his mother that he would go for the doctor. Though she fussed about the cost Iant assured his mother that Dad had paid his premiums and they would cover it. Iant was by no means certain that this was the case, but he knew that his father needed more than sal volatile. This was his mother's usual answer to most ailments

Iant was back from the village in under an hour, but it was afternoon before the doctor's horse and cart drew up outside. By this time Gwil was barely conscious. The doctor had lived in the village most of his life and was still adjusting to the idea that ordinary people could afford his services. He examined Gwil in a rudimentary way and pronounced that the next twenty-four hours would be crucial. Gwil might recover completely, but he might also lose some of his physical and mental capacity. He offered to prescribe a sedative, warning that the pharmacy in Corwen charged exorbitant rates. Iant took the prescription and saw the doctor out.

The next twenty-four hours were indeed crucial. Gwil did regain consciousness and tried to utter a few words. Iant glimpsed only tiny breaks in his mother's stoicism, though she seemed to age in front of their eyes as she watched her husband struggle to stay alive. Just before midnight on the second day Iant came into the room and could see from his mother's face that she thought Gwil had given up the fight. Iant felt for a pulse in his father's neck and then his wrist. There was little doubt, but for the second time Iant took the long walk to fetch the doctor.

Gwennie and Doy were naturally the most vocal in their grief. Despite his old-fashioned manner, Gwil had found small ways to show a kind of affection to his daughters. He could be strict but tended to undermine Megan with little treats if one of them had been very severely scolded. Even though his sisters were favoured by his father, it was still something that Iant found endearing. It had helped to soften the general view that he had held about Gwil.

His mother retreated further into herself. The few people that called to sympathise were not received very warmly, though Gwennie and Doy between them tried to fuss around with tea and sometimes a little cake. Despite his feelings for his mother Iant was pained by the way that she reacted. He could find no way of helping her and she seemed to resent all attempts at sympathy.

The following days were consumed with making arrangements for the simple funeral and keeping up with the rudimentary tasks on the farm. Now that he had to pay more attention it became even clearer to Iant that it had been a long time since the little area of land had been able to sustain anybody's life on its own. His father and mother had always lived simply, but without the wages that Doy and Gwennie were earning it would have been impossible to survive.

In the days before he became ill, Gwilym had begun repairing an old stone wall that had been crumbling for years. The length of time that it would take and the futility of the task had prevented Iant from assisting, but now he was glad of the excuse to escape the house for a few hours. First, he had to transport a supply of stones up to the top of the field in a rickety old wheelbarrow, a laborious task in the late summer sunshine.

As he completed the second of what would be a number of

147

trips he paused to take breath and saw a figure in the distance approach the house, but then turn and follow the way he had come with his heavy load. When Frances got a little nearer she half waved to him and he walked to meet her across the field.

'I wanted to give you my condolences Iant. I am so sorry to hear about Gwil.'

'Thank you.'

It had been nearly two weeks since they had sat together on the hilltop and they had not made contact since. This was not particularly unusual. Iant was not a regular in *The Grouse* and Frances had little call to venture up the lane to Iant's home. Yet both felt a slight unease between them. Frances tried to overcome it by offering an awkward embrace, but stepped back after Iant's discomfort became apparent.

'How is your mother?'

'It is hard to tell. She never shows what she is feeling.'

'Everyone has their own way I suppose.'

'Yes.'

'And your sisters?'

'They are not themselves. My Dad had a soft spot for them.'

'Yes, he did.'

'They would be glad to see you.'

Frances knew that they would not particularly welcome a visit from someone to whom they had never been close. Nevertheless, she understood that Iant wanted her to go and she took his cue to leave with a little dignity. Iant watched her walk back down the hill, ashamed again for his rudeness. He thought of running after and thanking her properly for her thoughtfulness. She was too far away now so instead he threw himself into hurling the remaining stones on the ground.

During the interlude before the funeral, the summer disappeared, as it so often did here in the shadow of Snowdonia. The thick grey clouds repeatedly massed and then deposited intense periods of rain on the Dee Valley. It was hard to get outside except to do the essential tasks such as tending to the hens. The sheep could take care of themselves and the vegetable plot looked beyond redemption.

By Thursday it had rained for three days solid and there was a little break in the clouds. Gwennie had borrowed some large umbrellas and they would ride to the village on the undertaker's cart. The tradition was that the mourners would walk from the chapel up to the little burial plot behind the cart that carried the coffin. It was something that Iant was dreading. He feared that his father's somewhat solitary nature would mean that few people would turn out and they would look a sorry bunch trailing up the village.

As they stopped outside the chapel Iant helped his mother down off the cart. Iant was surprised to see through the open doors that the place seemed to be full. The undertakers carried the coffin in first and the four of them followed with Megan holding Iant's arm. He could not help but realise that this was a rare moment when he had physical contact with his mother.

When they got inside they could see that the tiny chapel was indeed packed. Most of the village had turned out and there were many faces, even in such a small place, that Iant only dimly recognised. For the first time since his father had died, he felt close to tears. Behind him, he could hear his sisters breaking their hearts. He glanced at his mother and though she showed little outward sign of emotion he could see that she was affected by the number of people that had appeared in support.

As they sat in the pews, listening to the Minister's intonation of the simple funeral service, Iant allowed himself to think of Sara. For several days, he had forced himself not to consider how his father's death would impact them. He had even avoided writing to Sara to tell her that his father had died. Doing so meant facing the inevitable questions and dilemmas that it raised. Two days ago he had finally written to her, knowing that it would be weeks before she received the letter and much longer before he could read her reply. Iant had said little except to inform her of the news and to say how much he would have liked to see her at a time like this. He couldn't think beyond that.

His mother wore a short veil on her black hat and as he

looked across he saw that beneath it her face had collapsed. He felt the silent betrayal of thinking of Sara and compensated by putting his arm around his mother's shoulders. He knew that this would not be what she really wanted, especially in such a public place, but he felt compelled to make at least some kind of gesture. After a moment he put his arm back down by his side.

As the little procession made its way up the village Iant felt relief that so many were around them. Since his return, he hadn't really settled at all and he had felt that his experiences would never allow him to think of the village in the same way again. However, today, he understood that this place was not so easily dismissed. The idea of this being his home would not come so easily to him anymore. Despite that, today reminded Iant of something that he could not name. For the moment, he was grateful for that.

They buried his father, with the rain once again pelting down, in the little cemetery that clung to the hillside above a bend in the Dee. The last time Iant had stood at a graveside was in the baking sun and he thought of Oliver and all the comrades whose families would never get the chance to bury them.

After a week had passed since his father's funeral, Iant asked his mother if she minded if he walked to meet his sisters from the evening train. Inevitably, a kind of normality had begun to reassert itself in the house and his mother's tart reply to the effect that she didn't need him fussing over her every moment was a reminder of that.

Iant reached the station earlier than he needed to and paced the platform waiting for the Wrexham train. The little noticeboard near the entrance displayed timetables and various rules and regulations that no-one had looked at since the day they were put up. More recently someone had placed a poster over the top of these with the Great Western Railway Crest at the top, advertising for new guards and signalmen. An address was provided for men to apply in writing.

Iant had decided during the course of the last week that he needed to find at least some paid employment, whatever the

150

future held. He could not depend on his sisters being in work forever and his mother needed providing for. He had no idea if or when his injury would heal sufficiently for him to resume work at Ffestiniog, or indeed if they would automatically have him back. When the war ended the country would be full of men needing work. He took down the poster and folded it into his jacket pocket. At that moment the train pulled in and he waved his hand in greeting to his two sisters who were, at least, always pleased to see him.

That night Iant sat in the dim light at his mother's kitchen table and wrote a brief letter applying for a post as a signalman on the Great Western Railway. He thought that he might be disqualified as a guard if they found about his injury. The details he had to put in his letter brought back the battle on Pip Ridge and the loss of his sight. Iant had not dwelt on the details very much. He was grateful that he did not suffer from the terrors that he heard about from others. Despite this, the sheer physical discomfort of being on the mountain in the heat and sleeping on hard rock returned to him. The kitchen of his home had begun to feel cool in the evening as autumn approached, but Iant's memories of the Greek sun beating down on him and his comrades made him momentarily grateful for the breeze that blew down the valley.

Chapter 20

Sara's letter was the first that he had received for several weeks. It was clear from what she wrote that she had not received his news about his father. Iant cursed again the difficulty of maintaining contact with her, at least in any way that reflected what he felt for her. Her letter was full of the increased causalities at the hospital, though some ham-fisted censor had rendered any detail meaningless. She talked about the heat shrivelling her father's plants, her mother's numerous ailments and a marriage that had taken place in the village. She looked forward to the day of their own wedding and how they would make a feast that everyone would come to and dance until the next morning.

Perhaps for the first time, Iant really allowed himself to think about the impossibility of their situation. First, the war had to end, though the limited news in the Post had begun to take a more optimistic turn. Then there was the sheer physical difficulty of travelling. When he had journeyed to Greece as a soldier Iant had never thought about how it was done. He had simply been herded on to buses and trains and boats, as unthinking as any of the donkeys that travelled with them.

Perhaps he could enlist in the Merchant Navy he thought, before imagining the response that he would get if he asked if he could be transported specifically to Salonika. He knew enough that the nearest place from which large boats sailed before the war was Liverpool. Many families in the village had seen sons and brothers emigrate to Canada. Perhaps there would be a boat to Salonika from there. He could pack a bag, get a train to Wrexham and from there to Liverpool. Perhaps he wouldn't even tell anyone until he got there. Perhaps that would be the kindest thing to do.

His mother was dozing in the chair by the fireplace. It wasn't cold enough to light a fire in the grate, but this was where she felt most comfortable. The shirt of his that she was mending had slipped on to the floor and she snored gently. Since his father's death, she had changed little, except to withdraw even further into herself. Despite this Iant could not help but understand how dependent she was, and would increasingly become, on him.

He had heard from the railway company. He was to report for training at the Great Western Railway depot in Wrexham and he had to make an early start the following morning. He would have to catch the milk train at six o'clock and he was anxious that he would sleep through the old tin alarm clock on the chair beside his bed. His mother had surprised him by offering to rise early and make his breakfast, but he had told her there was no need.

The next morning as he rose and dressed quickly he heard noises downstairs. When he entered the kitchen his mother had made a pot of tea and put out bread and butter. There was a small parcel containing his lunch.

'I said there was no need Mam.'

'You would be off with no breakfast inside you knowing you.'

'Thanks, Mam.'

'Can't have you fainting and losing the job before you start.'

Iant ate hurriedly and in silence as his mother busied herself with a succession of jobs that could all have waited. He surprised her by giving her a peck on the cheek and he set off down the lane in the semi-darkness towards the station.

Because of his army training, Iant had been allowed to escape the time at the signalling college in Reading that trained men from across the country. Instead, he was to report to the station at Wrexham every day for a month to be trained 'on the job' and then, after that, he would be sent to work alongside an experienced man at one of the village stations until he was passed fit to have his own signal box.

Iant had visited the signal box in Carrog and asked to look around before he went for his interview. John Hughes the signalman had known his father and he promised to put in a good word for him. He liked the idea of working on his own in a cosy signal box. Mr Hughes had a little gas ring and a kettle for

153

his tea and a paraffin stove which made it warm and welcoming. He had even brought a bit of old carpet from home to give it a comfortable feel

When he got to Wrexham Iant was assigned to Ivor Griffiths a kindly middle-aged man who continually puffed and panted because of his weight. Iant wondered if an inactive life sitting in a signal box would send him the same way, but then he noticed how much Ivor ate and drank in a single day. His sedentary life was only the half of it.

The month in Wrexham passed quickly. It created in Iant a sense of this job's responsibility. Through the complicated maze of bells, whistles and semaphore he had to make sure that trains did not run into each other at high speed, especially whilst carrying children, babies, mothers and people innocently going about their business. Iant felt a sense of pride that he would be doing something useful and at the same time providing for his mother. Whilst it did not make him forget the journey he needed to make to be back with Sara, it filled some of the time and made him feel less guilty.

Ivor talked frequently about his own life. It seemed to Iant that he was content with his lot and had grown almost to love the railways. He complained a little about having been uprooted every so often, but once he had become a station master he had been given a house to live in and he was looking forward to retirement on his railway pension. What Iant liked most about Ivor was his good humour. Having grown up in a household that had been defined by a grim determination to survive, Ivor's gentle teasing and bad jokes came as a relief.

Iant's first job was to be at the little signal box that served the station at Llandrillo. The box itself was just outside the village on the road to Cnywyd. Iant was relieved to find out that he was not to be sent further away and he suspected that Ivor, knowing about his recently widowed mother, had put in a kindly word with those responsible for the postings. When he found out where he was to go Iant tried out the route on the ancient bicycle that had always hung about the farm. It was quite arduous, with several hilly stretches, but Iant thought he could make it in under an hour. His day would start at seven o'clock so this meant leaving his home no later than six, which he felt he could manage. He felt his ankle much less on a bike than he did walking.

On the first of November 1918, Iant set off in the dark for his first day of work as a signalman. He had invested in a dynamo and a pair of lights so that he could see the way but found that on the steeper hills the power he generated was barely enough to keep any light going at all. He also carried a puncture kit though he realised that his chances of mending a tyre in the dark of a winter morning were very small indeed.

Iant arrived early at the signal box and had to wait in the cold for the experienced signalman to arrive and unlock the door. After a few minutes, he saw a tall figure emerge from the gloom rattling keys. He shook hands warmly with Iant and introduced himself as Alun Lewis. Iant's first priority was to get the kettle on apparently and he was relieved to see that supplies were already in place. Alun told him that the first week's tea was on him, but after that, they had to go halves. He would bring the fresh milk for now as he didn't have far to go.

The first train was not due until seven-thirty so they had time to brew the tea and warm-up before the signalling system cranked into life. The box at Llandrillo was primitive compared to the one at Wrexham and even the one kept so well by Mr Hughes at Carrog, but it had all that was needed to serve the little line on the way down to Bala. Soon Iant was pulling levers and activating bells as Alun looked on, occasionally offering a word or two of advice as to the order of priority that Iant should follow.

Alun Lewis turned out to be distantly related to Iant on his father's side. Although this was not so surprising in this sparsely populated corner of the world, it helped to break the ice between them and Iant was soon at ease with someone who would be his constant companion for the next four weeks. After that, Alun was moving to Llangollen where he would have a slightly more responsible job and a pay rise that would help with his growing family. He already had two boys and a third child was on the way. They would be able to rent a slightly bigger cottage in the village of Acrefair, Alun said, and his wife was now looking forward to the move. 'After worrying herself to death', as he put it.

While he was adjusting to this new way of life, Iant's understanding of what was happening to the progress of the war had receded. He had a general sense, as had most people, that a surrender was probably coming. However, there was also a feeling at large that this had been rumoured so often that it was wise not to become too excited at the prospect. Meanwhile, the news was still full of young men dying across Europe. Iant did feel his good fortune, albeit heavily tinged with guilt, especially on sunny mornings looking through the window of his signal box. But he was also in turmoil about the impending crossroads in his life that he had to face.

As he cycled through Carrog on his way home, just two weeks into his new job he was surprised to see such a crowd waiting already for *The Grouse* to open. Furthermore, he saw both his sisters in animated conversation with a bigger group of village girls. When Gwennie saw him she rushed over:

'Iant, Iant it's really all over this time.'

'What are you talking about.'

'The war Iant. For God's sake man, has watching trains completely emptied your head?'

At this point, Doy rushed over too and in embracing him knocked him and his bike to the ground and they all ended up in a heap on the floor much to the amusement of the little crowd. Doy jumped up laughing too, but Iant got straight back on his bike and cycled as fast as he could up the little lane, much to the consternation of his sisters.

That night, lying awake Iant tried to make sense of his reaction to the war being over. Only a lunatic would have wanted it to continue for another second. However, the signing of the Armistice would soon bring Iant to a point in his life that he had been unconsciously hoping might never arrive. It was a point that he felt completely ill-equipped to deal with.

It was now some considerable time since he had heard from Sara and he, in turn, had not written since his father's death. He told himself that it was not his place to write until she had replied, but he knew that this was not good enough. When they had parted on the quayside in Salonika they had been very clear. Under the brightest blue sky and the hottest sun, they had promised to wait until the war ended. Then he would find a way to return to Greece so that they could marry.

There was no question that Iant still had the strongest feelings for Sara. If he made himself think of their times together, he felt nothing but happiness. Those memories in turn reminded him of what a bloodless life he was leading. Despite that, he had become relatively content in the little life he had started to shape. He had to make himself think of Sara, it did not come to him automatically. Life back at home seemed to have grown over him like a new skin and it was hard for him to feel anything through it. This is how Iant tried to justify it to himself.

It was another week before he received a letter from Sara. It reminded him again of the many reasons that he had come to love her so powerfully and so quickly. It was written before the news of the Armistice and in reply to his letter telling her of his father's death.

My dearest Iannis

It is with great sadness that I sit here writing to you about the death of your father. I know how I would feel if my own father was taken from us and it crushes me to think that I cannot even put my arms around you and try to take away a little of your grief. You spoke a little of your family and perhaps your father was not a man to show emotion I think? But I am sure that you know that he would have been proud of you and your bravery. He would have been glad to have you at home for at least a little while at the end of his life.

You must be a comfort to your mother now Iannis. She will be feeling all alone in the world and her son is what will keep up her spirits. It's normal I think for women to want to stop living when they lose a husband and you must be one of her reasons to live.

157

Now I come to a part Iannis that is so hard for me to write. I don't want to write it but I must, I know. I have thought about it for a very long time. It is hard because there is no-one that I can to speak to about it. No-one would understand, because no-one knew us together and the time we spent with each other.

Iannis I want to tell you so much, but I must now just tell you that I have to understand that your life has changed with the death of your father. It will not be possible for you to come here I think. My heart is very full but I have to say this Iannis. I cannot be selfish because I see how it would be if my father or mother was left on their own.

I want you to know Iannis that when I write this it doesn't change anything that I told you when we were together for that precious time. I write it to help you I hope.

I cannot write more now. I almost want to say to you not to write to me anymore, but Iannis I am too selfish for that. I think you will write to me again.

With love and much sadness too
Sara

Iant read this on his return from work and when he had finished he told his mother that he thought he had seen a break in one of the fences by the lane on his way home. It was pitch dark and without stopping to hear his mother's objections Iant walked quickly away from the house and towards the village.

Entering *The Grouse*, he was pleased to find that Frances was not there. He greeted one or two people perfunctorily and found a corner with his pint. He read the letter over and over again. The fleeting sense of relief he had felt at her understanding was now overwhelmed by something he had not anticipated; a terror that the most wonderful thing that was ever likely to happen to him now threatened to retreat into nothing.

Chapter 21

On the 1st of January 1919, Iant finally sat down to reply to Sara's letter. He felt nothing but misery throughout the first Christmas that he had spent with his own family since he had joined up. He tried hard to help Gwennie and Doy in their efforts to get their mother to attempt some kind of celebration, but it was half-hearted. There was no reason for anyone to question his mood. They all felt the loss of Gwilym and it was natural not to want to celebrate much this first Christmas.

In the weeks before he finally put pen to paper Iant had, a number of times, nearly embarked on a reckless attempt to travel. He thought that if he could get to see Sara again it would mean that a proper decision could be made by them both. Through his work, he obtained elaborate timetables of trains he could catch, first to Dover and then across to France. After that, he could find no information. He knew that he had to get to Marseilles and then catch a boat, but he had no idea if such a thing existed in peacetime.

He then wondered if he could travel by land and obtained an atlas of Europe from the little public library in Corwen. Poring over it by candlelight on his mother's kitchen table Iant even felt some sense of pride as he tried to follow and trace the journey that he had been on. Even his sisters and, briefly, his mother took some interest in this abstract representation of Iant's passage through the Great War. He enjoyed explaining to them the scale of the map and how that translated into reality. He traced a line with his finger and told them that just to get out of England was a journey the equivalent of twenty times as far as Bala. This was lost on them, but the exotic place names as his finger moved across Europe thrilled his sisters.

For a few moments, he forgot the real purpose of his borrowing the atlas, caught up in the deception that he wanted to show his family where he had been. When his family had grown tired of his explanations Iant tried to concentrate on how he might really make the journey. There must, he reasoned, be railway lines connecting the biggest cities. It was clear enough that he would go through Paris and then perhaps towards the Alps. He recognised the names of Geneva and Zurich. Would it then be towards Venice? After that none of the towns, even the countries barely meant anything to him.

That night in bed his head swam with names of places that he had seen on the map: Trieste, Belgrade, Sarajevo, Montenegro. They all seemed in roughly the direction that he had to travel, but on a school atlas, it was impossible to see in which order. Huge mountain ranges were marked in deep colours. How would any train cross those?

Then there was the question of money. Iant had tried to put aside a little from his wages each week. To do this he had to lie to his mother about how much he received. She had lost no time in indicating that she would control the majority of his finances while he lived at home and ate under her roof. Iant was acutely aware that without his money she would be unlikely to survive, but decided to leave her with her dignity. By the end of two months, the amount he had saved seemed pathetically small and Iant had no sense at all of what it might cost to make such an epic journey.

He had not slept well ever since his time in the hospital in Salonika apart from some brief respites through sheer exhaustion. Now, for days on end, his restlessness increased and he feared that he would become so worn out that he would endanger lives through his work. He had ceased to be supervised daily in the signal box, but Alun Lewis would be sent to call on him periodically to check on his progress. On one such visit, Iant could not stop yawning.

'What's the matter Iant? You been up all hours drinking and chasing girls?' Alun asked.

At that moment he felt weak in a way that he had never done before. His experiences in charge of men under fire on the mountainside had, of course, tested him further, but there he had a sense of how he needed to try and behave. Here, unable to tell

160

anyone about Sara or ask anyone how he should decide what to do Iant had reached a point that was close to complete despair.

'Come on, it can't be that bad – I'll make us a cuppa.'

His colleague's kindly tone was the final straw and Iant's face crumpled. His body became stiff and he could no longer prevent himself from sobbing uncontrollably.

Alun Lewis had known others who had returned home haunted by their experiences. His age and job had prevented him joining up, but he had developed a sense of what men had gone through. Few of them were willing to speak openly but he had learned enough to know that they had gone from this generally peaceful corner of the world and seen things that were beyond anyone's worst imaginings. He naturally assumed that this was what was happening to Iant.

'Iant, do you want to go home. I can cover for you. I can put off my other visit.'

Iant shook his head furiously.

'You're in no state to work though.'

'I am. I'm very sorry Alun.'

'Don't apologise for God's sake. Some of the things you've seen....'

'No. No, It's not that.'

Iant was suddenly anxious that Alun might report him as shell-shocked and not fit for work. He had heard of others who had lost jobs this way.

'What then?'

After months of secrecy, of going over and over what his future life might be in his head Iant could not contain himself anymore. He found himself recounting his story to this comparative stranger who, as luck would have it, was a sympathetic ear. As Iant finished his story he found himself fumbling in his coat pocket. As if to somehow prove that he was not mad, or a fantasist making the whole thing up Iant produced the ring that he had carried since he had left Salonika.

Without thinking Alun took the ring and held it up towards the window, letting the light shine through the stone. The furthest he had ever been was Liverpool and then only once when a cousin was taking the boat to live in Canada.

'And you are still thinking of trying to go back there you say?'

'I don't know. It seems impossible.'

'Nothing's impossible. Especially when you're a young man.'

'So you think I should try?'

'I didn't say that Iant. You have to look hard at what you want, but also what you think is right.'

'I know.'

'Your mam doesn't know about any of this I suppose.'

'No. Nor my sisters.'

'Just as well.'

They fell silent as a bell sounded loudly in the signal box. Iant was anxious to demonstrate that there was nothing wrong with his concentration and he responded promptly in a flurry of pulling levers and writing in the log on the big wooden desk in front of him. The slow train from Llangollen to Bala chugged past and they both gave the driver a wave.

After a while it was Alun that spoke:

'This girl. Would she come here?'

'No. I mean I don't think so. She couldn't leave her family.'

'But she wants you to do that.'

'No, she doesn't, she told me that I must stay here now that my father has gone.'

Iant had not recounted this last twist in his tale. Now he felt as though he had deliberately kept it back.

'Do you think she's trying to tell you something Iant?'

Iant felt a flash of anger but kept it to himself. How could a stranger know what had passed between them anyway? Sara was thinking of him surely?

'I don't think so.'

They were silent again. There was weak winter sun now and the little stove had made the signal box warm. Iant looked out on the field the other side of the line and the sheep brought down

162

from the hillside in anticipation of snow. Having got this off his chest he wanted Alun, kind though he had been, to go now, to leave him with his thoughts.

'You won't tell anyone about this?'

'No of course I won't.'

'I will be alright now if you need to get off.'

'Can you imagine telling your mam and your sisters?'

'Not really.'

'Could you do it?'

Iant thought about the coldness of his upbringing. Would he be so missed he thought bitterly? Deep down though he knew that this wasn't the whole story. Years of scraping a living and not showing weakness had made his mother what she was he supposed.

Alun began to put on his coat and scarf ready to leave. He took hold of Iant's hand and clasped his shoulder.

'How about getting yourself over to Acrefair on Sunday for your tea?'

'Thank you.'

'At about 3 o'clock?'

'I'll see you then.'

'Thank you, Alun.'

Iant watched the older man make his way down the lane. He had been glad of his kindness, but part of him also wanted to take back his story and keep it to himself. Now that he had let it out into the world, even if Alun kept his word and told no-one, the hard light could get at it and fade it.

That night, after he had eaten with his sisters and mother, Iant went to his bed early and got out the letter that he had written some days ago and read it for the umpteenth time:

My dearest Sara

I am very sorry that I have taken some time to reply to your letter. Since then so much has happened and finally, the war has ended.

This was the moment that we talked about and imagined that it would mean we would be together. When I got your letter, my heart sank and I imagined that you no longer wanted to be with me.

I now understand that you have written to help me. I can see in your words the person that I miss every day and who is so generous and loving.

I have thought so many times of just putting some clothes in a bag and setting off in my stupid way, not knowing how to get to you and I have looked at maps to trace how I would walk all the way if I had to.

I know though that if, somehow, I came to you, that you would see me differently. As a man that left his family when they needed him.

I know too that I cannot ask you to come here. I saw how much your family means to you and what you mean to them. I saw how much your village was part of you.

As I write this I still don't believe what I am saying. I think I can imagine us married and living somewhere that I do not yet know.

I think Sara that I will always love you, whatever else happens to me in my life. I hope that you might not forget me.

With all my heart
Iannis

He placed the letter in an envelope and got out the supply of stamps that he had saved. Before he could think any more and without saying a word to his mother or sisters he strode out of the house and down the lane.

The post box was at the top of the village and as he saw it dimly in the distance he quickened his pace. He knew that this must be done in a single action and he didn't stop or hesitate until the letter had been pushed through the slot. He then turned and walked quickly in the direction of *The Grouse* with every part of him straining to turn and perform the impossible feat of pushing his arm down inside the red box, pulling out his letter and tearing it into a thousand pieces. In his mind's eye, he could see them fluttering on the cold breeze and being borne away downstream by the Dee and on into the valley beyond.

Chapter 22

The next evening all that Iant could think of doing was to go once more through the few remaining belongings that were still with him from his wartime journey. He set aside the heavy greatcoat that he had returned home in, but the rest of his battle dress uniform he wanted to cut into rags or give it to his mother.

He knew it was there, but the shock at seeing Clara's address once again took Iant aback. He had not had any communication from her at all despite the letter that he had sent from Salonika. Iant realised that this had been before the battle and of course before he had met Sara. He was now a different man and the discovery of Clara's address reminded him of that.

Logically it should have gone in the rubbish bin with the other odds and ends that Iant had found. Tobacco tins, army issue scraps of bandage, insect repellent and quinine in a filthy little bottle were all taken outside and put on a bonfire along with any clothing that Iant could not imagine being used. It was supposed to be therapeutic though he could not really feel any noticeable effect.

By the end, Iant had only a coat, Sara's letters, the tiny ring and the scrap of paper with an address on it. It wasn't much to show for such a journey.

He had already considered the ring and what he really should do with it. Eventually, perhaps he should return it, but it was much too soon. Deep down he could not bring himself to believe that his hopes were finished. The ring could stay. It would be too painful to do anything now. It went into a tin with the letters. He was left only with the scrap of paper. There was a brown stain on one corner that could even be blood.

Iant's sleep that night was no better than it had been for some weeks and in the hours as he lay awake he started to form a plan to try and find Clara. He felt disloyal to even think of it so soon after he and Sara had abandoned their plans, but he had always been curious about what had become of her. That is all he wanted he told himself. It would give him something else to think about.

He had some time off owed to him and his railwayman's pass would give him the means to get there. It would be a long journey in a single day, but it would get him away from home. He would need to invent a story, but he had become better than he used to be at inventing half-truths. In the end, he settled on a story about receiving word from an ex-comrade who was still suffering from wounds he had received. It was the least he could do, Iant said to his mother.

On the train, he checked the piece of paper several times; Clara Johnson, 15 Penrefail Street, Rhyl. Iant had never been to Rhyl and didn't have much idea of how he would look for the street, but for now, he felt good to be doing something that had been at the back of his mind for some while.

The journey took him out of the familiar hilly countryside until the surroundings were flat and quite dull. His tiredness overtook him and he fell fast asleep. He woke up and he could see the sea in the distance getting closer and it was obvious he would soon be at Rhyl.

At the station, he tried asking the man at the ticket barrier, but he was quite off-hand claiming that he hadn't heard of the street that Iant named. As he left the station the wind was strong and blew fragments of what he thought must be sand into his eyes. For a minute he was alarmed as he was still supposed to take good care of his eyes after the treatment he had received in Greece.

His mind went back to his head being covered in bandages and the way that he had imagined Sara before he was ever able to see her. Inevitably his imagination had it wrong, but he was not disappointed. The memory of that day when he saw Sara for the first time would stay with him forever he hoped, despite the terrible disappointment that clouded the present. What was he doing here, he asked himself?

A few hundred yards from the station he found a small general grocers. As he peered into the darkened interior he could see that a man and a woman were busy serving customers. He waited his turn and then asked the man if he knew Penrefail Street. At first, he looked blank, but his wife overheard and suggested where it might be. It sounded some way to walk, and the woman's face suggested that it was not an area that she frequented very often. Iant brushed the thought aside and, besides he was glad of the walk after the train.

When he reached the seafront Iant thought to himself that everything today was conspiring to remind him of Sara. The only time he had spent time by the coast was in Salonika. The colours here were somewhat different. He remembered standing almost alone on deck as they approached for the first time and the blue of the Aegean. Here it was winter and the Irish Sea was brown, almost grey. Despite this, he breathed deeply and enjoyed the wind in his face.

He walked nearly a mile along the seafront, hardly seeing anyone else and then he saw the road he had been told to turn down. He quickly saw that the houses were grander here, but also that most of them had seen better days. The paint was fading on a number of them and the stone steps that led up to the front doors were crumbling.

Finally, he saw the entrance to Penrefail Street itself. The walk along the sea had taken his mind off what he was about to do, but now he had to face it again. He suddenly felt breathless and if he hadn't come so far he would have considered turning around and going back.

Number fifteen was near the end and as he got further down the street he could see that the general impression of decay was even more prominent as he neared what he imagined would be number fifteen.

But there was no number fifteen. Large wooden buttresses propped up the house next door and a patch of rough ground occupied the space where number fifteen once stood.

Iant had no idea of what he had been expecting, but the absence of a building of any kind made his stomach turn over. His first thought was that Clara had simply given him a false

167

address. Of course she had. And what an idiot he now looked, travelling all this way to find nothing. His emotional state had simply got the better of him. The sooner he pulled himself together and got on the next train home the better.

Stupidly he got out the piece of paper once more, as if to check that he had the right address when he quite clearly knew that he had.

As he stood there he realised he was being approached from a house across the road. An elderly woman dressed in old fashioned, black clothes asked, quite assertively what his business was and whether she might be able to help him. Help did not seem the first thing on her mind though, considering her tone of voice.

'I was looking for someone' Iant said.

'I can see that. Who are you looking for?'

'It's a Miss Johnson.'

'And what is her first name?'

'Clara. Clara Johnson.'

'And who are you?'

'I'm just a friend..'

'What kind of friend?'

'I knew her family. Before the war.'

'Did you now?'

'Can you tell me what happened to the house?'

'It collapsed. Dry rot they think.'

'That's terrible.'

'It had been falling down for years.'

'How long is it since anyone lived there?'

'It must be ten years now. Clara was just a child when they had to leave.'

The reality of the situation was dawning on Iant. But he was still not prepared for what came next.

'You do know she died?'

'Dead?'

'They hadn't lived there for years, but the people next door heard the news. Awful.'

168

Iant's face must have registered the shock he was feeling because the woman's tone softened somewhat.

'How did she die?' he asked

'I…I'm not sure.'

'Do you know anybody that can tell me anything else?'

'Some people in the street knew the family, but I don't think they would know any more than me.'

'Why did the family leave the house?'

'Do you want to come and sit down for a moment? I can make you a cup of tea.'

Iant nodded and followed her across the road and into her house. Inside it looked as if had once been quite grand, but the furniture was old and in decline. There was the smell of stale cooking and a cat rubbed up against Iant's leg.

'Don't mind her. She's on the scrounge for food.'

The woman took some time to make tea and gradually told her version of the story. A well to do family at one time. Coal merchants by trade but the business went into decline. The father found it hard to cope with the problems and eventually died quite young. The last she had seen of the family had been when the war broke out. They had been forced to give up the house and were going to stay with the woman's sister. Near Abergele, she thought. Clara had only been about fifteen when they left the house.

Iant asked very few questions, except that he could not leave without at least finding out what had happened to this young woman whose address he had so naively carried with him halfway across the world.

'There's never been a court case….'

'Court case?'

'They found her, poor thing, half-buried….'

'Where? Where did they find her?'

'In some woods. Near the army camp at Abergele.'

Iant couldn't speak for a moment.

'Did you know her well?' the woman said.

'No, no I didn't. A friend of mine did though.'

He felt ashamed at the pathetic and transparent lie, but he couldn't face getting any nearer the truth.

'I don't believe it myself, but the papers said that she was, well…you know…with soldiers at the camp. The story was that it was probably one of them, but there wasn't much of an investigation. what with them all being sent off everywhere. If it was he's probably dead himself by now.'

Iant could barely speak. He knew that the old woman was curious who he was but he needed to get away from there. He made an excuse that he could see she didn't believe and walked quickly back down the street.

He didn't stop or look back until he was some way down the seafront. There he found a vacant bench that looked out to sea and sat staring at the waves for a while. He still couldn't quite believe that this young woman who, very fleetingly, had entered his life and given him the affection he craved, was no longer alive.

What had his journey been for in any case? His proposed life with Sara had almost certainly turned to nothing in his hands and he had tried to return to a place where he had previously found comfort. He had been naively curious but also selfish. He felt as though he had lost all his self-respect.

As Iant made the long journey home he tried to focus his mind on Clara and the terrible thing that had happened to her rather than his own self-pity. He half-thought about trying to find the remains of her family. But he stopped himself. His naivety had already got him into this much trouble and his contact would give very little comfort to anyone. He must steel himself and grow up.

On the train, as he tried to turn his thoughts back to the memories of Sara, he realised how he had played a part in the sad ending to Clara's life. Not directly of course, but she would have taken all her grim experiences to the grave with her, never mind that a few sad fools like him wanted to think of it as something different.

Chapter 23

As the winter turned to spring Iant felt himself reluctantly respond to the warmth in the air. Since January it had felt as if he had lived with his teeth clenched and his face rigid. He became determined to get through his daily life without undue fuss. He threw himself into the routine of his job maintaining the family home.

He rarely ventured out unless there were errands to be run and his sisters tired of asking him to accompany them. However, on St David's Day, he agreed to take the bus with Gwennie and Doy into Corwen. There was a small eisteddfod taking place and a dance in the evening. Iant planned to leave at the end of the afternoon, but he had not yet told his sisters. He half-heartedly asked his mother to accompany them and was relieved when she refused. They were to meet Ben in Corwen. He would look after his sisters if he slipped away on the pretext of not leaving their mother alone too long.

The eisteddfod was to be held in a field just beside Corwen School and then there would be a torch-lit procession up to the town hall where the dance was to be held. After the misery of the war years Corwen, like many towns across the country, was making a special effort to celebrate as best it could.

As Iant and his sisters got off the bus they could already see small groups of people heading back along the high street towards the school. As they got closer they could hear a children's choir and they quickened their pace unconsciously so as not to miss anything. The singing and traditional dance competitions generated some enthusiasm among the crowd and, by the time they made their way back down to the main square to watch the parade, Iant could not help but be caught up in the atmosphere.

Dusk was starting to fall as they stood by the side of the road. By now Gwennie and Ben were caught up in their private conversation and Doy had met a friend to whom she was chatting animatedly about the dance later. Iant had begun to wonder if it might soon be possible to make his excuses when he heard a familiar voice behind him.

'Hello, stranger.'

'Hello, Frances.'

Iant realised that his greeting had not exactly been welcoming and he attempted to compensate by trying to make conversation

'You aren't working this evening?'

'No. My cousin was in the pageant so I asked for the time off.'

'It was very good.'

'No, it wasn't! But I like to see the children's faces acting all serious.'

'Yes, they do look funny.'

'Did you bring your mother?'

'No. She wouldn't come. She hardly leaves the house now'.

'It takes people like that sometimes.'

'She has never exactly been the joyful kind has she, Frances?'

They laughed together a moment at the thought of his mother's rather dour reputation and Iant realised how little humour there was in his life. It was a while since he had really enjoyed a joke with anyone. The beginning of the procession could be seen coming down the road and Iant made space for Frances to stand in front of him so that she could see better. The bigger children were allowed to carry the torches and in the gloom of the late afternoon, their faces were lit up as they paraded past. It had turned a little cold and the warmth from the passing flames was very welcome.

Frances moved back slightly from the edge of the road as the procession became a little wider and she leant against Iant for a moment. Part of him wanted to pull away but it would have seemed hostile. They stood like this for such a short while, though Iant felt a pang of guilt at the pleasure he felt from such small human contact.

The end of the parade disappeared out of sight and Frances

asked Iant if he would like to walk up to the *Blue Lion* and get out of the cold now it was getting dark. He found himself agreeing despite himself and the two of them walked the half-mile or so in near silence. Whether by chance or design, Frances had suggested the old hotel on the edge of town least likely to be frequented by people that they knew. They looked around and found a corner with their drinks that was tucked away off the main bar.

'So does the life of a signalman suit you Iant?'

'I suppose it does yes.'

'I wouldn't like to be on my own so much.'

'People come by now and then. And the drivers always give you a wave.'

'You don't talk to them though do you!.'

'No, but sometimes people only talk for the sake of it.'

'Do you think I do that?'

'No...no I didn't mean you.'

'I was just teasing you Iant.'

'Oh...I see.'

'You always look so worried.'

'Do I?'

'Well, you do when you are talking to me.'

They fell silent as Iant saw how transparent he was, but Frances was smiling and he was suddenly grateful for her company and good humour. He knew that he had not been easy to live with and that people made allowances for him, thinking it was what he had been through in the fighting.

'Would you like another drink?'

'Yes, I would. Then perhaps we could walk back. Unless your sisters are expecting you.'

'No, I told them I might make my own way. They'll catch the last bus I expect.'

It was a long walk but the moon was out so they could take a short cut across the fields where they knew the path was good. They laughed as the sheep scattered as they came near and some rabbits broke cover and made for the hedgerow. Frances had taken Iant's arm and he took her hand to help her over the stile. She sat for a moment on the wooden bar at the top so that they were the same height. The dark helped Iant feel less self-conscious when their mouths touched and they felt each other's warmth.

As they walked back along the lane the silence between them returned. Finally, they came to the top of the village and they could see Frances's home in the row of cottages on the right-hand side as the little road meandered down the hill past two chapels and *The Grouse*.

'You can leave me here Iant. You still have a way to go.'

'That lane will be the death of me. Every night I dread it on the old bike.'

They laughed together and Frances reached up and kissed Iant on the cheek. He watched as she almost disappeared into the darkness, but he could see that she had turned into her home and he began his ascent up the lane.

At breakfast the next morning Iant was relieved to find that Gwennie and Doy were far too full of their own gossip from the previous evening to have wondered where he had got to. Gwennie began to tease Doy about some boy that she said was sweet on her until Doy cast a pleading look in the direction of the back of her mother's head. All Iant had to do was keep quiet until it was time to wrap up against the cold morning and freewheel down the lane.

With the onset of spring the cycle over to Llandrillo had become steadily more pleasurable and the sun this morning had begun to take the chill out of the air. The trees were still bare, but a few primroses had begun to appear in the hedgerows along with the daffodils. Iant could see why Frances thought it strange that he would enjoy being so much on his own, but it suited him and the sunshine made him look forward to making a brew and looking out at the view from the box.

Iant felt the day and then the rest of the week pass quickly and on the Friday morning he told his mother that he might call by *The Grouse* on his way home and not to wait before eating. It was the first time he had done this in a long while. At six o'clock, as he rode down the street, he knew that he had been wondering all day if Frances would be behind the bar and how he should behave if she was. As he entered, the pub was not yet crowded and Frances had her back to him, serving someone. She turned to see him come in but immediately turned back to finish pulling the pint. Iant found himself watching her from across the bar, quickly turning his head away as she came over to serve him.

'Well sir, what can I get you?'

Iant was relieved to see the familiar smile, always looking to tease him.

'How have you been?'

'Well. Since we last met I have been very well thank you.'

'Good. I mean, I'm glad. I'll take a pint thank you. Will you have something?'

'Perhaps later. Thank you. I'll save it.'

At that moment a group of men came in and greeted Iant. Frances was soon busy serving them and Iant went and sat by himself in a corner. After a while, he was joined by two men who also worked on the railway in different signal boxes along the valley. Gruff was older and had not served in the army, but the other man, Lloyd had been in France and, it was said, suffered from some of the effects of being in the trenches. Iant had known both of them most of his life but had rarely spoken to either for any length of time.

'How are you liking it up at Llan Iant?' asked Gruff

'It suits me thank you.'

'A long journey by bike mind?'

'Keeps me fit.'

'Aye. I suppose it does.'

'Not too lonely up there Iant?'

Iant was surprised to hear Lloyd ask such a direct question. He had a nervous air about him and he made Iant feel anxious about his reply.

'No, not really. When you live in a house full of women. You know.'

175

Iant could see that Lloyd had really been talking about himself and felt that he needed to change the subject, but struggled to see how he might manage this.

'Not so many in here tonight.'

'Early yet.'

By now Iant had finished his pint and, flush from being paid, he stood up and offered to stand a round. As Frances approached to serve him her smile cheered him instantly.

'Are you enjoying the company?' she teased.

'They are all alright.'

'Men of few words.'

'We are managing I think.'

'Good. Do you want some dominoes?'

Iant realised that this might be a good idea and returned to the table with the box. As he collected the pints Frances spoke quietly.

'If you are staying I can leave in another hour.'

'Well, I can manage that.'

'Perhaps you could walk me up the street. It isn't far but you can come in for a cup of tea.'

'Alright.'

The dominoes were a success and Iant even found himself glad of the company. Little was spoken, that evening or any other, about the experiences that he and Lloyd had shared except for the trivia of long and uncomfortable journeys and the relief of clean sheets and socks. Iant noticed a slight tremor in Lloyd's right hand and a tendency to lack concentration. Gruff had never travelled even over the border into England, but to the untutored eye, there was little to distinguish between the three men. Two of them had seen and done things that nobody from this place had ever imagined before, but now here they were, playing dominoes as if the last six years had never been.

At eight o'clock Iant made his excuses and waited around the back of the pub. After a few moments, Frances appeared and the scent that she dabbed behind her ears preceded her. She took Iant's arm and they started off up the street. When they got to

Frances's house Iant suggested walking a little further. He wanted to clear his head from the beer and he did not look forward to the forced conversation and curious eyes of Frances' mother and father. He remembered for a moment the meal in Sara's house and the thought froze inside him causing his body to stiffen.

'Is something the matter?'

'No…no. I just felt a chill.'

'You just suggested walking. Make up your mind.'

'I'll be fine once I get moving.'

They walked down a side lane towards the river and then followed the gravel path along the bank. When they got to the ancient bridge they stopped under it and Iant reached around Frances's waist pulling her closer to him.

Chapter 24

In the weeks that followed Iant found himself able to relax more and more in the company of Frances. He realised that he had been foolish to shrink back from her confidence and he began to see the warmth and tenderness that was so much part of her. Above all, he enjoyed the fact that she made him laugh and stopped him from being so withdrawn.

Many times he thought of just telling her about Sara. It was not because he needed to confess anything, but simply she was one of the few people with whom he wanted to share something so important to him. He had been thinking of saying something to his family, one evening when he was getting ready to go and meet Frances, but Gwennie came out with news that drove everything from his head.

'Ben has asked me to marry him.'

Doy let out a squeal of delight and ran to her sister. When she had released her, Iant walked over and gave her a peck on the cheek only to be seized in a fierce embrace.

'Steady on Gwennie you'll break my ribs.'

His mother didn't rise from her chair, but Iant thought he saw a flicker of a smile pass across her face.

'And have you said yes?'

'I have Mam, but I would like to know that you all approve of course.'

'I think you should grab him before someone steals him off you.'

They laughed as it was as close to a joke as their mother was likely to make. Iant was ready to go out, but he felt he couldn't just leave so he suggested that they all go to *The Grouse* for once to celebrate.

'Come on Mam. There's quite a few ladies go in the parlour now. I'll get the cart out if you don't feel like walking.'

'I won't come, but you take the girls. I shan't mind.'

Iant had arranged to see Frances as she finished her turn at

The Grouse. Although Gwennie and Doy had teased him a little, it had not really been openly acknowledged that he was seeing Frances. He knew that his mother would be snooty about her, because she served behind the bar, and he was in no hurry to have that kind of confrontation.

As they entered the parlour Frances was still serving customers. Surprised to see Iant enter that side of the pub she was about to exclaim when she saw Gwennie and Doy come in behind him.

'Gwennie has some news' Iant said quickly

'Ben and I are going to be married.'

'Oh. That is good. I am very pleased.'

'Thank you, Frances.'

'He hasn't given her a ring yet. They're going to Wrexham next Saturday to choose' said Doy, keen not to be left out.

'That'll be exciting.'

Iant bought them all drinks. Shandies for the girls and a pint for himself.

'Will you join us when you finish?'

'Thank you. I will.'

When Frances joined them at the table they drank a toast to Gwennie and Ben. Iant remembered the night that he had brought Ben to *The Grouse* and he surreptitiously tried to look for a reaction in Frances, but he saw nothing. He was being foolish and old-fashioned he decided. Frances and Ben had clearly had a brief flirtation at some time. That is all there was to it.

His sisters were not used to any kind of drink and after an hour or so Iant suggested that he walk them home. He thought he would have to sacrifice his evening with Frances, but she surprised him by offering to walk with them. Doy and Gwennie exchanged glances and broke into a fit of giggles, but Iant ignored them.

While Frances was getting her coat, Gwennie, emboldened by drink, asked Iant outright if he and Frances were 'stepping out'.

'I don't know. Perhaps.'

179

'What do you mean "perhaps" Iant? Either you are or you aren't' said Doy

'I suppose so. It's nothing yet so don't go blabbing in front of Mam alright?'

'Of course not. It's just between us,' said Gwennie.

At this moment Frances reappeared and the laughter was stifled before they all four set off. It was a pleasant night, which was just as well thought Iant as he would need to take Frances back home after they had walked the girls to the door.

'Don't go waking Mam up now,.'

'In case she asks where you are?'

'Tell her I've gone for a walk.'

'Oh 'a walk' is it!' shouted Doy as Iant and Frances set off back.

'Take no notice. I'm sorry about my sisters.'

'I don't mind. They are just having fun.'

They walked on a little way in silence until Frances spoke.

'Your mother wouldn't approve of me would she?'

'Why do you say that?'

'You know it Iant.'

'Why does she need to approve of you?'

'She doesn't.'

Iant did not know how to help them over this. He was not so cowed by his mother that it affected what he thought of Frances, but it was a barrier between them that promised to become bigger. He was seized once more by the thought that he would tell her about Sara. It would be a confidence and it would show what he thought of her.

'I have something I need to tell you.'

Iant began by talking of his blindness which he rarely discussed. He found himself going back to the early moments of waking in the hospital in Salonika in a way that he had not done since he came home. The fear that he would not regain his sight was still vivid and terrifying. Eventually, he came to the Greek nurse that had been so kind. He told Frances how Sara had prevented each day being so full of fear and boredom. He found

180

it difficult to talk about Sara without being almost overcome by memories of her but forced himself to go on.

He went into very little detail about the weeks that followed his recovery, but after a lot of hesitation, he finally told Frances that they had agreed to marry, but that Sara had released him from that obligation.

Iant had talked for a long time now with little interruption. He had not spoken fluently though and he often struggled for the right words. When he finally came to a stop he wanted to search Frances's face for what she was thinking, but both the darkness and his own fear of what he might see prevented him. Eventually, she broke the silence,

'Well, you are a dark horse and no mistake.'

'I should have told you sooner.'

'Should you? And why is that?'

'Because I have become fond of you Frances.'

Again there was silence between them.

'It is a lot to take in, Iant.'

'Yes.'

'This Greek girl. What do you feel about her now?'

'We won't see each other again.'

'That isn't what I asked you.'

Iant struggled again to know how to respond. He had no wish to deceive Frances, but he feared that what he would say would make it irretrievably awkward between them.

'It would be a lie to say that I didn't think of her.'

'And what do you think Iant? When you think of her.'

'I think of her fondly. But I know in my heart that it is impossible to think of her as I did.'

'It is not impossible. Nothing is impossible.'

'It is finished between us. It is decided.'

'It is that easy is it? You can just decide not to care for someone anymore. Because it is not convenient?'

'That isn't fair. My father....'

'You don't have to answer to me Iant. I don't judge you like some chapel girl.'

181

'But you are angry.'

'I am not angry.'

'Then good. Things are the same between us?'

'I don't know Iant. I need some time to think about it. I thought of you in a particular way and now....'

'I am no different.'

'Of course you are. And I envy you.'

'Envy?'

'Yes, envy. You have been across the world and got yourself into a great romance while I have been stuck here pulling pints at *The Grouse*. So, yes, I do envy you.'

'I see.'

'Leave me here Iant. I'll walk the rest of the way.'

They were only about a quarter of a mile from Frances's house, but Iant felt uneasy leaving her, especially on such a note. He saw though that her mind was made up. He bent to kiss her good night and she offered her cheek.

'When can we meet?'

'I don't know. I will find a way of letting you know. Goodnight Iant.'

With this Frances walked briskly away from him. He waited until he could no longer see her and then a little longer until her footsteps died away. Finally, he turned and trudged back up the hill, hoping to find his sisters already halfway to bed when he arrived home.

A week passed and Iant understood from her silence that Frances had decided not to contact him. He felt that he had tried to behave honourably, but he knew he would be able to do little to change her mind. Indirectly, the shadow of the war and the way that it had tossed all their lives up in the air had thrown itself across his attempts to look to the future. He had once again been naïve and foolish and he would just have to suffer the consequences.

He fell back on the routine of his days and threw himself into the diligence and efficiency that were required in his job. When he was on the later shift the last train to pass along his stretch of track was at nine o'clock. He completed the last entry into the logbook and set about clearing up the box and washing up his cup and plate.

The evenings were drawing out, but it was almost pitch dark, so when he heard a tap on the glass pane of the door he could not see who or what it was. There had been an incident with some of the village boys playing a joke on one of the other lads, but he thought it was a bit late for that. He went to the door and peered out.

'Are you going to leave me standing here?'

Iant was so taken aback to hear Frances's voice that he did not speak for a moment but just opened the door. Frances came in carrying a canvas basket and proceeded to unpack what looked like a picnic on the desk facing the window.

'I hope you are hungry.'

'Well, yes, sort of. I had something earlier but....'

'I brought you a bottle of beer. I expect it's not allowed on railway property, but as you are not working I thought it would be alright.'

'Frances, how did you get here?'

'I got the bus to Corwen and then walked. It's not that far.'

'So, have you finished work for the night? Gwennie told me you would have done by now. No train after nine she thought.'

'Yes, yes that's right.'

Frances removed the tops from two bottles of beer and gave one to Iant. She drank and gave him a smile that made him feel that all was right with the world. He put down his beer and took her bottle from her hand and took her in his arms.

In Frances's bag was a blanket and she spread it on the floor of the signal box. She removed first her coat and then her dress. She wore very little underneath and Iant felt a powerful attraction to her pass over him. They both now knelt on the rug and Frances undid first the buttons of his shirt, and then his belt. As her hand moved inside his trousers, Iant pushed her back down on the rug and moved his hand along her bare legs.

Iant reached out and extinguished the hissing gas lamp that

183

made the signal box shine like a lighthouse across the surrounding fields.

Afterwards, they lay silently wrapped around each other for almost an hour before hunger made Frances bring over the food that she had brought.

Iant had a small supply of candles for emergencies and they ate greedily in the dim light. Frances reached over and gently touched one of the small scars on Iant's shoulder that had been left by the shrapnel on the ridge.

'Does it hurt?'

'No. Not at all.'

'What happened?'

'I barely remember. I was too busy thinking about my eyes.'

'And they don't trouble you?'

'I think I will need glasses soon, that's all. So long as I can tell red from green eh!'

'Will you write to her again?'

Iant was discovering that Frances had a disconcerting habit of changing the subject very suddenly.

'I hadn't thought to.'

'Will she write to you?'

'I don't know.'

'I don't understand.'

'Understand what Frances?'

'If I were so fond of someone that I agreed to marry them, I would follow them.'

Iant had no answer to this and he became anxious that someone might see a light in the signal box. He began to dress and clear away the remains of the food. Frances followed suit and a disagreeable silence replaced the warmth between them.

As they started the long walk back together, Iant pushing his bike, they talked a little more about Salonika. Iant told Frances about Oliver and Johnny and the earthquake, but the unease between them had returned and they could do nothing about it. It was a relief to Iant when they finally arrived back in Carrog and Frances kissed him on the cheek before going inside. As he got on his bike and began the steep ascent back up the hill Iant felt a sense of weariness come over him. For a moment he was tempted to stop his bike and find a comfortable place to lie down, but the thought of the damp grass and the questions he would face in the morning drove him on. He was relieved to find no-one had waited up and, as quietly as he could, he climbed the stairs and collapsed into bed.

Chapter 25

Iant heard nothing from Frances for the next two weeks. His work and the journeys he made were tiring and he found that he hadn't the stamina to make himself seek her out. He sensed that she had ended their evening together thinking less of him than when it had begun.

However, on the Friday of the second week, he hadn't felt like going home. At the very least he yearned for some company. Despite what happened between them, Frances was a person that usually cheered him up. He resolved to try and put it behind him.

As he entered *The Grouse*, he saw immediately that Frances was not behind the bar. He was partly relieved. It postponed a potentially difficult conversation, but he could not help but feel disappointed too. Gruff and Lloyd were sitting in the same spot as last time, about to start a game of dominoes, as if time had stood still. He bought his pint and joined them, hoping that Frances would be working later.

When eight o'clock had come and gone, Iant could see that Frances would not be coming. He thought of staying with Gruff and Lloyd, but their long silences, intent only on the game and their pints, finally drove Iant to the idea that he would call at Frances's home. He was reluctant to do this. Frances's mother would undoubtedly see it as of some significance, but he decided that it was worth the risk. He needed to see her and he badly needed some of the life that she seemed to inject into him.

As Frances's mother opened the door Iant could tell straight away that she was surprised to see him.

'Good evening Mrs Jones.'

'Hello, Iant.'

'I am sorry to disturb you.'

Iant was suddenly conscious of the beer on his breath and the fact that he had not been home to change his clothes after a long day working.

'I was wondering if Frances was at home?'

'I think you had better come in.'

Before she had said anything Iant could see clearly that Mrs Jones was struggling with her answer.

'Is she unwell?'

'She didn't say anything to you before she went?'

'Went where Mrs Jones?'

'She decided to take up the position that she'd been offered. She caught the train to London only on Wednesday. We are hoping she will write as soon as she is settled, but she will be busy I'm sure.'

'London?'

'She was asked to go and be a companion. To the Honourable Mrs Thompson. She is a cousin of the family from the Hall. Her last one went off and got married I heard.'

There was a long silence until Mrs Jones' embarrassment got the better of her.

'I am sorry that she didn't talk to you about it Iant.'

'It's…it's alright. I am sorry to have troubled you, Mrs Jones.'

'Would you like me to mention that you were asking after her when I write?'

'No…no, thank you.'

By now Iant was halfway out of the door and Mrs Jones was not inclined to detain him. Iant got on his bike and rather than head for home he pedalled hard downhill towards the river. For a long time, he sat overlooking the broad bank of shingle from where he had fished many a time when he was young. He was angry at Frances for not telling him, but angrier at himself for thinking that he had any hold over her. He knew deep down that he had always assumed that she pursued him and now he had got his comeuppance. He hurled stone after stone into the stream until he grew tired and began to pedal wearily home.

He received a letter from Frances just over a week later:

Dear Iant

I am sorry to have disappeared without at least a word to you. Truthfully, I am not sure why I didn't speak to you, except perhaps that I could not quite face complicated explanations.

Perhaps I said to you that I envied you getting away from home? I know that is selfish when the war brought so much suffering, but I felt I had to take a chance, so I did. I am really nothing more than a servant, so it isn't a big adventure really, but it's as much as I can manage now. I will see what happens.

I hope you find some happiness Iant – why not run back to your Greek girl eh? That would shock them!

Yours affectionately,

Frances

Iant decided not to write back. He had become fond of Frances, but his heart wasn't broken and he knew deep down that she had done the right thing in trying to see the world for herself. However, he was momentarily angered by her reference to Sara. It made him wonder again whether he was just a coward who could not grasp the one chance he would ever have to do something so bold.

That evening, as he sat trying to read by the light of the fire as his mother slept in the chair, he wondered again if he had it in him to make what felt like an impossible journey. Both Gwennie and Doy had recently lost their jobs as the munitions factory wound down. What jobs there were went to men coming back in droves from France. He was lucky to have got in early on the railways. If Iant went it would condemn Doy, in particular, to a life scrimping and scratching a living to care for their mother. Gwennie would soon be gone and Doy couldn't manage even the few sheep and chickens on her own. They would probably not be able to afford even the rent. They would end up in one of the places at the far end of the village that were not much better than pigsties.

That night Iant decided that he had to put it behind him. Although he and Sara had agreed to part some time ago, he had never really let the idea go. He hadn't been serious enough to grasp it though and live by his choice. He was torturing himself and it had infected his time with Frances. As well as that, people had begun to think of him as morose, another casualty of the war. The stories of the mental hospital in Denbigh, full of shell-shocked ex-soldiers, circulated widely and he resolved not to join them. By their standards he was fit, and it would be dishonourable to let himself wallow as he had been doing.

Iant knew that he had been neglecting the house and the little patch of land. He once again threw himself into the small tasks that needed doing whenever he was not at his work. He mended fences and whitewashed the outside walls of the house and the shed. He worked on the little garden that his mother tended, as best she could. He tried to turn it into something more manageable for her by laying paths and tidying the beds for the vegetables. He made sure that the sheep were all accounted for and sold at the right time and for the right price. He replaced some of the chickens and renewed an arrangement to sell the eggs to the village shop.

Gwennie and Ben were to marry next spring and Iant became set on saving a little money so that his sister could have some sort of wedding party. He set aside something from his wage packet each month before he put the rest into the household's expenses. Notionally his mother still regarded herself as in charge of this, but she depended more and more on Iant in practice. He volunteered for some overtime and weekends and began to feel more optimistic that he could save enough to hire the little village hall, lay on some food and drink and still leave enough over for the dress that Gwennie was hoping to buy from Holt's in Wrexham.

One Saturday Ben asked if Iant wanted to go with him and his friends to the Racecourse Ground. He had never been one for the football really, but he had been working hard and he thought he deserved an afternoon away. As he was walking down the platform on Wrexham station he felt an enormous thump on his back followed by a huge bellow:

189

'Iant!'

It was Gethin. The last time he had seen him was on the Ridge.

'I didn't know if you were dead or alive.'

'Gethin. Oh my God man!'

'What happened to you?'

'I ended up in hospital in Salonika. Blinded I was. What about you?'

'Prisoner of bloody war – don't ask me about Bulgarians right? I haven't been home that long – took months for them to sort us out and get us back. You going to the match?'

'Aye. I'm meeting my brother-in-law. Or I will be soon.'

'Bring him up to *The Seven Stars* – I'll be there until just before kick-off. Christ man it's good to see you!'

'It's good to see you too Geth.'

'So, see you in a while eh?'

'Alright. *Seven Stars.*'

When he saw Ben he was with a group of friends, so he arranged to see him in the ground. *The Seven Stars* was full because of the game, but as soon Iant got inside he heard his name being called across the crowded bar. Before he knew it, he had a pint in his hand and Gethin was talking nineteen to the dozen. Iant realised how much he had missed not just Gethin, but anyone that had been with him during the war. His mind had been so much on leaving Sara behind, that his life in the army had almost been forgotten.

Gethin told him about the surrender on the mountain and the long march into the south of Bulgaria. They had a few men die just from exhaustion and hunger before they got to the camp, and even more when they got there. Gethin's memories of being a prisoner were worse, he said, than of the fighting. At least then you could do something. In the camps, he told Iant, you were powerless and made to work with not enough food. He said that he felt lucky though. He was only there a few months. They had met Serbs and Romanians who had been there longer and were nearly dying from hunger. The Bulgarians seemed to treat the

190

British and French better for some reason.

They didn't have long before the match started and Iant would have liked to stay. They arranged to meet up the following week and went their separate ways. He found it difficult to concentrate on the game when he met up with Ben. The conversation with Gethin had taken him back to somewhere that he had imagined that he would not want to go, but for everyone, the war had been a complicated experience. Some of the best times of his life had been while he was in the army. The war had taken him away from the village and given him experiences he would never have had. His life had been endangered, but, as well as Sara, he had met people that he now missed. He thought of Johnny and whether he was back in London.

In the coming months, Iant and Gethin became firm friends. Whilst Iant would never have Gethin's appetites he enjoyed getting drunk with him from time to time and, in turn, Gethin would come to the house at weekends and help out with things that Iant could not manage on his own. Gethin charmed Iant's mother with a smile and a bit of cheek and he became something of a fixture around the table whenever he could get away.

Iant felt the benefit of his renewed friendship and became more and more determined to try and get on with his present life. As Gethin's visits up to Carrog became increasingly frequent he also began to see that they were not completely motivated by wanting to go out and shoot a few rabbits and pigeons.

As the flirtation between Gethin and Doy became more and more overt, Iant felt some anxiety that he had brought a man into their home that would not be right for his younger sister. He knew how much Doy was desperate not to be the one to be stuck looking after their mother and he worried that this would lead her to rash decisions. He had grown fond of Gethin, but he also remembered him in Salonika as a different person and not one that would be inclined to offer his sister the kind of stable home that he imagined for her.

Iant agonised for some time about speaking to Doy about

191

Gethin, but he hadn't the heart. He could see how she smiled when he came into the house. Who was he to interfere when he had his own secrets? As time moved on it was clear that the moment had passed and Gethin asked if he would mind if he and Doy stepped out. He took her to a dance in Wrexham, to the pictures and eventually to his mother and father's house for tea one Sunday. The following weekend Gethin called when Doy was out and asked, very politely if he could speak to Iant's mother. A few moments later he emerged smiling and declared Iant his future brother-in-law.

It had been barely three months since Iant had met Gethin again and he was now part of his life forever. Gethin said that the war had made him impatient to get on with his life, and Iant found it difficult to argue. They would stay engaged until after Gwennie's wedding next spring and then think about a date. He made himself feel happy for them both, but he could also not help a creeping feeling of dread at what his own life might soon become.

Chapter 26

Over the coming months, Iant saw the future begin to take shape. He went more frequently to Wrexham with his prospective brothers-in-law to watch football and drink in their local pubs. They helped him and his sisters up at the house and on the fields and they became a new kind of family. This had a lot to recommend it. His mother, especially when 'the boys' were around, became happier and more inclined to smile occasionally, while he found himself enjoying some regular company.

Gwennie and Ben were married in May 1921. The wedding party was small, but it was a happy occasion. Iant walked his sister down the aisle wearing his Lance Corporal's uniform for the first time since he got off the train after the long journey from Salonika. Gethin too got out his old uniform and after the little wedding breakfast was over they drank the health of the comrades they remembered, especially Oliver.

Iant helped to pay for two nights in a tradesman's hotel in Barmouth for the married couple and a little group walked them down to the train the next morning. Despite a slightly sore head, Iant felt happy to see his elder sister start a new life and hoped that Ben would be a husband that she could rely on and who would look after her. His mother, Iant was surprised to see, looked on benevolently as the train pulled out of Carrog station. It would not be long, Iant thought, before Doy and Gethin set a date and he would be waving them off somewhere.

Long after he had become the one person to who he had told the story of his 'engagement' Iant had maintained a friendship with Alun Lewis. Periodically the older man would invite Iant over to Acrefair where he would eat a meal surrounded by Alun's growing family. They would sometimes also take walks together leaving Alun's wife, Mary, with the children. A favourite was a longish hike up to Horseshoe Falls with a view over Llangollen and the valley most of the way. If they timed it right and it was a Saturday, they would stop at *The*

Chain Bridge Hotel and sit outside sipping their pints overlooking the river.

One hot Saturday in July after Gwennie's wedding Iant arranged to meet Alun at the Falls and walk back to Acrefair. The heat had made him keep to the shade whenever he could. He had lost almost all the tolerance for heat that he had developed in Salonika. Alun took a seat on one of the benches outside while Iant went in to get the beer. The hotel's landlord was always behind the bar and was not always the most cheerful sort.

Out of the bright sunlight, the hotel bar had a dingy feel to it. The landlord managed to contribute to this with his hangdog expression. Iant could not wait to get out again into the sunlight. The landlord called out to the back room and a young woman came out and cleared away some glasses and wiped the table. As she turned she glanced very briefly at Iant, but the hint of a shy smile passed across her face before she was back out of sight.

'That'll be a bob and a penny.'

'If my wages went up at the same rate as the beer I'd be a rich man' joked Iant.

'If I had a bob for every time I heard that one, so would I' said the landlord before turning away and putting the coins in his till.

'How is smiler?' asked Alun as Iant sat down beside him.

'He'll be on at the Llandudno Empire yet.'

They sat in silence for a few moments savouring both the beer and the rushing water below them. They had managed to find a seat out of the direct sun and Iant thought that there was no better place to be when the weather was like this. He thought of the young woman's smile and caught himself grinning while Alun was talking.

'What is so funny Iant?'

'Nothing…just something my mother said this morning.'

Doy and Gethin lost no time in setting a date for their wedding. Gethin had a little money saved and they booked a reception in the *Owain Glyndwr* hotel. The thought passed across Iant's mind that Gethin had a streak of one-upmanship in him.

His wedding had to be better than Ben and Gwennie's. He had seen this in the army when Iant had been promoted over him. However, he could see that his younger sister was happy and that was what was important. The wedding was to be the following spring.

Ben and Gwennie had rented a little house in Wrexham. It suited them because of Ben's work, but Gwennie told him that she missed the hillsides and often grew bored cooped up in the house. She talked of trying to find some cleaning work, though Ben was not keen on the idea. He thought she could do better than, as he put it, skivvy for someone else. In the end, common sense won through and Gwennie began cleaning three times a week at one of the big houses on Ruthin Road near Belle Vue Park.

Iant saw less of Ben now, even Gethin as he was supposedly saving for the wedding. Every now and then though they would meet for a drink, usually in Wrexham. One night, as Autumn began to set in, he met Ben on his own in *The Nag's Head*. It was cold for the time of year and after they left the pub Ben hurried off home while Iant headed for the station, anxious not to miss the last train. He knew a short cut that took him down some of the back alleys off the High Street.

As he went to turn down one he saw a man and a woman with their hands all over each other and he quickly took a different route. Who was he to spoil their fun he thought with a smile? A noise from behind him made him half turn and as he did so he caught the slightest glimpse of Gethin's face in the streetlight.

For a second or two, his instincts told him to rush back and confront him. He wasn't sure whether Gethin had seen him or not, but the coward in him rushed on to get his train. He wasn't afraid of Gethin, but he hated the idea of such a public confrontation. All the way home on the train and on the long walk back up the hill he seethed with a mixture of anger and shame. How could he not just have rushed at him and knocked his bloody teeth out? As he got nearer the house he prayed Doy

195

would not be up and when he saw that she wasn't he crept silently to his bed.

The next day Iant dashed straight to work without seeing anyone. As the morning wore on he came to realise that he had to do something. Apart from his need to look after his sister he knew that he would not be able to let it lie for his own sake. He could think of little else and worried that he might make a mistake over a signal.

At the end of the day, Iant didn't go home. He went straight to the station and caught the train to Wrexham. His mother and Doy would be worried where he had got to and then angry that he made them worry. It could not be helped, he needed to settle this, whatever the consequences. As he walked from the station towards Gethin's house he realised that he had little idea of what he was going to say or do. He had spent so much time seething about what he saw as Gethin's betrayal both of his sister and of himself that he hadn't got to the part where the matter was resolved. He could not think straight so he just kept on walking until he found himself knocking on the front door of the small terraced house where Gethin's family lived.

'Iant, hello love.'

'Hello, Mrs Williams.'

'Come in Iant, take your coat off.'

'I'm not stopping thank you Mrs Williams. Is Gethin at home please?'

'Gethin. It's Iant.'

He saw Mrs Williams' face begin to register that this was not a normal social call, but he could not bring himself to engage in small talk as he would usually have done.

'Is everything all right Iant. Doy isn't unwell is she.'

'No. She's at home with Mam. Everything is fine thank you.'

By now Gethin had appeared behind his mother and she left them to it.

'Iant, man. Have you come to drag me out for a pint.'

'Yes, I have. Hurry up and get your coat.'

As he waited on the doorstep Iant could hear hushed voices.

196

When Gethin came back with his coat on they walked off down the street without another word. At last Iant could contain himself no longer.

'What the hell do you think you're playing at Gethin?'

'What are you talking about?'

'So you didn't see me then?'

'What do you mean?'

'Last night, you didn't see me?'

'What...?'

'You were a bit busy I suppose.'

A grin passed across Gethin's face despite himself and Iant lost his temper pushing Gethin into an alley and then up against the wall.

'You think its funny do you Geth?'

Iant was much the smaller of the two of them and he knew that he would be no match for Gethin if it came to a proper fight, but his anger got the better of him and Gethin remained pinned to the wall.

'So what have you got to say for yourself?'

'Iant....'

'Never mind 'Iant'. How bloody dare you? You've not been with my sister for anywhere near a year and you are all over some tart!.'

'Have you told her?'

'What would you care?'

'Have you, Iant?'

'So now you realise what you have done do you?'

'It was nothing man. I hardly know her.'

'Is that supposed to make it better you bloody idiot?'

'Don't tell her Iant.'

'Why shouldn't I? Do you think my sister doesn't deserve to know that she is being made a fool of by you?'

'Don't tell me you haven't got drunk and chased a bit of skirt Iant.'

This enraged Iant further, partly because it had a small grain of truth. It had been some time since he had thought about Clara

197

and his discovery of how short and sad her life had been. He had told himself often that he and his comrades didn't know what was going to happen to them back in the camp, that they were just grasping at something that they might never otherwise have ever experienced. He had been genuinely fascinated by Clara, otherwise, he would never have tried to seek her out after the war. But he had still been part of the miserable life she had been forced to lead.

He grabbed Gethin by the throat now and he didn't resist.

'I wasn't engaged to someone's sister. I hadn't made any promises to anyone you bastard.'

Gethin pulled himself free, coughing from the choking effect of Iant's grip.

'It won't happen again, Iant.'

Iant remained silent, not knowing what to do next. He remained furious, but grabbing at Gethin had made him feel foolish more than anything.

'If you tell Doy it would just make her unhappy.'

'Yes, it would.'

'So let it be can't you? I've told you it was nothing and it won't happen again.'

'If it does it'll be the last thing you do boy.'

As soon as he had said it, Iant saw how pathetic the words sounded, but they were all he had. He wanted now to be away from here, from Gethin, but also the ridiculous situation. He hated confrontation of any kind, but he had known that he could not just forget what he had seen the previous night. He began to walk rapidly away in the direction of the station.

'Iant man. Come on, let's have a pint. Don't go like this.'

He didn't reply. Let him stew Iant thought. He had made up his mind that the lesser of two evils was to not tell his sister. She would have felt humiliated and he couldn't face that. For the moment though he had no intention of having a matey drink with Gethin as if nothing had happened. He needed to get away from him and compose himself.

On the journey home Iant talked himself through the

deception that he had to carry out. Not just this evening when he would be confronted with the anxiety of his mother and sister about where he had been without telling them, but one that would always be there. Perhaps it was, as Gethin insisted, something trivial, something that he had to put aside in favour of Doy's future happiness. He steeled himself to do that and by the time he reached home his story about sheep straying on to the track was perfectly straight in his mind.

Chapter 27

In early November there came a spell of uncharacteristically warm weather. The hillsides were still vivid with colour and one Saturday Iant set off on his bike telling his mother and sister that he was going to meet Alun in Acrefair.

He left his old bike at Carrog station and travelled to Llangollen. The train was busy with people going to the market and he had to stand the short way into town. It was under an hour to walk to *The Chain Bridge* but Iant found himself dawdling on the way and stopping to look at the view over the town rather more than he might normally do. He told himself that he needed to rest the ankle but in truth, it only occasionally gave him any difficulty now.

The hotel bar had not long opened when he arrived and was still quiet. The landlord's face, as ever, indicated his apparent displeasure at actually having a customer, but Iant bought his pint and took a seat in one of the windows that looked out over the river. Although the weather was warm the hotel didn't get much of the winter sun and sitting outside was not an attractive idea. Besides he needed a seat that gave him the best chance of doing what he had come to do.

He hadn't arranged to meet Alun Lewis at all that day. On a whim, he had engaged in a mild deceit motivated by the faintest of memories of a girl's smile some weeks ago.

Since his last walk with Alun Iant had often found his days spoilt by the encounter with Gethin. He had tried to be less censorious about what he had seen that night in the alley but had felt let down by the breach of trust. Alone in the signal box all day he had a lot of time to deliberate.

He had decided the previous day that he needed to do something to shake himself out of his pre-occupations. In recent months, it had felt that he had worked hard to make his mother feel secure in her home and to help give his sisters a start in life. Despite his current feelings about Gethin, he felt glad to see

Gwennie and Doy begin the lives they wanted. At nearly twenty-six himself though he struggled to see his own future.

Iant was just considering a second pint when the young woman appeared from a door behind the bar carrying plates. She walked through the bar and on into the adjacent dining room which, at weekends, was open to non-residents. She was gone before Iant had a chance to catch her eye, but only moments later she returned and, yes, there was the faint, shy smile that had stuck in his head.

'Lovely day' Iant found himself blurting out, but not quite loudly enough as she was gone without a pause. He went to the bar and bought another pint and found himself fervently hoping that the young woman was not the landlord's daughter. At least there was no resemblance and her gentle smile was the opposite of the landlord's stony face. In fact, her face was the opposite; the kind that brightened up a room when she came into it. She was pretty Iant thought, but in a way that was quite understated. As well as that smile he had noticed her smooth, pale skin and her contrasting very dark hair.

On a sign by the bar, Iant noticed that the hotel stopped serving lunches at two o'clock. He decided to drink his pint and take a walk up to the Falls and back. It would be better than nursing his drink for an hour or, worse still, knocking back a couple more and get unsteady on his feet.

About ten minutes to two Iant found a flat rock to perch on by the river just upstream from the hotel. From there he could see the little road that wound up the entrance. He had tried to think through what he might say, but he was still far from clear. The advantage of where he sat he thought was that he could always pretend to be staring across the valley if his nerve failed at the last moment.

Iant's options became more restricted when the young woman finally emerged from the back entrance of the hotel and, instead of turning down the road towards Llangollen, as he thought she would she turned in the direction of where he was sitting. Before he knew it she was just a few yards away and

201

without seeming very rude Iant had no choice but to speak.

'Beautiful view, isn't it?'

'Yes, it is. I don't notice so much since I have worked here I suppose.'

'No, I suppose you wouldn't.'

'Have you been walking?'

'Just up to the Falls. Have you finished work now?'

'Until this evening, yes.'

Somehow Iant managed to both ask her where she was going and then ask if she minded him accompanying her the short distance to her home. As they strolled the half-mile to her house Iant discovered that her name was Nancy and that her father worked on the estate in the Eglwyseg Valley. She lived with her father and mother in one of a small terrace of cottages in the little hamlet of Pentredwr. Iant found that Nancy was the kind of person that made him feel at ease. She spoke gently, but easily, without leaving awkward gaps in the conversation. He couldn't know this yet, but Iant felt sure that he had met someone who was naturally kind and generous by nature. They were not completely alike, but there was no doubt that Iant was reminded of how he had felt on the walks with Sara during his recovery.

When they reached Nancy's home they politely shook hands and Iant rather awkwardly said something about seeing her again when he visited the hotel.

As he walked back towards Llangollen a breeze had got up and Iant quickened his pace. He wasn't sure whether his trip had been successful or not. He was glad that he wasn't walking home feeling ridiculous or deflated which would have happened if he had failed to catch a glimpse of Nancy. The person that he had already begun to think of as the girl with the smile.

Over the next month, each Saturday was, for Iant, taken up either by shifts in the signal box, essential maintenance at the house or a prearranged visit to Alun Lewis. The latter could also have included a visit to *The Chain Bridge Hotel*, but when Alun suggested it Iant declined, opting instead for a freezing cold walk up to Pen-y-Bryn. There was no doubt in his mind that he would like to see Nancy again, but the idea of meeting her when his friend was present and then be subjected to a barrage of teasing questions, was too much to face.

Eventually, six weeks after they had exchanged a few words and walked up the road to Nancy's home, Iant set off on the train to Llangollen. He had some errands to do including replacing a much-mended saw that had once been his father's, so he did not have to resort to deception. He made his purchases and arranged to leave them with the stationmaster before setting off on the road towards Horseshoe Pass and the hotel.

Iant had considered writing a note addressed to Nancy but he still felt cautious. He couldn't deny that he still had thoughts of Sara and often wondered what she was doing and whether she ever thought of him. He also knew how badly he had handled what had taken place with Frances. He sometimes thought that their relationship could have become closer if he had not been so inept.

He grew more and more anxious as he climbed the hill. Perhaps she would not be working that day? Perhaps also, given that several weeks had elapsed, she might have taken offence that he had not called or made any kind of contact? Worse still, another passing stranger may have walked into the hotel and returned that smile with much more confidence than he had.

On this visit, Iant later reflected, the gods were with him. Without even encountering the landlord Iant almost walked into Nancy as he entered the hotel. She was returning from serving some diners and was just passing the door as he opened it. With the minimum of fuss, they arranged to meet when she finished work around two o'clock.

Rather than sit waiting in the bar Iant left the hotel and walked on up the hill. He felt some relief that he had met Nancy again and that she had at least not been displeased to see him. Iant had a plan of sorts which was to invite Nancy to go with him to the Christmas bazaar organised by the chapel attended by Alun and his wife in Acrefair. It was to be the following Saturday

203

and, he hoped, would be convenient for her if she finished working at the same time.

This plan, however, involved something of a decisive step for Iant because it would involve letting on to Alun and his family that he had met someone that he was keen on. He recoiled at the thought of the embarrassment of this and the inevitable need to say something to his mother and sisters. However, it had to be got over because Iant realised that he genuinely wanted to see and get to know this young woman. It was based on little more than a warm smile and the ease he felt as they walked to her house a few weeks ago, but it could not be ignored.

At five minutes before two o'clock, Iant waited at the side of the hotel. Nancy emerged on time wearing her thick dark winter coat and what Iant noticed was a blue scarf that matched her eyes. She looked so naturally pretty and Iant felt his attraction to her take a strong grip on him.

Iant wanted to get the difficulty out of the way, so he asked her if she would consider accompanying him to the bazaar the following Saturday. If she would, he would walk her there and back of course and make sure that she was not late if she was working that evening. Nancy's face coloured, but she agreed conditional on her father giving his approval.

At this moment Iant understood how his recent life had changed him. Growing up in the village that was so dominated by the chapel he would once have taken it for granted that a father would have needed to approve nearly every move. Now he was momentarily taken aback that Nancy would need to ask permission for such an innocent venture. He wouldn't make it a barrier between them. His life had thrown up experiences that he would not once have imagined. If he had to be patient, then so be it.

'I think it would make it easier if you were to come in with me if you have time' Nancy said, as they reached her house.

Iant had not been expecting this and felt ill-prepared, but there was little choice and he followed Nancy through the front door which led direct to the front parlour. Her mother and father were sat in the back room either side of the black range which was lit making the room very warm. Her mother looked very small and was dressed in the old-fashioned way that he remembered from his grandmother. By contrast, Nancy's father was quite a large imposing man sitting with his shirtsleeves rolled up. He had on a brown waistcoat with his watch-chain strung across his stomach.

'Who have we got here then?' Nancy's father said.

'This is Iant, Dad.'

'Iant is it? You're not from around here are you?'

'No…no my family live outside Carrog. On the way to Corwen.'

'I know Carrog. Fishing.'

'Yes, there's some good spots there they tell me.'

'You don't fish then?'

'No…no I don't.'

'Iant has asked me to go with him to the Christmas Bazaar at Acrefair next Saturday. He's come in to ask if that is alright with you.'

'The chapel, is it?'

'Yes, that's right. My friend Alun Lewis and his family go to that chapel. We'll all go together if that's alright with you?'

'I suppose it is, yes.'

'I will walk Nancy back afterwards of course.'

'Will you have a cup of tea?'

It was the first time that Nancy's mother had spoken or moved since they had come into the room.

'No, thank you. I won't disturb you anymore. I'm sure Nancy needs to rest before she goes back to work.'

As Nancy was seeing him out she gave him a reassuring smile. When they were out of earshot he told her that he had no idea of her family's name. All the time he had been struggling with how to address her father.

'Its Roberts. My Dad is Dilwyn and my Mam is Catrin.'

'Nancy Roberts.'

'That is me.'

205

'Well, Nancy Roberts I will meet you next Saturday with your Dad's permission.'

'You will.'

Iant went back down the little road smiling at the memory of the twinkle in Nancy's eye and the flash of something that was half-teasing him. He was already looking forward to the following weekend.

Chapter 28

As Iant gradually got to know the Roberts family over the following weeks and months he grew fond of Nancy's mother. He liked her father but knew he was someone not to cross. Dil Roberts was a man more respected than liked. He had many skills and could turn his hand to anything. As a consequence, people from many of the surrounding villages would often call on him in a variety of small emergencies. He was therefore variously seen as an untrained vet, a carpenter, even a layer-out of the dead. He was capable of great kindness, but also of impatience and bad temper.

Catrin on the other hand was a very shy, but also a very generous person who, especially when Dil was not around, welcomed Iant into her home with great warmth. Having grown up with a mother who found it difficult to show sympathy or affection, Iant found himself looking forward to the reception that he invariably received when he called for Nancy.

Gethin and Doy were to be married at the end of May and Iant had thought for a long time about whether to ask Nancy if she would come to the wedding. People saw it as a mark of serious intent to ask a girl to accompany you to a wedding, but eventually, Iant cast off his caution and Nancy accepted the invitation.

It had only been a few months since Iant had first accompanied Nancy on their first modest outing and, mainly because of the distance between their homes, they had still not spent very much time in each other's company. Despite this Iant felt the ease that he had sensed from the start grow between them. His time with Sara had already shown him what it was like to feel great passion and desire. With Nancy, he felt something quieter, but which was bringing him happiness. He thought that the same was true of Nancy, but, so far, she hadn't expressed much of what she felt.

As his younger sister's wedding approached Iant made every

effort to put the episode with Gethin behind him. He saw that Gethin was attentive towards Doy and that he saw the need to be a dutiful son-in-law. While there remained a wariness between them, Gethin resumed helping Iant with jobs that needed doing and there were even evenings when they met others for a drink. This had not extended to the two of them meeting on their own and Iant wanted it to stay that way.

After they were married Iant reasoned that he would see little of Gethin in any event. To Iant's surprise, Gethin had got a job with the Ministry of Labour which meant working in the new Labour Exchange in Rhyl. Although it meant living some distance from her family Doy was excited about the move to a seaside town and some relatives of Gethin's had helped set them up with some respectable digs until they got settled.

Thinking about Rhyl made Iant spare a thought for Clara and her wasted life, but much more pressingly he also thought of what his wedding would have been like in Greece. Strange, certainly, and he would have missed his family, but Sara would have helped him through it, he was sure of that. For some time the day before he thought he might have to tell Nancy that he had made a mistake and that she should return to her parents. The dreadful idea of doing this and the upset it would have caused stopped him in the end, fortunately, but he remained distracted all during the last-minute preparations.

Although it was over three years since he had been discharged from the army, his sisters had pressed him and Gethin to put on their uniforms once more for the wedding. As he walked down Corwen's main street on his way to collect Nancy from where she was staying with relatives Iant felt self-conscious. His uniform inevitably took him back again to Salonika. Sometimes he would struggle to bring Sara's face clearly into his mind. He didn't want her image to disappear altogether though he felt guilty at trying so hard to keep this memory clear. He felt nothing but happiness when he thought of their time together and had never really stopped wondering what might have been had they lived different kinds of lives. The ring with the green

208

stone still lay in the box in which he also kept her letters.

By the time he knocked on the door of the house in which Nancy had spent the previous night Iant was doing his best to concentrate on the fact that today was his sister's wedding day and that this was where his thoughts should be. When Nancy herself answered the door he found himself thinking, really for the first time, how lovely she looked. She was wearing a simple dress printed with small red and yellow flowers tied at the waist with a red sash. On her head was a small straw hat. He wanted to tell her that she looked a picture but became stupidly tongue-tied.

Nancy surprised him by saluting as he stood there and they both laughed. After passing the time of day with her relative they walked down the street with Nancy holding Iant's arm. The sun was shining now and, dressed in his heavy army jacket, the warmth sent a trickle of perspiration running down Iant's back, but almost despite himself, he felt a rush of happiness.

Compared to Gwennie and Ben's wedding this was a lavish affair. After the chapel service, there was a buffet at the hotel with some beer for the men and a punch for the women. Iant had introduced Nancy to his mother and both his sisters. Gwennie was just starting to show the signs of expecting her first child and she stood talking to Nancy about her pregnancy and how fat she felt. Later Iant looked over and saw Nancy sitting beside his mother. She smiled and nodded her head as his mother spoke and he even saw a smile pass occasionally across the older woman's face.

Later in the afternoon some of the tables were cleared away for dancing. Someone played the piano in the corner of the hotel dining room while Gethin and Doy moved awkwardly around the room. Eventually, others began to join them and Iant thought now would be a good moment to rescue Nancy.

As they shuffled around the room with a handful of other couples Iant's hand lay barely touching the small of Nancy's back. He had not drunk very much but he was suddenly conscious of the smell of beer on his breath. In the time he had known Nancy they had exchanged only the briefest of kisses and Iant was not sure why. All he could say to himself was that he had sensed that this was what she had wanted. His hand on her back pressed a little more firmly and Nancy moved a little closer to him.

As the evening finished Iant arranged for his mother to get home safely and he walked Nancy back to her relatives' house. It was cooler now and Iant gave her his jacket to drape over her shoulders. They walked hand in hand up the street, both slowing to delay the moment when Nancy must go inside. Iant suggested that they took a detour along the path by the river and they sat for a while on a bench and listened to the water. Nervously Iant turned and took Nancy's face in his hands and they kissed, at first awkwardly and then with warmth and tenderness.

'I need to be back, I think, Iant.'

'Yes. I'm sorry. I don't want to make you late.'

'I don't want them telling tales back to Dad.'

'Did you enjoy the day?'

'I was a bit nervous, but people made me welcome.'

'I hope they did.'

They walked a little quicker now and when they arrived at the house Iant kissed Nancy very lightly on the cheek. They hastily arranged to meet for a walk on a Sunday in a fortnight's time and she was gone. It crossed Iant's mind how quickly and naturally he had become intimate with Sara, but he managed to suppress the thought.

Iant had expected his mother to be inquisitive about Nancy, but he was not prepared for the level of interest she showed. She had, in her own way, obviously taken a liking to Nancy and she brought her into the conversation whenever there was an opportunity. She had already found out from someone in the village that Nancy's father worked on the estate as a maintenance man but wanted to know more about her mother, whether she had brothers and sisters and what kind of house they lived in. More surprising was her lack of disapproval about Nancy's job in a licenced premise. There had been many a time when Iant's mother had suggested the unsuitability of such a thing for an unmarried girl, but having met Nancy this was apparently all forgotten.

During the rest of that year, Iant saw more and more of Nancy. The long evenings made it possible to visit on a weekday and Nancy began to stay the occasional night at Iant's mother's house once her father had become convinced of the utmost respectability of the arrangement. Once or twice they journeyed to Wrexham to the picture house and attended village fairs together near each other's homes. Iant was aware that it was a slow courtship and sometimes he couldn't help thinking of the makeshift swimming pool that he and Sara had swum in. The feel of her body under the water that day had stayed very vividly in his mind and it fuelled his imagination more often than it should.

However, after a time in his life when he had not known where to turn, he began to welcome the peaceful rhythms of his time with Nancy. Their relationship gradually became more physical, but it was not just about that. Iant began to love the gentleness that Nancy brought to his life and the kindness to him and his mother that she seemed to show very naturally.

In late September Iant and Nancy rode back on the train together to Llangollen after she had visited his home for tea. They were alone in the carriage and Iant, after thinking of nothing else all day, plucked up the courage to ask Nancy to marry him. He would of course talk to her father, but he wanted to know what she would say first. Her quiet reply confirmed that he had found the right person for him. She didn't exclaim out loud or cry, she produced the shy smile that Iant had first seen nearly a year ago and said very calmly that, yes, she thought they would work very well together. After a moment, she leaned over and kissed him gently on the cheek.

This, what Iant had always imagined would be one of the most important moments of his life, had passed almost unnoticed. Nancy had entered his life in the quietest way and now they had agreed to spend their lives together. When he was alone again Iant realised with a start just how little he and Nancy knew each other, but it did not make him regret asking her to marry him. He felt a strong trust in her that was not based on any factual understanding and he decided that was how it had to be.

Within just a few weeks Iant and Nancy had agreed that they would marry soon. They would live with Iant's mother as she was alone and she would stop working at the hotel. His wages would support them and Nancy would make the most of the garden and perhaps have a few more animals to make a little extra money. To Iant, it sounded a simple life, but one that would offer some hope of happiness to them both. He had experienced great disappointment, but he also felt lucky. He had survived a war that had taken so many, even in this small corner of the world. Despite the memories that still overtook him sometimes, he felt ready to try and make his happiness and the happiness of those that depended on him, in this, the quietest of places.

On St David's Day the following year, Iant stood with Alun Lewis in the Methodist church on the outskirts of Llangollen. Any moment Nancy would come through the door on her Dad's arm. Dil would probably be looking serious, but inside he would be nervous and already missing his daughter. Iant looked across the aisle and smiled at Catrin Roberts who looked lonely sitting on her own. Nancy's one brother, Bob, had emigrated to Canada just before the war only to be sent back as part of the Canadian army. He survived the trenches and now lived in a small town in Ontario. They would all drink his health later.

The man playing the upright piano began to play and there Nancy was in a dress that he hadn't seen before, a blue straw hat and new black shoes. Always that smile Iant thought and he turned to face forwards so that the handful of guests wouldn't stare at him. Alun placed a reassuring hand on his shoulder and soon Nancy was beside him. She had already become the person around who Iant felt most at home in the world.

Chapter 29

A honeymoon spent in the little spare room of Gethin and Doy's house was not as perfect as Iant would have wished for. A combination of close proximity to other people and natural nervousness did not make for an ideal start to the intimate side of his life with Nancy. Despite the fact that he had had sexual encounters with two women Iant did not feel experienced. He tried to take a lead but also be gentle. Nancy, like most young women of her background, had only the most limited idea of what was expected of her. From Sara, Iant knew that both of them should experience pleasure and eventually, with some difficulty they began to manage this some of the time.

Nancy had already become firm friends with his younger sister and this helped to make up for the awkwardness that Iant still felt around Gethin. In truth, Iant had been reluctant to take up the offer of a few days in Rhyl for their honeymoon, but he could see that Nancy was excited about the prospect of being by the sea and he felt unable to refuse.

They took long walks along the seafront and the March winds nearly blew them off their feet. The town was quiet and Iant and Nancy often felt as though they had the town and the view over the grey seas to themselves. They spent a lot of time at the town's pride and joy, Marine Lake. It contained a funfair and a miniature railway, but the fair was closed at this time of year. They wandered in and out of the rides and once climbed on board two horses on the stationary carousel and urged each other to imagine that they were moving.

However, the little narrow-gauge railway was running, and they rode it several times, laughing at the absurdity of a railwayman spending his honeymoon on a train. The little train gave them both pleasure, perhaps something to do with being squashed together into the scaled-down carriage Iant thought. There was a kind of magic for both of them of chugging along around the artificial lake with almost no-one else around, that is apart from the ducks and swans swimming in endless circles.

Along the seafront stood *The Royal Alexandra Hospital* and every day, as they walked past, Iant was reminded of how lucky they were to be strolling along on their honeymoon. The hospital was really intended for sick children and the pathetic sight of them being pushed by mothers and fathers in wheelchairs was made even worse by the addition of men still convalescing after the war. This long after the end of the war, the hospital only contained men who were the most seriously wounded, many of them unlikely to make a full recovery or return to a normal life.

Iant had, by and large, chosen not to dwell on his time in battle. It was a short if painful time in his life. He had been terrified when he thought that he might not see again but had been well cared for and the memory of that fear did not haunt him. As he walked along the grey windswept seafront, he understood that it was the memory of his time with Sara that haunted him more than his time as a soldier. It was not that he wished himself elsewhere, or that he wished that his life was with Sara rather than Nancy, it was the thought that something like that could have happened to him and that he had let it go.

On the last day of their holiday, Nancy caught him looking across at the men in wheelchairs, wrapped tightly against the wind, and squeezed his arm more tightly. Iant knew of course that she thought he was remembering the war and he felt ashamed. What would be the point of telling her about something that would soon be a distant memory? He tried to tell himself that it would only hurt her for no reason, but he knew that it was a stupid and cowardly lie. He thought of the ring that he kept at home and imagined one day the hurt that Nancy would feel if she found it. He would choose a time, he told himself. When they were settled back at home.

To Iant's great surprise and delight, not very long after they returned from honeymoon, Nancy had walked halfway down the track to the village to meet him as he cycled home. She told him, very shyly, that was almost certain that she was going to have a baby. Although shocked Iant found himself almost

214

overwhelmed with pleasure in a way that he had experienced before. It was happiness that started in his stomach and came up to bring tears to his eyes. When he embraced Nancy though he could sense a holding back and she told him how worried she had been that people would think that they had to get married.

When Iant laughed out loud it was the first time that he had really seen Nancy's face cloud in anger. He did not understand, she said, that this was the world she had grown up in and that making her parents ashamed in any way would spoil the happiness that the baby would bring. If she delayed telling them, she reasoned, then perhaps they would not jump to the same conclusions. Iant, though, was bursting to tell the whole world but knew that he could not propose telling anyone until Dil and Catrin had been informed. The news would have mysteriously travelled down the valley to Llangollen and then up to the Pass before they could blink. By the time they reached home Iant had persuaded Nancy that they must make the trip to her parents' home the following weekend. If her parents were as pleased about the news as they surely would be then they would have nothing to fear.

In the intervening days, Nancy became so anxious that Iant feared it might affect the tiny beginnings of a child inside her. He did his best to calm her and make her realise that her fears were baseless, but her upbringing had been such that he could do little to affect her. She told him about a woman in the chapel whose father had forbidden her marriage because he had found out that she was expecting. The man had been forced to leave the area and look for work in Liverpool. No-one had seen the woman for the last two years. The fact that they were already married did not seem to count in the weighing up of Nancy's fears.

As the two of them walked up the hill towards Nancy's house the following Sunday Iant could see that the colour had drained from her face and he felt completely at a loss as to what he could do about it. In his heart, he felt sure that the news would surely only bring delight to Dil and Catrin, but he could not be certain.

215

They had not had time to send word that they would be coming and when they knocked on the door Catrin's pleasure at seeing them was mixed with some anxiety at why they had come unexpectedly. This was compounded by her instantly recognising her daughter's concern. By the time they had entered the back room where Dil sat in his usual place, Iant had become almost as troubled as his wife.

They had decided in advance that it would be Iant that spoke. He had volunteered and been surprised when Nancy agreed. At this moment, he regretted offering at all. He decided to get it over with as quickly as possible.

'Mr and Mrs Roberts, we have come over today with some news.'

'We didn't think you'd come to take the air on the mountain boy.'

'Iant can you call us by our names do you think.'

'I'm sorry. I will try.'

'So what is it then? Is it that railway moving you to the other side of the country?'

'Oh no, no nothing like that.'

'Well?'

'Dil…er…Catrin…Nancy and I are very happy to be able to tell you that we are blessed to already be expecting a child.'

There was a brief silence and then to Iant's enormous relief the first sound he heard was a great sob of happiness from Catrin as she embraced her daughter with such tenderness that Iant himself felt on the edge of tears. Out of the corner of his eye, he saw Dil move from his chair and before Iant could think the worst, he was shaking him by the hand and congratulating him. Dil was a man much too terrified of ever losing control of himself for tears, but Iant would later maintain that he saw a moistness around his eyes.

If the ordeal of telling Nancy's parents their news brought only a welcome surprise, then telling Iant's own mother brought less dramatic but also surprising consequences. Since his engagement to Nancy Iant had witnessed a thaw in his mother's disposition that he had would never have been able to bring about alone. In his more cynical moments, he wondered if his mother was simply being self-interested. With both, his sisters gone his mother perhaps saw Nancy as the one who would look after her into old age. After they announced that the baby was due however, his mother slipped back into her old ways. It was slow and almost imperceptible at first, but gradually she scolded Nancy more for some domestic oversight and began to withdraw more and more into her darker moods where she talked little, sometimes for days. There was no doubt that his mother's own upbringing had been harsh and now he felt that, sadly, the consequences of this would be felt by them all forever.

His mother was, though, not enough to spoil Iant's happiness. He and Nancy spent as much of the summer as they could out of doors, taking advantage of the long evenings to walk higher up the on the hillsides. Sometimes this was under the guise of a small job which required Nancy's assistance, sometimes they just walked and managed to ignore their sense of guilt at leaving Iant's mother alone on her own. Besides, she frequently gave every sign that she preferred it that way.

Nancy was as tolerant of Iant's mother as he had expected she would be. She had an ability to ignore her petty slights and to return them with kindness. This, in turn, seemed to encourage his mother to step up her efforts until occasionally Iant's patience deserted him and he could not help coming to Nancy's defence. At times, it felt like a war of attrition and despite his happiness with Nancy Iant wondered at the wisdom of them starting their life together like this. Nancy never gave much sign of objecting and brushed off his questions when he asked her about living with his mother. She was getting old now, close to her seventies, and needed them. There was nothing to discuss.

Iant's nephew was born in the autumn. He and Nancy visited a few days after he was born and the sight of Nancy holding the tiny creature filled Iant with anticipation. He longed for the birth of his child and secretly hoped for a son. He wanted to be a father less harsh than his own and for his child to grow up more secure. His job would mean that they worried less about money than his parents had been forced to and that there would not be the threat of a war hanging over them all. Gwennie and Ben called their son Tomos and they all looked forward to their children growing up together.

The baby had not come easily, but any details were confined to whispered conversations between Gwennie and Nancy. Iant knew that his sister had a gift for exaggerated detail and he hoped that she would not fill Nancy's head with things that would make her anxious. He need not have worried, Nancy approached childbirth with the same sense of quiet self-possession that she did everything else.

As Nancy had no sisters both Gwennie and Doy had volunteered to be around when the baby was expected and, to Iant's surprise, his mother naturally assumed that she would be the one in charge. Arrangements were made for the old household to be reassembled for a period around the date when Nancy was due, and Iant felt gradually relegated to the periphery of things. He did not particularly object as this seemed to be the way of the world, but he also wanted to somehow make sure that a thing of such importance did not slip from his grasp.

By Christmas of that year, Nancy was becoming less and less mobile, though she refused to have her condition prevent her from doing her everyday jobs. In Iant's eyes, she had become very beautiful and it was a surprise to him to find that physical intimacy had not ceased with Nancy's pregnancy. He had thought, perhaps, that sexual relations were something that had to stop until the baby came, but just as the prospect of the baby had brought them closer together, so too did it seem to open up a physical passion in them that Iant had feared might not be part of his marriage. Sometimes they lay together dripping with sweat and laughing at the effort they made to keep the sounds they made low enough not to disturb his mother.

Iant and Nancy spent Christmas Day with Dil and Catrin. Iant's mother was to spend the day with Gwennie and Ben. Doy and Gethin would be in Wrexham too. Iant was relieved to get

218

away from his mother and so was Nancy though she never said as much. In Nancy's old home Christmas was simple, but the pleasure that her parents obviously felt at the prospect of a child lifted the mood. They walked to and from chapel where Dil was part of a choir that sang carols unaccompanied. They returned to a meal that Catrin had obviously taken some trouble over. A chicken had been found and cooked and there was a pudding full of fruit.

That night, as they lay squashed together in Nancy's childhood bed they talked quietly of Christmases to come and how they would try to find the means to give their child times that they would remember. It was now a matter of weeks before the baby was due and if Iant and Nancy felt remaining anxieties they had been drowned out by a sense of anticipation. Iant looked to the future more optimistically than at any time in his adult life.

Chapter 30

From the side of the hill, he could hear her screams. Part of him was glad he been banished up here by his mother and his sisters, but he also wanted to comfort her if he could. She had been like this for many hours now and he was worried that she wouldn't bear it.

Nancy was strong though. She had shown this in the way she put up with his mother and remained kind to her. Iant saw how increasingly petty and cruel his mother was becoming. Now he had to trust that she would look after her and the child that was taking so long to come. His sisters would help, but they were afraid of their mother too and he had allowed himself to be shooed away by them all. The midwife had come out from Corwen, but she was young and inexperienced.

He was a coward over such things, he knew that, but he was no worse than other men he thought. After everything perhaps he was entitled to some cowardice, in this at least.

There emerged a different sound now. Higher pitched and even more frightening and mixed with Nancy's screams. Afraid though he was, he forced himself down the hill toward the little farmhouse. Halfway down he heard the train whistle as it approached Carrog station. The whole world seemed to be screaming.

Gwennie was by the door. She'd seen him running across the last field. He tried to read her face to see if she had bad news.

'A boy', she said.

'Is he well.'

'I think so. I came out when I saw you.'

'Nancy?'

'Well, I think. Exhausted. It's been twelve hours. The midwife has left already she was tired out.'

Twelve hours. He hadn't realised. He must have slept through some of it though he couldn't remember. He had developed a knack for sleeping through things in Salonika of course.

'Are you going to see?'

'Am I allowed?'

'It's your wife and child Iant.'

'I know that, but....'

'Get upstairs for goodness' sake.'

Despite the remains of his limp, he took the stairs quickly. The crying had died down, though he could hear noises that the child made. The idea that he had a son suddenly overwhelmed him and when he entered the room and saw Nancy he forgot, at least for a moment, the terror he had felt up on the mountain. Even his mother could not quite resist a half-smile when she saw him, though she did her best to hide it.

Nancy spoke first: 'Evan' she said.

'Yes.'

'That is what we said?'

'It is.'

'Could Iant hold him?' said Nancy.

'Don't drop him' said his mother, but handed him the infant nevertheless.

'Evan' he found himself saying aloud, though he felt foolish with the two women watching him and quickly gave the child back to his mother.

'Is he well?'

'We are both tired' said Nancy, 'He doesn't want to feed.'

'You have to persevere' said his mother 'It won't happen by itself.'

She handed the child back to Nancy and left them alone in the room. Iant sat carefully on the side of the bed and stroked his wife's cheek which was wet with sweat.

'I heard his cries from up on the hill,' Iant said. 'Lungs like his Nain.'

'He's quiet now though,' said Nancy 'He seems to have no interest in what I have to offer.'

'His hair is thick.'

'Yes.'

'A son. It's a blessing,' though he added quickly 'A girl would have been welcomed just the same.'

She smiled at his discomfort, but in a world so short of men such feelings were openly discussed.

Nancy's eyes closed involuntarily and he placed an arm under the infant, barely touching either of them. The child was certainly very still, but its chest rose and fell and he felt just a little peace.

Soon his mother returned and busied herself with the minor scoldings in a way that had become her life-long habit even at moments like this. He was happy to remain so that he drew the fire from Nancy and she could get some rest.

What had he been doing while he waited for the baby to come? Wood for the fire would not chop itself, baby or no baby. And some were talking of snow later in the week. Whilst he resented his mother's constant barrage, nothing could quite take away from the sheer wonder of the idea that he now had a son and inwardly he smiled to himself, as the implications began to sink in.

He had some good memories of life with his own father, though he was a harsh disciplinarian at times. He hoped that he might find it in him to be a little different with - he hesitated to link the name with the reality of the baby - his Evan.

Part of his father's life had been adventurous, and this set him apart a little from most of the other men. Building a railway halfway across the world in Patagonia and then coming back to the Dee valley was a difficult adjustment to make and one that his father had never successfully managed. He wondered whether this had helped make his mother the person she was. Marrying her when he returned had probably always seemed like second best to his father and she would always know that. It was an infection that always existed in their lives together.

The result was a perpetual impatience that very occasionally erupted into violent outbursts. He had never done serious damage to anyone, but the sight of his large brown belt being unbuckled was imprinted on Iant's consciousness. There would be no belts in Evan's life he thought optimistically.

He was brought back to the present once again by his mother, 'Iant, put the baby down now. It doesn't do to let them get used to being held all the time. You'll never be able to put him down if you hold him too long.'

Reluctantly he laid his sleeping son in the bed he had made out of a drawer from an old chest. He felt his clumsiness as he struggled to support the baby's head and not wake him at the same time. Finally, he let go and stood back to watch anxiously, trying, as every new parent has ever done, to be sure that he could see him breathe.

Re-assured he felt anxious to get away from his mother's critical attention. He slipped quietly out of the door intent on providing more wood for the fire to avoid the inevitable sniping that would come later if the pile by the hearth fell below the level that his mother deemed sensible.

He looked up at the sky as he moved across the yard. It did look like snow and he felt an irrational loathing for his mother's ability to always be right.

That night he slept in the chair by the fire to try to let Nancy rest. The baby woke frequently but remained reluctant to feed and as dawn came all three of them were exhausted. Iant's frame of mind was not helped either by his mother's continued insistence that she knew best and that Nancy must continue to try and feed. By mid-afternoon, the baby had taken a few drops of milk, but seemed more content and fell asleep.

Iant must have dozed off because he felt himself awoken by shouting. He rushed upstairs to find Nancy practically hysterical and his mother almost wrestling the baby from her.

'What's going on?'

'It's nothing. It's normal after giving birth. The silly girl won't listen to me that's all.'

'Mam, don't talk to Nancy like that, especially when she is so exhausted.'

'Iant, it's his colour. He doesn't seem right.'

Iant looked at his tiny son and realised straight away that he needed to go for the doctor. He called for Gwennie and asked her to sit with Nancy and the baby. Then he ordered his mother from the room.

'Don't you speak to me like that.'

'Mam, you are upsetting her, can't you see?'

'What would you know about it?'

'There isn't time to talk like this. I want you to promise me that you will stay out of the room until I get back.'

His mother didn't respond but just turned away.

All the way he prayed that the doctor would be at home, but he was attending an elderly patient the other end of the village. When Iant found him and described his son's condition the doctor immediately stopped what he was doing and arranged with Iant that he would drive the cart on ahead and that Iant should follow on his bike.

The steep lane back home meant that Iant was ten minutes behind the doctor when he arrived back at the house. He could hardly breathe with the effort of cycling. When Gwennie met him at the door he knew immediately that the news was serious. She didn't say anything but took him by the hand and led him upstairs. The doctor was standing over Nancy who was holding Evan and looking down at his tiny face. When Iant entered the room the doctor turned towards him.

'I am sorry Mr Evans.'

Iant went to Nancy who would not take her eyes off her son. He wrapped an arm around her shoulder as the doctor continued to talk.

'It was probably a faulty heart. It's very common in new-born infants. There would have been nothing anyone could do.'

The room was silent for a long time.

'I would try to persuade your wife to put the baby down.'

'Why? She will have long enough without him won't she.'

The doctor turned to leave and spoke quietly to Gwennie, though it was easy for Iant to hear.

'I'll write out the death certificate downstairs, you'll need it for the undertaker.'

Iant guided Nancy across to the bed and they sat down. Nancy held Evan very tightly and Iant made no attempt to prevent her, just reaching out his other hand to stroke his cheek which was still warm. A few moments later there was a tap on the door and Gwennie came in.

'I think that you need to speak to the doctor Iant. I'll stay here for a minute.'

Iant went downstairs and the doctor stood in the front room. His mother sat in the chair by the fire. The doctor looked slightly embarrassed and Iant realised that he was waiting for payment. Iant fetched his wallet and the doctor handed him a handwritten bill with two items. One was for being called out and the other for issuing the certificate. Iant took out the notes and coins and placed them on the table and turned to leave immediately. He realised that, as well as everything else that he was feeling, he could not stand to be alone in the room with his mother.

Chapter 31

In the weeks and months that followed the death of their son, Iant could see that Nancy struggled even to make the effort to open her eyes each morning. He knew this but he saw Nancy again and again struggle to make sure that no-one else was disturbed by what she felt like inside.

Iant too struggled to make a complete return to his daily routine. He was not officially allowed any time away from his work except for the day of his baby's funeral. In truth, he did not really want time away. The numbing routine of forcing his bicycle up and down the familiar roads and paths, followed by concentrating on his job was a help to him. More than anything he craved relief from thinking and his daily tasks granted him this, however inefficiently he carried them out.

Iant now also had something else to deal with. Up until now, he had felt a strong feeling of duty towards his mother, despite the lack of warmth between them. It was the main reason why he had given up the idea of happiness with Sara, something which previously he only rarely resented. Now though he found that he could only barely tolerate his mother's presence.

It was not that he could blame her in any way for his son's death. There was no logical connection. However, he could not easily forget her unthinking obstinacy in the hours after Evan's birth and his mind turned over, again and again, an image of what her behaviour might have been in the final moments of his son's life. He could not bring himself to ask Nancy. He cursed the fact that he had been absent, even though he knew that he had no choice but to have gone for the doctor.

The daily life of the household returned to its familiar routine, but it was one that was now conducted almost in silence. His mother knew enough not to try and impose herself anymore and Iant's hostility created a wall of resistance so that even if she had been inclined to be the sympathetic presence that could have helped them at such a time, he would have hated it even more.

Each day he turned over and over in his mind how he might help Nancy back to the person that she had been. She did not shut him out in any hostile way, but he found it impossible to reach in himself what she needed from him. It hurt him deeply that he was so helpless, until one day as he cycled home through the rain he reached a decision. He wanted them both to leave his mother's house. It was, after all, the place that was full of reminders of the loss of their child. More than that, though Iant could scarcely admit it, he longed to be free of his mother. He had accepted his responsibilities when his father died, but he found now that he was unable to carry on. Moreover, it felt like something that he was able to do for Nancy though she would never have asked it of him.

As the two of them lay awake in bed that night Iant told Nancy of his plan. He knew of course that she would object, that her natural disposition would be against such a thing, but he felt strongly that he had to persuade her. He would continue to contribute financially to his mother, he would visit as much as decency demanded, but he could no longer live under her roof. If he did he felt somehow that she would drag him and Nancy into her life of misery.

Iant had already formulated a course of action. It was as if this decision was freeing him to begin to act, to move on from the tragedy in their lives. He had heard of a little house to rent in Llandrillo. If they still supported his mother as well, it would be difficult, but he was determined that they would manage. Perhaps Nancy could get a little part-time work. He knew that deep down she too would like the chance to get out of the house. He thought this might help to persuade her that this is what they should do.

At first, Nancy was adamant that they could not do this. She would never forgive herself if anything happened to his mother because they were no longer around to look after her. Iant did not respond with his true feelings because he knew that it would not appeal to Nancy's kind nature. Instead, he argued that his mother was much more capable than he had once thought.

Didn't she after all spend most of her time ordering them around and showing who was really in charge of the household? As for the demands of looking after the smallholding, he would approach the landlord and ask that they reduce the size of what they rented so that it was just the house and surrounding plot. He would still come and do the heavier jobs in the garden when it was strictly necessary. They would be free of the sheep and perhaps the chickens too if his mother felt she could not cope.

Nancy could see from his passionate tone that he had it all worked out. After their third night of talking, she consented to Iant at least approaching the owner of the cottage and the landlord of his family home. No decisions should be taken yet, but she agreed that he could at least explore the idea. Iant did not, of course, tell her that he had already begun doing this and he was confident that it would work, at least for them. He could wait another few days.

A little over a week later Iant arranged with Nancy that she was to visit her parents. He wanted to tell his mother of his plan while they were alone. Partly because of Nancy's urgings he would not present his case in anger. They were to leave because the endless cycling between his work and home was taking its toll. In truth, the nagging pain he experienced in his leg had become more severe whenever the weather was cold, but he felt dishonest using this as an excuse. In addition, Iant planned to say that he and Nancy needed a little time together on their own, that things had not been easy since the baby had died. It was not a year yet since they were married, and they needed to think about starting afresh. He had not told Nancy that he would say this.

He had written to Gwennie and to Doy. They were not to worry he said, he would not be shirking his duties, but he also had obligations to take care of Nancy. He trusted that they would not relate this back to her. He asked that they increase the number of visits that they made to their mother when it was possible and, more reluctantly he asked if they could spare just a little to contribute financially. Despite everything, he could not bring himself to abandon his mother's needs entirely.

'Mam, I need to talk to you.'

'Yes.'

'Will you come and sit?'

'I can listen to you here.'

His mother was engaged in one of the tasks in which she seemed to take most pride. Blackening the grate with lead was an almost daily job. It seemed one of those through which his mother could show them both how hard she worked and how much she resented it. Iant thought of the hundreds of times that he had seen her do this and felt a pang of regret for his mother's sense of her wasted life, though it was not enough to deter him from what he was about to say.

'I want to talk to you about Nancy and I...'

'I will manage on my own.'

He had not anticipated that she would know so quickly what the conversation was about and he struggled with what to say next.

'You can understand why we need to live on our own?'

'It makes no difference what I can understand or not. I told you that I will manage and that is an end to it.'

She had barely paused in the relentless business of applying the black lead and moved to reach for the cleaner rag to start the polishing.

'The long ride is not helping my leg....'

'Yes. I had noticed you limping more the last few days.'

Iant saw what his mother was implying, but could not bring himself to rise to the provocation. Instead, he saw little alternative but to move on to the practicalities. It would have to be done soon enough.

'I have heard about a little cottage in Llan. Near the station.'

He knew that he would get little or no response so he went on, telling her that they planned to move in just over a month. He would visit weekly to attend to the various jobs that she could not manage, that he would find ways to fetch her to visit them. She expressed no enthusiasm for the latter and told him he need not trouble himself about the jobs. Finally, he told her that he would cover the rental on her house and that Gwennie and Doy were to help as much as they could. For the first time in the conversation, he saw something involuntary pass across his mother's face which he recognised as a realisation of her own helplessness. If she could have resisted taking anything from him she would have done so.

Despite her misgivings about the move, Nancy could not help but be excited about the prospect of making a home for the first time. As Iant had hoped she began to emerge slowly from what had consumed her completely since they had buried their son. They had visited the little house, one of several in a row opposite the village school, and Nancy had immediately begun planning what they would need. Some sticks of old furniture came with the house, but Nancy's ideas were about turning the little place into a proper home.

Not only did this prospect give Nancy a new sense of life, it did the same for her mother. Catrin had been thrilled to think of her daughter finding happiness and devastated that the baby was buried without her or Dil having seen him. Helping Nancy find bits of left-over material and turn them into curtains, cushions and bedspreads reassured her that she would recover and that the young woman of whom she was quietly so proud was now properly starting out on her life.

The day they moved their few possessions from the old house Iant had borrowed a horse and cart. As he drew up outside he caught a glimpse of his mother looking from an upstairs window. When she saw that he had seen her, she moved rapidly away. Iant felt the old anxiety rise in him about what would become of her, but he knew that this must be done. He had come to realise that it was stupid to lay the blame for everything at the door of his mother, but that nevertheless, she was part of the reason that his life after the war had become increasingly narrow. He must try now to imagine it differently. What they were doing was not such a drastic step and he was determined that they should seize this moment.

At Iant's request, Doy had come to stay with his mother for

two nights, but she had not been made welcome. Still, Iant thought, at least he would not have to worry about her today. When the cart was finally packed up Iant was surprised to see that his mother had, after all, come to the door to wish them farewell. She beckoned to Iant as he prepared the horse for the journey and when he approached she handed him an old brown envelope.

'It isn't much.'

'Mam?'

'Don't make a fuss. I always kept a few coppers back.'

As Megan hurried inside Iant mounted the cart to join Nancy. He showed the envelope to her who suggested that she must go back and say thank you. Nancy had already tried her best to say goodbye and Iant said that his mother would prefer it if they left with nothing more said. It was, for her, a gesture of some significance and he was overwhelmingly pleased that she had made it, but she had done it in her own way and they should allow her that dignity.

As the old horse began the journey they waved to Doy standing on the step and Iant was reminded that she had done that as he came home on leave before being sent abroad. Since then so much had happened to him and this short journey, barely ten miles, was tiny by comparison with those he had made during the war. In truth, though, Iant felt as though it marked a moment when he had begun his life again. He had followed his instincts and he felt a sense of freedom. He looked at Nancy sitting beside him, still clutching the brown envelope and felt determined to build a life with her that was based on more than a sense of duty. They had little money and were only moving to a rented cottage in a small village, but they could plan together, have a family and give them some sense of the world's possibilities.

Chapter 32

Within six months of moving to their new home, Nancy announced to Iant, less anxiously than the first time, that she was expecting another child. In the middle of their delight and jokes about their fertility came a natural nervousness about how they might prevent their past ordeal being repeated.

Apart from having little money to spare the little terraced house was everything that they had hoped it would be. Nancy took a little work cleaning up at *Palle Hall* and despite the mundane nature of the job, she felt better that she could contribute to their new household. Though it was now back in the hands of the family that owned it Iant felt strange about the place. It had been used as a hospital during the war and he was inevitably taken back to the time he had spent in the hospital in less grand surroundings. Nancy's job involved cleaning the huge number of bedrooms that not so long ago had housed men like him, invalided back from France.

When the news of the child came Iant was adamant that she stop work immediately, but for all her quiet and calm personality Nancy found ways to assert herself and it was decided that she continue until her condition became too obvious. When it did she would in all probability be prevented from working in any case.

In many ways, Nancy's announcement was not a surprise. Freed for the first time from the eyes and ears of Iant's mother they had begun to find real pleasure in each other. For some time after they had lost their son neither of them approached the subject of sex, though they frequently clung to each other in the darkness. Now without either of them saying very much, making love took on an importance in their lives that surprised and delighted them. At weekends they loved to find time to go to bed in the afternoons and take pleasure in looking at each other's bodies properly before their mouths and tongues explored in ways and places that they had never done before. They longed for each other and were considerate of each other and they patiently discovered a whole new dimension to their life together.

Their daughter was born in the spring and they named her Eleanor, but gave her a second name, Megan, after Iant's mother. They hoped that she was pleased, but found no conclusive proof. Iant had found out that his job with the railways gave him a limited entitlement for some medical bills and Eleanor was born in the maternity hospital in Wrexham. The first child in either family not to have been born in their own home Iant's mother had remarked. Iant had insisted that if anything was wrong with the child, then a doctor or nurse could more easily be found and Nancy was willing to help quiet his worst fears, even though she felt uncomfortable among so many strangers.

Eleanor had been born without complication and the early days of her life that Iant had fretted about for so long were peaceful. The hospital, though offering no privacy and numerous small indignities, did give Nancy some quiet to become used to her daughter. They made the journey back to their home after a week with Eleanor having taken to feeding as easily and voraciously as all the young animals that Iant had watched from childhood.

During the latter stages of Nancy's pregnancy, Iant had, he knew, avoided visiting his old home more than he should. He reasoned that his priorities had to be elsewhere, though he knew he was glad of an excuse. One Saturday, some three weeks after the birth of his daughter, Iant knew that he could put off the journey no longer. He set off on his bicycle to make a journey that was so familiar to him and which he had made daily for so long, but which now felt daunting.

In the time since he and Nancy left he had thought that, as far as he could tell, his mother had changed little. Her life was restricted, but then it had always been that way. She had elected to keep the chickens and seemed to be managing them. Once a week someone collected eggs to sell to the little store in the village.

His mother was yet to see her granddaughter, but Nancy

233

made him promise to tell her that they would bring the infant to visit before the month was out. Iant spent most of his visit busying himself outside, finding small tasks that he thought his mother might not manage or notice, though he took some tea and a slice of a freshly baked loaf that she offered. Now that he was no longer under her roof Iant had gradually come to find it easier to be civil to his mother. He tried to reflect more often on the hard life that his mother had lived. Her gift of money to him and Nancy was a flicker of generosity that he hoped indicated that she might have a more content old age. He hoped so for his own sake, but also for her's.

The last mile of the journey back home was the easiest and Iant whistled as he rode along. He was looking forward to seeing his wife and daughter and to shake off the demands of the day with his mother by telling exaggerated stories of her to Nancy. She would both laugh and tell him off at the same time.

As Iant entered the room Nancy was seated, holding Eleanor whilst also holding something in her other hand that she was encouraging her daughter to follow with her eyes. The green stone caught the light and the baby's eyes followed it back and forth, seeming to squint to make sense of this new and delightful object.

From almost the first moment that they had met Iant had meant to tell Nancy about Sara, or at least as much of the story as he could manage. There was after all nothing that he should be ashamed of. In fact, it was Sara that had first suggested that it was impossible for them to be reunited after his father had died – he had been devastated, but had not behaved dishonourably. What could anyone object to what he done all along? And yet he had never found the moment to tell Nancy.

At first of course he had not wanted to scare away a woman that he considered to have led such a sheltered life. What would Nancy make of someone who had conducted a passionate affair with someone from somewhere so exotic and removed from her understanding? He blushed now at his arrogance. But then they had been set on marriage so quickly. He had convinced himself

234

that he could not jeopardise such an easy and natural relationship. Then there was the tragedy of their son. He remained sure that he could never have told her during such a time. It was perhaps the only part of the story that he had continued to tell himself that was true.

Iant had not consciously sought to hide the ring from Nancy, or from anyone. He had simply kept it in the tin box that was one of the few things that had survived from his time in the army. The ring had been inside a small brown envelope that he had found in his mother's house and had simply lain in the box alongside some insignia from the army and some trinkets that he had picked up in Salonika. These included a small plaster of Paris model of the white tower and two postcards of Mount Olympus. Iant had to admit to himself, that he had worried about the box when they were about to move to their own house. He had placed it at the bottom of a tool bag in which he had gathered a small selection of implements that he hoped would cover his future needs. The bag had lain in the cupboard under the staircase and he only touched it to retrieve a hammer or a screwdriver when he wanted them.

How on earth could Nancy be showing the tiny ring to their daughter? It made a delightful picture and Iant felt only stupidity had led to him looking at them open-mouthed rather than enjoying a scene that he had been looking forward to all of the day. Instead of starting the process of making things better, he made them worse.

'What's that you're showing her?' he said

'I found it in that old box. The back door had begun to stick and I was looking for something to help mend it.'

'You should have left that for me.'

'Well it's still sticking, so you can try now if you like.'

'I'll look later.'

'Where did it come from?'

There was no suspicion in her voice, just a natural curiosity. Until that is, Iant remained silent just long enough for Nancy to realise that Iant's possession of the ring meant something to him.

'Iant?'

'It belonged to someone that I met during the war.'

'A girl?'

'Yes, it was a girl.'

Nancy's face betrayed no hint of jealousy or admonishment. She giggled and teased him about all the old sweethearts that she didn't know about. For Iant, though something had been opened up and he decided that this was his moment, not simply to be honest with Nancy, but to face up to what his time with Sara had been and what it had meant. He remembered the look, almost of scorn, that had passed across Frances's face when he told her. He knew that Frances would not have brought herself to tell him, but that deep down she had despised him at that moment. She had despised him for passing up his biggest chance to have a different life. A life that defied what he had been born to.

At that moment Eleanor giggled to herself. She had a wonderful laugh. The light kept playing on the green stone and sending patterns on the walls and ceilings of the room. Her chubby baby's legs kicked and squirmed making Nancy cling on to her to stop her rolling on to the floor. Iant half-turned towards the door before speaking.

'Her name was Sara. She was a nurse in the hospital in Salonika.'

'When you lost your sight?'

'Yes, she helped me a lot when I was recovering.'

'Was she in the army?'

'No...she was...is...Greek. Her family is from Salonika.'

Without meaning to Iant had allowed the conversation to take on a more serious tone. Nancy's face was no longer as relaxed and she looked down at her child who was suddenly starting to look sleepy. She placed the ring on a table in front of her.

'Do you write to her?'

'No...no...I did write to her when I first came back. Not for a long time.'

'It sounds very romantic.'

236

'Well…during the war…you know.'

'Not really Iant. My brother said one or two things I suppose.'

'Nancy…we were engaged to be married.'

Something in Iant had pushed him towards this small piece of bravery. It would have been possible to laugh along with Nancy at the stupidity of a flirtation with a pretty nurse, but Iant realised that he needed to properly acknowledge the enormity of this thing in his life. There was no doubt in his mind that he was happy with Nancy, especially now that they had a child. But it also rushed over him for the first time in a while, how much he had been in love with Sara. It also reminded him that he would always think himself a coward for using duty as a reason for not attempting to pursue such a difficult thing as leaving his home behind.

Nancy was quiet for what felt like a long time. Long enough at least for Iant to decide to sit down in the uncomfortable little armchair that was nearest the fire.

'Does your Mam know about this? Or your sisters?'

'No…no I haven't spoken about it to anyone.'

Another lie he realised, though he knew that now was not the moment to try and untangle that part of his recent past.

'Did you break it off?'

'We just agreed that it was impossible. And my father had died.'

'I am just wondering why you did not tell me Iant.'

'I have always meant to.'

It wasn't much, but Iant saw that he had created just the smallest of cracks in the trust that they had placed in each other. Nancy was not foolish, or prudish enough, to become jealous of a sexual relationship that had happened in his past, especially one so far away. She had come to see their life together as something based on mutual ease rooted in knowing the other person and all their faults. They had been fortunate in this so far as Iant could see, compared at least to the marriages made by his sisters which sometimes looked like uneasy truces. Now he had introduced something big enough to threaten, if not their marriage itself, then its basis.

A feeling of dread came over Iant. He was disgusted with himself for causing Nancy hurt, but he was also afraid of stirring up memories of Sara. Was it just that she was the first person to whom he had become properly attached? He doubted it. Their time together had astonished him and he should not deny it. But to find a life together had proved impossible. He was suddenly horrified by the idea of admitting to himself that somehow he had settled for second best. That was something he certainly could never admit to Nancy.

Nancy did ask one or two more questions, but they were perfunctory. For different reasons, neither of them wished to talk in much more detail. They went about their domestic evening as normal. There was nothing different about it to the outside eye, but for Iant, it felt full of lurking dangers, most of them imagined. He was glad when it was time to be in bed and to extinguish the little oil lamp that flickered badly because he hadn't changed the wick for too long.

He half expected to hear Nancy's voice in the darkness, but after they had kissed goodnight she had appeared to sleep. They both knew that Eleanor would only give her a short time before she wanted to be fed and Iant did not want to break the silence by testing if she was awake. In the darkness, he remembered with a start the letters that he had kept and wondered if Nancy's curiosity naturally aroused, she might now come upon them.

Before he left for work Iant decided that there was one thing that he could do. After finishing his breakfast much faster than usual he went straight to the cupboard in which Nancy had found the ring. He had thought there were more, but in the old biscuit tin in which he had kept the very few official papers that had marked his life, he felt underneath his army discharge papers and his certificate of training from the railway and found the small handful of letters that Sara had written since they had parted that day on the quayside.

Instinctively Iant held them up to smell them, perhaps for

the last time, but he detected only the scent of damp that always filled the cupboard. He returned to the kitchen where Nancy was bathing the baby in a ceramic basin. He longed to stay at home and try, gradually, to ease them all back to normal. Instead, he carried on with the course of action upon which he had set his mind as he lay in bed in the early morning.

On the table, Iant placed the letters which had been tied up with some old rough string that he had used in his mother's garden.

'These are some letters I have kept Nancy.'

'From Sara?'

He flinched momentarily as she used her name.

'Yes. I am going to leave them here. You may do anything with them. There isn't anything else about it all to hide.'

Before she could reply Iant kissed her and Eleanor and was out of the door. As he walked down the lane, past the school and on to the main road, he glanced furtively back at the window, but he saw nothing and was glad. This morning a light drizzle caused a mist to obscure even the closest of the mountains and he hunched against the damp as he walked slowly to the signal box.

That evening when he got home he greeted Nancy as usual but his eyes were inevitably drawn to the pile of letters on the table. They were tied up with string, but the green ring had been placed neatly on top.

'Did you read them?'

'I did.'

'Shall we burn them?'

'They are yours, Iant. I cannot say, but if you ask my opinion I think you should keep them.'

'Why do you say that?'

'Do you want to pretend again that this didn't happen to you? That you loved this woman who sounds so wonderful?'

Iant blushed deeply and looked away.

'I am not saying this to punish you Iant. One day you would regret it if you threw all this on the fire. If you had really wanted that you would have done it by now. It is, whether you like it or not, part of who you are.'

He decided that no more was to be said. He fetched the biscuit tin from the cupboard and placed the ring and the letters inside. This time he did not hide the letters under anything. He placed the tin back in the cupboard and by the time he returned, Eleanor had woken and was crying.

'Go and pick up your daughter Iant.'

He collected Eleanor and sat on the settee trying to soothe her. He knew that she would not be pacified for long because he did not have what she really wanted. He could not yet tell whether this episode in their lives was over yet, but he knew enough to reflect on his luck at coming upon someone with as much wisdom as his wife.

Over the coming weeks and months, Iant and Nancy eventually returned to where they were. Thanks to Nancy, Iant came to think that a person's life is not so simply shaped. His could contain both the truth of what he and Sara had been and the growing contentment of the life that he and Nancy were living together. He should think himself lucky for that and that is what he made every effort to do.

Part 3

Chapter 33

In quick succession, Nancy gave birth to two more girls and they called them Annie and Nia. Annie's second name was Catrin after Nancy's mother and Nia had the name Mared after one of Nancy's grandmothers who had died many years before. Gwennie and Doy who both had two sons teased him about being surrounded by girls, but Iant revelled in it. He doted on his daughters to the extent that Nancy had to overcome her own gentler instincts more then she would have liked or else the girls would have grown up like savages.

Iant thought sometimes of Evan, who would now be nearly ten years old. He longed to know how he would have grown up and what he would have thought of so many girls around him. He never said this to anyone but he also wondered if having no boys was a kind of blessing. They would never have to worry in the way that so many had done as they saw their sons and brothers off on trains and die in their thousands in the trenches.

He wondered too if Evan would have had to go far away, even to Canada like Nancy's brother, to find real work and a future. More and more men were being laid off at Ffestiniog and the smaller farms seemed to be closing every week. Ben had a good position but was always anxious about his future. Gethin at the ever-expanding Labour Exchange felt safe and Iant thanked the injury that had made him look to the railways after the war. For the moment at least it was making his family secure.

Alun Lewis had suggested more than once that Iant should be looking to move upwards himself. He had done his job well for several years and he could think of even being a station master on one of the small branch lines if he wanted. Iant had so far resisted. He was happy being in charge of himself and his signal box. Sometimes the sheer physical effort of moving the heavy levers made him exhausted at the end of a week, but he took pride in the idea that his care over his work kept others safe. He had read about a terrible accident in Ireland that had killed so many children and he shuddered at the thought of being responsible for such a tragedy.

Sometimes if the evening was fine Nancy would walk the girls up to meet him when he had finished work. Nia still walked quite slowly, but Ella would race on ahead with Annie failing to keep up just behind. Iant loved the sight of them rushing up the road and would hold his arms open ready to sweep them up as they arrived puffing and panting. One evening, just as he was about to lock the door and see if the girls were coming the telephone that had been newly installed in the box rang insistently.

Iant disliked the telephone. The railway still used the telegraph for all the signalling because it was seen as much more reliable, the telephone was supposed to be for urgent messages, but already Iant had experienced people using it for all manner of things, including practical jokes. Reluctantly he turned back into the box and picked up the receiver. He felt so awkward talking into the mouthpiece, but you never knew if someone was checking up on you so he tried to speak as formally as possible.

To his surprise, it was the signal box in Carrog calling for him. It was against regulations, but they were passing on a message about his mother. They said he should come now if he could. They were not very clear how she was, only that someone in the village had run down the hill to see if they could catch him before he left for the day. Iant glanced up the door and saw the smiling faces of Ella and Annie peering in. He smiled at them and held up his hand for them to wait just a moment while he finished talking.

As they made their way back down the lane to the village to fetch his bicycle Nancy was the calm presence that he always relied upon, it seemed from their first moments together. He could not, however, prevent thoughts of his mother rushing through his head and stop him focusing on what needed to be done. He only knew that the person who went to collect the eggs

244

had found her after a fall. They could not say how long she had been lying there, nor what state she was in. He had the impression that it was a favour that they had used the telephone to contact him and that he was not to ask too many questions.

He never regretted leaving his mother's house for even a second, but he had often imagined something like this moment, though the telephone had not played a part in it. In truth, his mother had mellowed very slightly in the last few years as far as she was able. The part played in this by her grandchildren could not, of course, be underestimated.

As he arrived at his old home he saw the doctor's horse and cart outside. The last time that he had seen him was the night that his son had died. Guiltily the thought of the doctor's bill passed through his mind. He leant his bicycle against the wall of the house and dashed inside.

His mother was laid flat on the old ottoman and the doctor stood up from examining her. Eluned the neighbour who took the eggs each week hovered nearby. He noticed that his mother showed no sign of reacting when he came into the room.

'I am almost sure that she's suffered a stroke. Probably quite a severe one.'

Iant knew the word but didn't fully understand its implications. He had heard of others in the village who had died from what had been described as a stroke.

'I am afraid that she isn't likely to recover.'

'What can we do for her doctor?'

'I could get her taken to the hospital in Wrexham, but I don't think it would be worthwhile.'

Iant glanced across at his mother and he could see that one side of her mouth drooped and she was very pale.

'You need to keep her comfortable if you can. Would you like me to call back tomorrow?'

Iant knew that he would have to pay him again, but he felt unable to say no. After the doctor left he asked Eluned if she could stay, while he returned home for some clothes and to make arrangements. He would have to stay with his mother, at least for now.

Despite his protestations, Nancy insisted on returning with him. The two older ones could stay with Catrin and Dil for a few nights while Nia and she would stay with Iant and look after his mother. He could not be away from work for much more than a day or so. He went to the village post office and sent short telegrams to Gwennie and Doy.

Nancy and Iant took it in turns to sit up with his mother during the night. She showed little sign that she was aware of anyone being there, but it didn't feel right to leave her alone. During the second night, just as Iant felt himself drifting into sleep his mother opened her eyes for the first time and made a noise that was only just audible.

'Mam?'

She made no response but seemed more agitated so reached over and dabbed her lips with a wet sponge as the doctor had suggested. Iant realised that it had been a long time since he had really looked at his mother. She had been, almost since his childhood, someone whose gaze you avoided and who avoided the looks of others. Lying there now she looked much older than she really was. Had she ever been young Iant thought?

Megan had talked little about her family and Iant barely remembered his grandparents who had both died when he was young. He remembered talk that his grandfather was not well-liked and he had heard talk of other women. In general, the impression was that his mother had not had a happy childhood, made worse by having no brothers and sisters. She married Gwilym quite young and Iant supposed that she looked to get away from home. His father had not been that much of a catch, but he was reliable and his travels to Patagonia had made him determined to settle. Between them, they had built a life that was about survival. Perhaps he and his sisters had not been grateful enough for that thought Iant, but his mother had never made it easy to feel gratitude.

His sisters arrived the following day bringing their children. Suddenly the old house was more alive than it had been for years, probably forever. It was a full-time task stopping the young ones from making noise in the place where their grandmother lay, though practically it made little difference. None of them could quite bring themselves to think that she didn't deserve at least a little peace at the end of her life.

On the fifth night after Iant received the telephone call the inevitable happened. He had been sitting with her alongside Doy. They now took turns in pairs, because there was more of them. He hadn't had the chance to spend much time with his younger sister in recent years and the two of them had been laughing quietly at some shared childhood memory when a small but definite change in their mother's breathing made them stop. They waited a few moments before Doy went to wake Gwennie.

It was at least another hour before the rattling in Megan's throat finally slowed and then stopped. For the first time since she had been found their mother had looked disturbed and uncomfortable and at first it was with relief that they realised that this had stopped.

It was best not to wake the children and so Gwennie put on the kettle and made tea. The three of them sat with their mother and talked of her life, finding the scraps that made them smile such as her pleasure in her grandchildren, whilst also feeling sad that she had found it so difficult to find sustained happiness.

Soon it was dawn and the first child to wake could be heard upstairs. They needed to be practical and to start on the round of arrangements that always followed anyone's death, even someone who had lived so determinedly out of sight as Megan Evans.

Eventually, the house would go, thought Iant. In many ways the sooner the better. The rent and the upkeep had been a drain on him, and to a lesser extent on his sisters. All they had left, apart from the house was the little garden and the hens now. Sometimes though Iant walked through the hilly fields that his father had once rented. He would, on balance, be glad to see the place go, but what kind of human being does not feel sadness when facing the loss of their childhood home?

247

One day, hitching Nia on to his shoulders Iant took the three girls on a walk up to the highest field. At the top of the ridge, they sat near a spot where once he had lain on the ground and clung to Frances when they both needed nothing more complicated than the warmth of another person. Annie had begun to complain about the climb halfway up, but he praised her and Ella for doing so well. He felt in his pocket for some barley sugar and they all sat in silence sucking on the sugary sticks, looking down on the village some way below. Iant felt a surge of feeling towards his girls and a renewed determination that they would not live in the gloominess that had infected so much of his childhood.

'Is Nain going to be in the ground?'

Ella had understood well enough what had happened, but Annie was obviously still working things out for herself.

'Yes, cariad, she is.'

'What about heaven then?'

Iant was not quite prepared for such a demanding conversation.

'She will be in both places. When someone dies, they can do that.'

Annie seemed content enough, only holding her puzzled expression until he produced a second barley sugar stick. This was going well beyond the usual rules, but it was a moment that demanded that Iant felt.

He could not claim that the rising feeling he had in his throat was really for the loss of his mother, or indeed of the prospect of not sitting here again looking at his childhood home. But both of those things were part of a general and suddenly intense feeling of how fragile the world was. Nancy, the three little girls, intent on their sweets, this valley and its settlements that lived out their routines so far from Salonika or Flanders or London all seemed vulnerable to him and he turned his head away from his daughters. When he turned back he managed a smile because they had, of course, remained entirely oblivious.

Chapter 34

A few months after they buried his mother Alun Lewis came to see him up at the box. Iant was pleased to get the chance to catch up with his old friend. He didn't get over to Acrefair very much anymore, what with the children and his garden to sort out in any spare time that he had. When they did venture that way, it was to see Catrin and Dil who occasionally needed some help, though Dil strongly resisted such an idea.

Alun had risen up the ranks of the GWR and now worked at a desk in Llangollen which Iant teased him about a little as he went through a familiar routine of hauling on the heavy levers that changed the points.

'Well, that's partly why I've come all the way up here. You don't think I came for the good of my health do you?'

Even though he wasn't old enough Iant had come to see Alun as something of a father figure. He had been sensible and kind to him at a difficult moment in his life and he was always grateful for that. Iant thought that he knew what was coming and though he slightly dreaded it he was also flattered.

'So you know they want some new station masters don't you?'

'I had heard something.'

'And you are going to put in for one aren't you?'

'I don't know Alun. We are very settled here and they can send you anywhere.'

'Not to bloody Timbuktu they can't. Come on man, you're still young and it won't be the ends of the earth.'

Iant had to break off to change the points again but as the two carriages rumbled past the window Alun continued to press him.

'You can't spend your whole life stuck up here in the back of beyond. You've been halfway across the world man.'

'That's why I want to spend my time in the back of beyond.'

They both laughed at his logic. There was a time Iant

thought when all he wanted to do was work out how to get himself to a place a very long way from here.

'Promise me that you'll at least think about it. Talk to Nancy. She might surprise you.'

Iant agreed to do what his old friend suggested and Alun walked off to get his train home.

That evening after the girls had finally settled into bed Iant spoke to Nancy about Alun's visit., Nancy thought that he should at least look into the idea so Iant had little choice, otherwise he would have felt a coward yet again.

A week later Iant sat at the kitchen table looking over a pile of papers that had arrived headed with the grand coat of arms of the Great Western Railway. There was a solemnly written account of the duties and responsibilities of a station master, grade 2, a form to apply for internal promotion and a declaration of fitness to be perused and signed.

Iant had not been an exceptional scholar but he had coped with school as well as most that had gone through the motions, knowing that their lives would not require of them many of the things that they were taught. His life in the signal box had made him more precise and correct in his daily routine and as he looked at the pile in front of him it did seem that it would not need a great leap of his intellect for him to be able to do the job as it was set out.

He did wonder what it would be like to lose his precious solitude for much of the day. In the years after the war being alone had undoubtedly suited him. The combined effects of the war, life in crowded conditions and the loss of his vision of a new life had made being a signalmen suit Iant. Had Nancy and his girls made him more at ease with himself and those around him? The job of a station master would require him not only to work with others but be responsible for their work. It would not be on a grand scale. Perhaps just himself, a porter and a booking clerk with a signalman just down the line, but it would still be a responsibility.

In the end, it was the blackmail of fatherhood that pushed

Iant into filling in the forms in his best copperplate and sending them off to the regional offices of the GWR in Chester. First Alun Lewis and then, very subtly, Nancy, had sown in his head the idea that the lives of Ella, Annie and Nia might be improved by his seeking some advancement. It was not simply that he would be paid more, but that they would live somewhere else, in more substantial accommodation and meet people that had not been born, bred and confined into this small corner of the world.

Iant knew that he was lucky to have such a choice to make. Bob, Nancy's brother, had written from Canada to say that although his job was safe for now, Toronto's streets were full of people begging, many of them come from the provinces in the West that were suffering great hardships. Here the Daily Post told similar stories about Liverpool and, in Wrexham, Ben and Gwennie fretted all the time about how they would manage if he was out of work. If he moved up, he reasoned, then someone else would have a chance perhaps.

The letter, inviting him for interview came more quickly than he expected. Nothing had yet been said to the girls. There was nothing to be gained by unsettling them, though as the day approached the two eldest especially knew that something was going on. Nancy took pleasure in making sure Iant made the best of himself, and they engaged in an endless debate about whether he should wear his signalman's uniform or the old suit that, remarkably, still fitted him after all these years. Iant worried that the uniform would remind the panel that he was, after all, really a signalman. Nancy tactfully steered him in the other direction by saying that it made him look loyal to the company. In truth the suit had seen better days and although it fitted him the waistcoat had begun to pull across the middle.

Two weeks to the day after the interview another letter with the familiar crest was dropped through the door of the Llandrillo house. Although desperate to open it Nancy left it until it was time for Iant to finish work and set off to meet him with Annie and Nia. Ella had reached an age when other things pre-occupied her after school.

251

As they set off back from the signal box the two girls ran ahead and Nancy retrieved the letter from her bag and gave it to Iant without a word. He held it in his hand a moment and, to Nancy's amazement and annoyance, put it in his inside pocket.

'What are you doing Iant?'

'I can't open it here.'

'Why? I've been waiting all day.'

'I can't just open it as we walk along. And the girls…'

Silently they agreed that he would wait until they got home. But then Ella was upset because she could not manage some sums that she had to do and then it was time for tea. It was seven o'clock before Iant sat in front of the stove and sliced open the envelope with his little penknife. Nancy was out of the room settling down the younger girls and Iant wanted it that way. He didn't want anyone looking at him, even Nancy.

The last time he had been confronted with any thoughts of promotion had been in the heat of Salonika. Then he had not sought it but tried to rise to the responsibility. For the first time in a while thoughts of his time with Sara came flooding back. What, he thought, would he have been doing with his life by now if he really made the journey back to Greece. He realised with a half-smile that he had not given such practical matters much thought. As he had tried to pick out Sara on the quayside from the deck of the enormous ship he hadn't thought of anything except that he loved her and that nothing would prevent him returning so that they could be together.

As she walked back into the room Nancy could see the letter open on Iant's lap, but found it impossible to tell from his face what it contained. He stared into space, lost deeply in his thoughts.

'Iant?'

'Where is Crudgington?'

'What?'

'Crudgington, where is it?'

'Can you just tell me what's in the letter Iant?'

'I have been offered the job of acting station master in

252

Crudgington.'

Nancy rushed and embraced him. She told him how proud she was of him and that he should have believed her and Alun when they said that he could do it. Iant managed a smile and kissed her on the cheek, but both of them were of course really pre-occupied with the idea of Crudgington.

'Doesn't it say anything about where it is?'

By now Nancy had taken the letter and was looking through it herself.

'It says that it is on the Wellington to Market Drayton line, in Shropshire.'

'Shropshire isn't very far is it?'

'I'm not sure.'

Iant fetched the old atlas. The last time that he had looked at it in earnest, he had been planning his route across Europe to meet Sara. He found Shropshire easily enough but had to look hard for Crudgington. A pinprick on a map of this scale, but just there nevertheless because of the railway. He traced his finger backwards on a line first to Shrewsbury and then all along the trunk road that passed through Llangollen before driving through the mountains towards the Irish ferries on Anglesey. On the atlas, it was still called Watling Street, the old Roman Road.

'It looks a long way cariad.'

He rarely used the word and it made Nancy put her arm around his shoulder and press him to her.

'Not so far by train. Even from here. Look – change at Llangollen and then again at Shrewsbury. We'd be there in no time.'

He knew then that he must show some simple courage and embark with his family on this modest adventure. If he did not, he had to accept that his whole adult life would be defined by caution and fear. If Nancy could embrace it, actively reach out for it even then surely, he must too.

The Great Western Railway proved as impatient as the army when it came to posting. No sooner had Iant written back accepting the job than he received notice that in a month's time

253

he would be moved from his signalling duties and take up his new post in Crudgington. He was to spend a week helping to train his replacement and when he got to Crudgington someone would be there for one week to show him the barebones of the station and his duties.

It seemed to Iant an impossibly short time but, as always, Nancy was reassuring. It was decided, for the children's sake that they would finish their school term so Nancy would stay behind with them while they gave notice on their house. Iant went on ahead to start his new job. It was only just over six weeks and he would be able to make visits home she supposed.

Iant wanted Nancy to see their new home with him for the first time so she asked Catrin if she and Dil would take the children for a night so that she could do that. They left the children with her parents quite seldom because Dil was not in the best of health, nor always in the best of humour. His bark was much worse than his bite though, and Catrin loved the chance to have the three girls.

Nancy's parents had lived lives that had contained so little change until their son left for Canada that the news of the move had been an enormous shock to them. When they were told that their daughter was going to live over the border in England they did not initially take it well. Nancy had to explain many times that Crudgington was just a short, albeit slightly complicated journey away. She explained it several times but could see that it was all too much, especially for Dil.

On the 1st June 1931, Nancy and Iant set off on a train with a large leather suitcase containing clothes that would last Iant for as long as possible and the things that Nancy would need for a stay overnight. They were about as excited as they were apprehensive and Iant was relieved that Nancy was making this first journey with him. The previous day he had removed his few possessions from the signal box for the last time. He remembered vividly the night that Frances had visited him there. It had all ended strangely but today Iant remembered most Frances's turning up unexpectedly and the blanket she had brought for them to lie on. The last he had heard she had remained in London and was married to someone that she had met in service.

In the carriage, after they had changed at Ruabon, Nancy sat close to him and leaned her head on his shoulders. This was, as far as Iant could remember, the longest that they had been alone together since Ella was born. For a while, as the scenery flashed past and they passed from Wales into England they forgot the momentousness of the journey and became again the young people that had rushed headlong into marriage and children a dozen years or so ago. Finally, after the slow train had meandered through numerous tiny halts with barely a platform they were in Shrewsbury and set on finding the correct platform for their next train.

'Come on Iant bach, you are a station master now. Which way are we going?' she'd said grinning broadly.

Iant smiled back, but inside he felt more than a flutter of nerves, not because he was to be a station master, but because they had launched themselves towards a new life that he had no certainty would be the best thing for them.

'Well, what are you waiting for?'

She was right of course, what was he waiting for and he strode with affected purpose in the direction of Platform 3, train to Wellington, in fifteen minutes.

Chapter 35

Although Iant and Nancy had been tired after their journey the effect of being alone in what was to become their new home had made them feel once again like honeymooners. This time though they had none of the anxieties that turned so many honeymoons into the first and most difficult test of a relationship.

As they arrived at the stationmaster's house it was late afternoon, but the sun was still warm and sent shafts of light through the leaded windows. These caught the dust that swirled up as they stepped across the wooden entrance floor, though the house was not dirty. It was completely empty as they had expected, except an old cooker and an enormous wooden bed that they had purchased from the last occupant for a few shillings. Iant's suitcase contained some sheets and pillowcases and the railway had supplied some blankets, the cost to be deducted from his first pay packet. The house would remain almost as bare until the few belongings that Nancy and Iant had accumulated were brought on a railway lorry in six weeks' time. Ella and Annie were already excited about travelling in the lorry with the men.

The house was far from perfect, it had only been cleaned perfunctorily and looked so bare without their possessions, but it was much bigger than where they lived in Llandrillo and had a garden that ran all the way around. All in all Iant and Nancy felt thrilled with it, despite the shock of the first train that passed which felt so close it could have been in the room with them.

They lit a fire after it got dark, not so much against the cold but because it made the place seem less empty. They had brought a few provisions and ate some bacon and eggs in front of the fire.

They made the big old bed up and put out the oil lamp, barely able to keep their hands off each other until they got under the blankets. They had always tried to make time for each other, but it had not been easy once there was five of them in a small house. There was no-one around to hear them, but they could not shake off the habit of trying to keep as quiet as they could, laughing uncontrollably as the ancient bedsprings creaked and groaned. Nancy said that her body was showing all the signs of being the mother of three children and insisted that the lamp remain off. Iant complied but told her, as he helped remove her nightdress, that she felt as soft and beautiful as the first time he had touched her.

Iant especially longed for this little interlude to go on indefinitely, but he had to begin his new working life and Nancy had to return to their children. Iant had instructions to spend some of his free time scouring the area for some sticks of furniture to supplement what they already had and to find out the best places for them to get their supplies. Nancy was instructed only to smother the girls with kisses from their dad and to take good care of herself. Iant was to visit in three weeks and until then they had to learn to manage apart for the first time since they were married. At nine o'clock Nancy got on the first Sunday train to Wellington just outside their house and began the long journey back.

The weeks, until he was joined by his family, hung a little heavily on Iant. He tried to busy himself with his new job, getting to know the two men that worked for him and establishing a routine, but he found it difficult. He could not get away from the idea that John Matthews, the elderly booking clerk, and Michael Thompson the porter were scrutinising him and judging him as being inferior to his predecessor. In many ways the work was easier than what he had experienced before, certainly, it was less physically demanding, but it did carry many new responsibilities.

The number of travellers that passed through the tiny station was very small, but this was a big farming area and the amount of freight was considerable. The large creamery just a few hundred yards from the station meant that the platform was constantly crowded with supplies coming in and the products of the dairy farms going out to market. Much of Iant's time was taken up by keeping track of the paperwork associated with this

257

traffic and several times in the first few weeks he lost milk churns or sent a crate of butter in the wrong direction.

It wasn't too long though before things began to settle down. John Matthews was a much more affable presence than he had first appeared and he invited Iant to the working men's club in Water's Upton and once to *The Bear* at Hodnet. Cycling home from *The Bear* Iant crashed his bike into the hedge after drinking more than he had become used to. He did not make as much headway as he would have liked in finding furniture, but he bought a big rug from one of the local farmers and acquired an armchair that had seen better days from someone in the village.

Finally, it was time for the family to join him. Iant worried that the youngest children would struggle to settle in the little village school and, even worse, that Ella would find it hard travelling each day on the train to the grammar school in Wellington. At home, they had spoken both Welsh and English, but Iant and Nancy both worried about the children adjusting to a place and a school where Welsh was a foreign language. At least they would see Ella safely on and off the train without much trouble.

When they arrived, the girls tore through the place exclaiming about its size and squabbling about who was to sleep were. Annie and Nia were to share a room and Ella, for the first time, would have the tiny box room all to herself. As Nancy supervised the men from GWR unloading the old rail lorry, Iant showed the children the garden and walked them up to the crossroads from where the two youngest could see their new school, just down the main road. They had most of the summer left before they started, and the house was full of their excitement at exploring a new place. Iant felt his spirits as high as he could remember for some while as the children were finally settled down for the night.

Some weeks after the children had begun their new schools Iant was supervising the loading of empty milk crates on to the goods wagon when he noticed that a passenger was getting off the train further down the platform. This was in itself unusual in the middle of the day, but after squinting to see who it was Iant's heart beat faster as he recognised his sister Doy, closely followed by her two boys. She struggled dragging a large suitcase behind her and Iant abandoned what he was doing and ran to help. Doy's face instantly told him that this was not an unexpected social visit.

As they approached the house, Nancy came out, her face attempting to hide her concern and trying instead to make her sister-in-law feel welcome. The kettle was boiled and plans made for Ella to move in with her sisters so that the boys could share a room for the night. It would be a squeeze, but they would manage. Eventually, the boys, Bryn and Emris, drifted outside to play in the garden and they were able to talk to Doy.

When she began to speak Doy became distraught and had to begin again several times. It was clear that something had happened concerning Gethin, but it was some while before she was coherent enough for Iant and Nancy to understand.

Three days ago, Doy had sent one of the boys with a message for their father. It was innocent enough; Gethin, who was now one of the under managers of the labour exchange in Rhyl, had gone back to work after his tea to prepare some paperwork that he had neglected during the day. This had happened regularly of late, but Doy was pleased about her husband's promotion and thought little of it. That evening though, after he had left to go back to work, one of Gethin's friends from the club had called round and asked if he could fill in on the darts team. They had a match and someone had cried off at the last minute. Doy had sent Bryn to give a message to his Dad. It would be good for him to have a night out, he had been working hard.

It was a good ten-minute walk to the labour exchange, but Bryn liked to see how fast he could run. He was there in five minutes and he had a trick of climbing over a side gate and going round the back to his dad's office instead of knocking on the front door. The light was on and the blind was down, but not

259

quite pulled to the bottom. Bryn had peered in making a funny face for his dad, but had instead been confronted with something that it had taken some while for his mother to get out of him.

Bryn was back in the house not much more than ten minutes after he had left. He ran upstairs and straight into his room without a word. Doy followed him and for a long time, he refused to speak or say whether he had given the message to his dad. She assumed that he must have been picked on by some boys on the way home, though he didn't appear hurt in any way. She was about to leave him to it when Bryn blurted out that his father had been 'lying on top of someone'. He was afraid that he had been hurting them.

Without saying a word Doy got her coat and told Bryn to watch his brother. She rarely left them alone together as they were always fighting, but she was out of the door before Bryn could reply. Doy could see the front door of the labour exchange from the entrance of the alleyway where she stood. She had initially thought to go and hammer on the main entrance, but at the last minute, her courage had failed her. She had been standing in the spot for some five minutes before first Gethin emerged looking up and down the street, followed by a young woman she recognised as Martha Williams, a clerk from the office that her husband managed. As Martha passed Gethin to walk down the street his hand rested on her hip and, giggling, she walked in the other direction.

For Iant of course memories of the evening in Wrexham came rushing back. And beyond those, Gethin's reputation in Salonika which at the time Gethin had gloried in. He should have said something to his sister when she and Gethin first met, but she wouldn't have thanked him for it and at the time he had felt that he was being prudish and old fashioned. Now here was his little sister sitting in front of him with her heart half-broken.

Doy had not told Gethin where she was going, or indeed asked him about what had happened. She had suspected him a few times before but had never been confronted with any evidence. What had upset her most Doy said was having to lie to

Bryn and thinking of him seeing what he did through the gap in the blind. So far she had no plans but had just known that she had to get away while she thought about what to do. She hadn't gone to Gwennie because she felt Ben might not have been very sympathetic. He had always been very friendly with Gethin. So she had turned to her brother.

That night after they had all retired to bed with Doy stretched out on the couch in the parlour, Iant and Nancy discussed what they could do to help. Part of Iant had just wanted to rush up to Rhyl and confront Gethin. He felt his trust had been betrayed almost as much as his sister's. He knew that this would not improve anything, though in the end, he knew that he would need to speak to Gethin. By morning Iant had decided to suggest that he would go to Rhyl. He wanted to knock Gethin's teeth out but instead, he agreed to tell him what they knew and see what his reaction was. They would all take it from there and Doy agreed.

He managed to arrange a day off with the GWR by telling some half-truths about his family needing urgent assistance. It was not scheduled to be a busy day, so he felt safe leaving the station with John in charge and Michael assisting. He had his free rail pass now, and if he got up very early he could go with the milk to Shrewsbury and then a train to Rhyl. He could just about make it there and back in a day.

Doy had told him that the Labour Exchange closed at one o'clock for lunch and that Gethin usually went home for something to eat. He got to the place at about twelve forty-five and waited across the road. It was market day and the town was full of people. Iant was afraid that he wouldn't be able to see when Gethin emerged, but at just before one he spotted him. At a safe distance, he followed him back through the side streets to the house where he and Nancy had spent their first nights together. It seemed a lifetime ago.

He let Gethin enter the house and waited a few moments before crossing the road and knocking on the door.

'Iant, man. Bloody hell, what are you doing here?'

261

In a split second, Gethin realised the connection between Iant's sudden arrival and the fact that his wife and sons had not been in the house when he arrived home last night. Luckily this made him drop his hale and hearty tone because it set off a fury inside Iant that might have threatened his promise to stay calm and talk rationally to Gethin.

'So she's run off to you has she?'

'That's up to Doy to tell you if she wants to.'

'What's she been telling you then?'

'Did you know your boy came to give you a message when you were working two days ago?'

Gethin face flushed immediately, though he kept up the pretence just a few moments longer.

'What are you talking about Ianto.'

He hated Gethin calling him that. Familiar.

'You know what I'm talking about Gethin.'

To Iant's temporary satisfaction Gethin turned away from him. He couldn't look him in the eye and his embarrassment showed on his neck and in his scalp.

'What am I going to do Iant?'

'You have to ask me that?'

'Yes. I don't know what I should do.'

'You admit it then?'

Gethin turned away again, but Iant was determined that he would face him.

'Say it to my face. Come on. It's the very least you can do.'

Gethin turned to face Iant, his eyes flickering to everywhere except Iant's stare.

'I have been stupid Iant. I didn't want to hurt her, it was just fooling around.'

Iant lost his self-control and ran across the room at Gethin, knocking him to the floor. Before either of them could think Iant was sitting astride Gethin and talking so close to his face that he could see his spittle land on Gethin's face. Normally Gethin was the stronger man, but there was no possibility of him being able to push Iant away.

'Fooling around Geth? Is that what it was? Do you want to tell that to your lad that looked in the window and saw God knows what? Do you want to tell it to his little brother who's wondering why his dad hasn't gone with them on the bloody train ride? Do you want to tell that to my sister who's breaking her heart and doesn't know which way to turn? You fucking bastard. You complete fucking bastard.'

Thinking that Iant was about to strike him in the face Gethin made a final effort and managed to dislodge him from his chest. For a minute they both lay on the floor, exhausted by their efforts until Iant jumped to his feet and headed for the door.

'Where are you going?'

'Where do you think? To tell my sister what a useless piece of dirt she married. To say sorry to her for ever introducing her to you.'

'Don't do that.'

'Why wouldn't I? Tell me Geth, go on.'

After a long silence between them, Iant couldn't stand it any longer. He turned and walked out of the house and down the street. He could hear Gethin shouting after him, but the loathing he felt at this moment kept Iant walking. After a few minutes, he realised that he had turned in a direction that he didn't recognise. He was lost, but he couldn't stop walking. Eventually, he reached the promenade and sat looking at the sea.

For a moment he was back on the mountain in the baking heat. Gethin had stuck up for him when his authority with the other men had faltered and now he hated the fact. He couldn't stand to feel anything but disgust for Gethin and he fought hard to put the memory from his mind. But instead, he thought of Sara. She still came into his mind more often than he cared to admit and he had never shaken off the idea that it was him who had let her down. She had never suggested that in her letters, but it did not stop it being something that would always gnaw away at him.

He tried hard to remember where the station was and, after a while, set off in what he hoped was the right direction. He

263

didn't have long before he had to catch the only train that would get him back that night.

The wind had got up and it had begun to feel like a proper autumn day. Iant trudged along the prom as the sea got greyer and the sun disappeared finally behind a bank of cloud. He had little sense of what he would say to Doy when he returned, but he had a long train journey ahead to think about it. He quickened his stride as he finally saw the spire of the church that he recognised as being quite close to the station.

Chapter 36

Doy and the boys eventually stayed in Crudgington for more than a month. He would never have said it to his sister, or even to Nancy, but Iant bitterly resented this intrusion on the new life that they had only just begun. Instead of enjoying the space in the new house it now felt very crowded with every corner seemingly filled with squabbling children or drying washing. Ella, who had been looking forward to her own room was back in with her sisters and not able to start to act the grammar school girl that she now was. She was tearful and complained that she was already behind with her homework.

Nancy never complained and Doy was very grateful for the refuge. But Iant could not help what he felt. He was sympathetic to his sister and would never have seen her without anywhere to stay, but he channelled his anger into what he thought about Gethin. He hated having to feel the small amount of gratitude he felt for his behaviour in Salonika, and now it had been overwhelmed by his disgust at what his sister had told him. He turned over and over in his mind the scene that his young nephew would have been faced with and the effect that this might have on him, perhaps for the rest of his life.

The first letter from Gethin arrived just a few days after Iant had made his trip to Rhyl. Gethin's writing was fluent and expressive and the letter was predictably full of protestations of how sorry he was and how much he missed Doy and the boys. Iant was pleased to see it torn into shreds not long after it had been read, but many others followed, many of them asking permission to visit. Eventually, Doy asked Iant and Nancy if Gethin could visit, but only for a day. She would not ask them to have him in the house.

Eventually, it was agreed. The visit would be on a Saturday and Iant and Nancy would take the two boys off on an expedition. It would be too unsettling for them to see their father and Iant felt repulsed by the idea of seeing Gethin again so soon.

He was very much against the idea of Doy seeing Gethin at all, but he knew that it would be stupid to even try to forbid it. He was not her father. He wanted to protect her from coming to more harm, but she was an adult and would make her own decisions.

Iant and Nancy took the boys and their girls to Shrewsbury on the bus. Being with five children meant that it was an exhausting day and Iant's mind kept wandering back to his sister. They had agreed to stay out until five o'clock and that Gethin had to be gone by then. As they walked up the road from the bus stop Iant found his heart racing. The last meeting with Gethin had brought out something in him that he hated, and he did not want to be reminded of it. He wouldn't have put it past Gethin to refuse to go in time, but when they arrived at the house Doy was alone.

'I'll make tea' said Nancy as soon as they entered the house. 'The children will be alright for a while. We had ice cream as well as their sandwiches.'

Iant was left alone with Doy. Nancy had, all along, respectfully avoided giving any advice. She was kind to Doy and a good listener, but she felt that it wasn't her place to tell her what to do. In private she spoke about it to Iant, but she felt that now was a moment when Doy needed to speak to her brother alone.

'He came then?'

'Yes, he did.'

'Did he behave himself?'

'Yes. He was like a little puppy dog.'

'I suppose he would be. He wants something.'

Iant had been determined not to be too quick to speak, to let his sister talk, but he hated the thought of Gethin turning on the charm again.

'He wants me to come back to Rhyl of course.'

'Yes.'

'He kept talking about what's best for the boys.'

'Bastard. He should have thought about that before....'

'I know.'

'And what did you say?'

'I said I would talk to you and think about it.'

'You know that you and the boys have got a home here for as long as you want?'

'I know that Iant, thank you.'

'I need to go and check on what Matthews has been up to.'

Iant knew that he should have stayed and talked some more with his sister, but he was angry and didn't want to upset her. Every part of him told him to urge her not to return to Gethin. He would never trust him again and he thought that Doy shouldn't either. He knew though that her choices were very hard. He meant it when he said that he would look after her and the boys and that Nancy would wholeheartedly support that, but that didn't make for a very appealing future.

Later that evening Doy made the three of them a cup of tea after the children had all settled down. Wearily she told Iant and Nancy that she had decided to give her marriage another chance. She did not mention Gethin by name. Iant could not bring himself to press her on her motives. He knew how hard it would be either way. All he could do was reassure her that there would always be somewhere for her to fall back on if it went wrong again as in his heart he felt it inevitably would.

The following weekend Iant saw Doy and the two boys off on the early train. They were weighed down both with their possessions and the baking that Nancy had done to 'tide them over'. Gethin was to meet them at the station in Rhyl. Iant knew that he should have gone with them, helped them in the two changes that they must make in Wellington and then in Shrewsbury, but he could not stomach the thought of seeing Gethin again. Indeed, he could not stand the thought of ever seeing Gethin again.

A week after their departure Doy wrote to say that they had settled back reasonably well, that they were not to worry and thanking them profusely for all that they had done for her and the boys. Iant did not want to speak about it anymore, but he

267

knew that the bad taste in his mouth and his lingering sense of guilt would stay with him for a long time.

Nancy especially was anxious that the girls especially should feel settled after this disruption to their lives. She made great efforts to overcome her natural shyness and to get to know the few families that lived nearby. She paid attention to Ella's school work and took care to ask her about any friends that she was making. The two younger girls were already more settled she thought with their easy walk to school and playmates in the scattered houses that made up the village.

Iant decided he must concentrate on his work. It was a small station, but he had not yet completely adjusted to being responsible for so many pieces of paper and for two other people. Michael Thompson was a good-natured young boy, but very apt to try it on with Iant when he could. John was much easier but ageing and set in his ways. Mainly things ticked over but Iant was conscious that any mistakes would be seen as his doing and wanted to make a good impression on the bigwigs that occasionally dropped in on him at his little station office.

In the years since the war had ended, Iant's thoughts about his time in Greece had, of course, been dominated by his relationship with Sara. Now, as he assumed more responsibilities, he thought often about his time in training and combat. He seldom talked about it, but sometimes the physical dangers that he had experienced came back to him. Most often these involved the slit trenches that had offered almost no protection, followed by the intense pain of the gas as it reached his eyes and ears. Sometimes he would be lost in these memories when he should have been concentrating and this added to his anxieties about failing in the job. He wondered if this was the same for the millions of other men who went through such experiences and worse. It was only Gethin that he knew to any extent and he would be the last person he would discuss such things with.

As well as his employers Iant had to maintain good relations with the station's nearest neighbours at the giant creamery that he could see from his window. It had been set up as a co-operative by a group of local farmers to help sell their butter and cheese and it was the station's biggest customer by far. The few passengers that used Crudgington station had to compete for space on the platform with crates and milk churns as well as building materials. The creamery was thriving and it was important that Iant had the confidence of the people who ran it.

Most significant of these was Colin Rogers, a burly man who managed the co-operative on behalf of the farmers. He was friendly to Iant in his own way, though inclined to strut around the place issuing orders. John and Michael thought him pompous and made fun of him behind his back. Iant thought it more prudent to maintain friendly relations which sometimes included the offer of being bought a pint or two at *The Lion* at Water's Upton.

As far as he could, Iant made himself put aside his memories of the war and his anxiety about his responsibilities. He could see that Nancy and the girls were thriving in the extra space that the house and garden offered and he enjoyed working so close to them all. The girls often put their heads around the door of his office and, although he made a show of reminding them that he was at work, he loved them bringing him presents of things that they had picked up or a scone that Nancy had baked.

One Saturday, in early March, Iant was up earlier than usual as Colin Rogers had given him warning of a special delivery that would be arriving on the first train, just after seven. It was a very large metal water tank that was to be installed at the creamery. The tank's bulk had meant that a special open goods wagon would be used and a crane-like contraption would be needed to lift it off the train and on to a flat-bed lorry that would take it the last few hundred yards to the creamery.

It was a very clear spring morning which lessened the blow of rising earlier than normal at a weekend. After the hills around Carog and Corwen, the flat north Shropshire landscape could look bleak and featureless but on a clear morning like this, the green fields stretching to the small Wrekin hills beyond looked perfect. The Wrekin itself, no more than a small wart on the

269

landscape, looked much bigger against the flatness of its surroundings and Iant sometimes imagined it as the volcano that it had once been several million years ago.

Just before seven, there was a loud knocking at the office door and Colin Rogers barged in.

'Just checking that you are up and about Evans bach.'

The sentence contained two things that Iant didn't like about Colin Rogers. One was the pompous use of his surname and the other was the slightly mocking use of Welsh from one who clearly thought it ridiculous. Colin Rogers was one of a breed that had lived life close enough to Wales to pick up some of its simpler idioms, but who thought it clever to poke fun at the survival of this quaint old language just over the border.

'So the crane will be on the waggon too?'

'It'll be on the one behind Colin. Your tank takes up a whole waggon to itself.'

'No wonder it's costing us a bloody fortune to get it here then.'

'Well by all accounts it's a big piece of metal.'

At about five past seven the goods train rumbled into the station and the open waggon carrying the tank pulled up alongside the station office. Iant found himself staring up at an enormous slab of black metal that blotted out all the daylight. For a moment, all that anyone standing on the platform could do was stare in awe at this object so out of scale with the station.

There was a gap of three hours before the special goods train had to be moving again and Iant realised that this would be not a moment too long. Four men had travelled with the tank, but there would, in theory, be little lifting to do as the crane would do that. There was though a lot of attaching of heavy chains to be done and manipulation of the tank off the train and onto the lorry that had now arrived and was reversing to the end of the platform.

Colin Rogers was clearly anxious that such an expensive piece of equipment be handled properly and he kept fussing and interfering. Iant thought to himself several times that he would

270

have been better to leave the work to the men, himself and Michael who had also come in early. Daft as he sometimes could be Michael was experienced at manoeuvring very heavy objects, though not usually anything as big as this.

The crane was put in place quite smoothly and then the chains began to be put in place on the tank. This seemed to take much longer than expected and there was difficulty attaching them to the corners. Colin Rogers became more and more impatient, at one point climbing up on the wagon to see what was going wrong.

At last, the tank was ready to be moved which involved lifting it in the air and then swinging it around in a half-circle on to the lorry that had all its sides down ready to receive the enormous object. As the handle on the crane was turned by two of the men there was a shout to stop because one of the chains had slipped slightly. Once again Colin Rogers mounted the wagon and fiddled with the chain himself. He jumped down and pronounced it secure.

Before anyone could contradict him, the vast object was on the move. It swung away from the waggon slightly before, to Iant's horror, he heard a terrible sound of metal slipping on metal. The tank slid remarkably quickly and at an angle first out of one set of chains and then, pulling the crane with it, out of the other, one corner hitting the concrete platform with a sound that no-one who heard it would ever forget.

The sound was so deafening that it took a split second for Iant to realise that Colin Rogers had not moved fast enough out of the path of the tank. Once the echo of the impact had died down the absolute silence was terrifying and was enough to confirm the horror of what had happened.

Chapter 37

Over the following weeks, Iant remembered the brief second of silence after the tank hit the platform above everything else. It was so short, but in Iant's memory, the silence overrode all the terrible shouting and screaming that followed. This in turn, though he could not recall how long it took, was followed by endless sirens. The fire engines were first to arrive, closely followed by an ambulance and finally the police.

Iant remembered thinking that he might be arrested. It was, after all, his responsibility. He was the station master, the one in charge. No matter that everyone saw how Colin Rogers had charged around like a bull in a china shop, or that someone had not fastened a chain properly to the enormous tank. In the end, he, Iant, was the one responsible. Why had he not ordered Colin Rogers out of the way, told him that he was endangering them all and for him to leave it to the experts?

Iant could not free himself from feeling responsible. His mind moved endlessly from the horror of the terrible accident to his inadequacy as a lance corporal in the mountains when Gethin had rescued him. He even tortured himself with thoughts of his decision not to return to Sara. Was it all part of the same strain of weakness that now had led to the tragic death of a man in front of his eyes on his station.

Iant was never arrested. He did though have to endure endless speculation, both from those he met and in the pages of the newspapers. *The Wellington Journal* was the one that took the most interest, though the local papers all over the Midlands covered the story. Nancy tried to suggest that Iant did not read any of the accounts, but he insisted on doing the opposite, accumulating heaps of cuttings from all kinds of sources. Nancy was right, he was torturing himself, punishing himself by going over and over what the papers had to say.

Much of the writing was just repetition of the bare facts embellished by what reporters had managed to get local people to say. One detail though was repeated again and again in ways that many claimed had sickened them, though Iant sensed that a taste for the truly horrific had been aroused in many. As the firemen supervised the lifting of the great tank it became clear that Colin Rogers had been decapitated. This terrible detail of what was, in any case, a tragedy, seemed to spread like wildfire and, shamefully in Iant's view, formed the basis of at least one newspaper headline in the days that followed.

As the crane started to lift the tank away from Colin Rogers' body Iant had felt horrified that his children might see what had happened and ran towards the station house shouting for Nancy to keep them away and not to let them go near the windows. In the following days, some criticised him for this. He should, they said, have been concentrating on the rescue. Iant knew though, from the terrible silence onwards, that there was not going to be any rescue and he could not help but think of his girls. As it happened Nancy had, from a distance understood very quickly what might happen. Having run out of the house at the terrifying sound of the tank hitting the platform she very quickly distracted the children and took them to a neighbour. She knew that Iant would need her and she was right.

No-one was able to fault Iant over what he did next. Having faced the horror of what lay beneath the tank, Iant knew that he had to be the one to walk the quarter of a mile across the main road and several fields to the house owned by Colin Rogers. He spoke to the fire officer and the police and the ambulance man who only had smelling salts for anyone who felt faint. The policeman tried to suggest that he must inform Miriam Rogers of her husband's death, but Iant was so determined that he must face this himself the policeman relented. He was only a young country bobby and was secretly glad to be relieved of such a task.

Iant had only walked a few yards away from the scene when he felt a hand in his.

'I'm coming with you.'

'No, no I don't want you to.'

'Iant, it will be easier for her if a woman is there.'

273

At this they fell silent, all the time conscious of the policeman walking a respectful distance behind them. Iant had in his mind that Miriam Rogers may have heard the commotion and already be readying herself to come down to see what was happening, but as they got closer to the old farmhouse there was no sign of anyone.

They walked around the back and Miriam was crouched down pulling weeds from around her plants in the pretty garden that she had created in the shadow of the industrial buildings that made up her husband's creamery.

'Iant....'

She had only a moment to look up before the policeman appeared behind Nancy and after that, a quiet life in this little country backwater was changed for all time. Nancy tried to hold Miriam, but her body went stiff and she settled for holding her hand as the young policeman intoned more official-sounding condolences. From somewhere a small dog appeared which began yapping at Iant's ankles and he bent to quieten it, glad of something to do.

For several days no trains were allowed to stop at Crudgington. Officially the tiny station was closed, but Iant felt compelled to sit in his office, fussing over bits of paper. Nancy did her best to tell him that he should take the advice of the doctor to rest, but Iant could not. Besides, there was endless paperwork to complete including a lengthy witness statement that he kept starting and then putting down.

The girls sensed his mood and came to see him more frequently, usually one at a time. Iant could not find a way to talk to them about the accident, though there was no way of preventing them knowing that someone had died. As he sat with one of them on his knee at the office window Iant's eye kept being drawn to the stain on the platform that he had scrubbed at again and again. It was less prominent now and almost certainly would not have been noticeable to anyone not looking for it, but Iant was conscious of his children's natural curiosity and desperate that they should not see it or, worse still, remark upon it.

The day of Colin Rogers' funeral the Great Western gave permission for the station to be completely closed for the day as a mark of respect. The tiny chapel was packed and people stood outside in the drizzle. Iant tried as best as he could to hide away at the back, but outside was approached again by a newspaper reporter who asked questions that should never have been asked anywhere, never mind at a poor man's funeral. Nancy said that they must go for a short while across to the Rogers's house where there was tea and sandwiches.

Iant had not spoken to Miriam Rogers since the afternoon of the accident. He had written to her and her family expressing his sadness and offering to help in any way that he could. He had no reason to expect hostility from the family and none was forthcoming. Nevertheless, he spent the funeral tea in agony and was hugely relieved when he and Nancy left.

The date for the inquest into Colin Rogers' death was set for the 25th of June, some three months after the accident. Iant had been subjected to several visits from railway big wigs. At first, these seemed sympathetic, but Iant became more and more aware of how anxious the company was to exonerate themselves from any wrongdoing. If this meant sacrificing one of their employees, especially if there was any suggestion that they had been personally negligent, then they would have done this. Nothing so explicit was ever stated of course, but Iant's statements were pored over endlessly for any sign that the company had been at fault.

Iant was only required to be at the inquest to give his evidence, but he took some of his holidays to attend for the week. He felt he had to hear everything and he hoped it would help to put it all straight in his mind. In the three months since Colin Rogers had died Iant's sleep had become a mixture of waking anxiety and confused, terrible dreams that were sometimes about the accident and at others about situations in which his competence was exposed in different ways. In one nightmare he took the girls out on a picnic only to see one of them close to a quarry edge and him too far to do anything. In another, Doy pleaded with him for help and he just walked away. Once, a train pulled out of the station with a door wide open and a child perched on the step of the carriage.

The inquest itself was almost an anti-climax. Iant was in the witness box for only a short time and the expert witnesses all agreed that the crane had not been suitable for the job. This had been compounded by the impatience of Rogers which resulted in insufficient time being allowed for the chains to be reattached to the tank. Iant felt little relief and desperately sad for Miriam Rogers who had not only lost her husband but now heard that his personality had contributed to his death. Part of him wanted to cry out that it was his fault, that he should have asserted himself and taken charge, but he knew it would have achieved little. After the coroner's verdict had cleared the GWR of all blame, Iant received a letter thanking him for the clarity of the evidence that he had given. He tore the letter into a hundred pieces and put them into the official company bin that sat in his office.

Iant tried very hard to put the accident behind them. Nancy gently reminded him of how much the children needed him and he tried to focus on the great luck he had in being surrounded by his beautiful girls. Ella was starting to take on some of the habits of a young woman, and was the one that needed more of his attention. She had been older when they had moved and therefore with the most to give up from her earlier life.

Iant decided to make Ella feel special by turning her box room into a place where she would feel comfortable and private. Never having had a room of his own Iant could only imagine what it would mean, but he thought that Ella would like some shelves for her books and perhaps a colourful chair on which she could sit or drape her clothes. He set about finding and making things in secret so that one evening when Ella came home she found her room transformed. Nancy teased her that its tidiness would last five minutes, but Ella's pleasure stayed with Iant for weeks.

The dreams and the wakefulness persisted despite the pleasure he took in seeing his girls grow and the reassurance he always received from Nancy. He still suffered flashbacks and reminders of the battle on Pip Ridge, but they were not the ones that plagued him most now. The sounds from that morning on the station platform came back to him again and again.

Towards the end of the year, Nancy tried to persuade Iant to visit the doctor and eventually he agreed, though the kind, but old-fashioned village doctor had little sense of what could be troubling Iant. He had heard of shell-shock of course and suggested that the noise that Iant described may be akin to that. Iant returned home with a preparation of fine white powder to be dissolved in water once a day. When he discovered that it made him want to sleep during the day he refused to take it anymore. He was terrified of losing his concentration, especially at work.

Iant decided that what he must do, at all costs, was to hide what he felt. He would not have this terrible accident affect the lives of his daughters, or, as far as he was able, the life of his wife. He could not control his dreams or his sleep, but he would no longer talk about what he had experienced.

Through an enormous effort of will, Iant was able to achieve this, but it was at a cost. Though never outgoing or gregarious Iant's marriage and children had made him a calm and cheerful presence. But now he became anxious and inclined to introspection. Around his daughters, he tried hard not to scold too much and to play with them whenever he was in the house. He helped Ella with her schoolwork and managed to joke about her becoming much cleverer than he was. But, as Nancy confided to Gwennie on a rare visit to Wrexham, it was as if a part of Iant was not present anymore.

At first, Nancy tried to broach her fears with Iant, but she saw how deeply it troubled him and how he just worked harder to hide what he felt. After first a year had passed and then two, Nancy knew that she had to settle for something. Iant remained a man that she could love, someone who was gentle and

277

considerate. Only she really knew how much was missing from him and occasionally she allowed herself to miss him as he once had been.

Chapter 38

1938

As he waved Ella off on the early train to Wellington, where she worked at *Bates and Hunt's* the chemist, Iant felt a strong sense of his age. With one daughter going out to work and, he suspected, a boyfriend or two, and the other two just a couple of years from finishing school he wondered where the years had gone. Iant knew that everyone felt like this as they got to middle age, but this didn't make it better somehow.

As always, he tried to count his blessings. The easy companionship that he enjoyed with Nancy was not something that he took for granted and he knew that in recent years he had not always been an enjoyable companion. More recently he could go for months at a time and feel just like his old self, but then something would come over him and it was all he could do to get through the working day and remain civil to everyone. After years of trying to coax him out of it, Nancy had taken to leaving him to find his way. Iant knew that this is what she had to do, but selfishly he sometimes resented it.

He had wondered whether he should try and find another posting. The railway had expanded despite so many out of work and Iant was now an experienced station master. In many ways, he longed to get away from this place where every day he had to walk past the site of the accident. Inside his office, he looked out onto the platform and he lived that morning over and over again, though mercifully the pictures in his mind had become less vivid.

But every time he thought of moving, he was reminded that his girls would be uprooted again and about how Nancy had worked hard to make the station house a comfortable home. Sometimes the company themselves moved men around with little notice, but Iant came to think that Crudgington had an aura of bad luck about it, so the GWR was content to leave it as his responsibility. Best stay put and try to count your blessings he thought with resignation.

The previous Christmas had been the first since the accident that Iant could remember enjoying. With both sets of parents now gone, Nancy had been determined that Gwennie and Ben, Doy and Gethin would come with all the children. Iant had felt his heart sink at the prospect. Just the sense of having to be jolly around so many adults and children for a few days was enough. Then there was Gethin with whom he had only accepted an uneasy truce over the years for Doy's sake.

When it came to it though things had turned out quite well. Iant avoided too much time in Gethin's company and had been able to get out of a Christmas Eve drink with him and Ben down at *The Lion* because he had to get up before them on Christmas morning to carry out some checks. There had been no passenger trains on Christmas Day, but there were some engineering works on the line and someone needed to be on duty for a couple of hours. Half-anticipating needing an excuse, Iant had volunteered so the others could spend an uninterrupted day with their families.

Iant shared the Christmas Day washing up with his sisters and realised how few times he had been alone with them both since he had joined the army. They had always been co-conspirators in the long struggle against their mother's disposition and they now laughed together as they reminisced over her scoldings and seeming inability to ever really enjoy herself. They even grew misty-eyed at the thought of how long it had been since she had passed. Iant realised again how fond he was of his sisters and he resolved to make sure that their families remained close, despite any differences.

On Christmas night he and Nancy had lain on cushions in front of the fire as the rest of their family were crammed as best they could be into the nooks and crannies of bedrooms upstairs. Among blankets that they lay under was one that Iant had brought back from the army and they laughed as they squirmed against its roughness. In the fading light from the fire in the grate Iant had reached under the blankets and drawn Nancy towards him. For a long time, they had lain still, glad of the physical

280

closeness that had not always come easily to Iant in recent years. As Nancy had turned to face him Iant felt his desire for her mingle with an overwhelming sadness that he had allowed his state of mind to limit their life together. For a brief moment, his mind had gone back to another blanket on an unforgiving surface, in the ruins surrounding the Church of the Rotunda where he had asked Sara to marry him, but Nancy had been determined to keep Iant in the present, though she had no idea what part of the past he had drifted towards. They made love passionately sometimes slightly forgetting how sound travelled through the thin walls.

Afterwards, Iant had slept more than he had done for years and they both only awoke when they heard the sounds of people getting up in the rooms above them.

That Christmas was a time that Iant returned to many times in his mind. He did so again this morning to stop himself imagining a life away from this place and a time that he would never fully escape, whatever he did. As Ella's train disappeared out of sight Iant turned to go up the path to the house anticipating breakfast. As he did so he felt one of the sharp pains in his side that he had grown used to for some time and he slipped a Rennie into his mouth chewing slowly.

Annie and Nia were already at the table squabbling and he hushed them gently as he sat down. Nia smiled at him but Annie was developing a scowl that was appropriate for her age and Iant pulled a face at her. A flicker of a grin quickly emerged and then disappeared lest it ruin her composure. Even Nancy lost her temper with Annie sometimes and Iant knew that she would be a match for anyone as she got older. He took a quiet pleasure in this even though he was glad that it would be another man who would have to find an accommodation with Annie one day.

Nia was the gentlest of his children, the one least likely to take offence or worry about her problems. There was still time for that to change of course, but Iant saw Nia as the most like her mother. A peacemaker who would try and make the best of a situation and not worry for too long if things did not go

281

according to her plans.

Iant would sometimes be made fun of about living amongst women or asked if he minded not having a son. People were not to know about Evan and these days he rarely saw the need to explain to anyone who didn't know. Once the sadness of his son's death had faded Iant had felt the good fortune of being surrounded by daughters. They teased him mercilessly, but they also cared for him, mothered him in a way that his mother had never done.

'Have you made an appointment yet Iant?'

Nancy's voice brought him back to the present and made him look at his watch. Come on Annie bach, I'll put you on the train.'

'I've told you, Dad. I'm not a parcel.'

'Well if you were, you would be in the guard's van, instead of a nice Great Western Railway comfortable seat. Now hurry up or you'll miss it.'

'Iant?'

'No, I haven't yet.'

'Use the phone in the office for once.'

'Do you want to get me sacked woman?' he joked.

After he had seen Annie on to the train and waited in vain for a cheerful wave, Iant returned to the office and, while John Matthews was outside, picked up the phone and made an appointment to see the young Dr Morgan. At least he wouldn't remind Iant of the accident and hopefully wouldn't share the old doctor's bafflement regarding anything but the simplest physical ailments. He would be able to talk to Dr Morgan of the persistent pain in his stomach he had after eating a meal without fear that it would be put down to his 'nerves'. Nancy had reminded him again and again over several months and the persistent traces of blood on the lavatory paper that he had noticed several mornings running made him ignore even the wrath of those that scrutinised the use of the railway's telephone.

Over the coming weeks and months, as Iant submitted first to simple tests in the doctor's waiting room and then to more invasive procedures at the cottage hospital in Wellington and then to radical surgery at the *Royal Shropshire Infirmary* in Shrewsbury he tried to hold on to the only useful idea that had carried him through his recent life. That he was, in most respects a lucky man. He told himself that and he told Nancy, though he stopped short of telling his daughters for fear of baffling them. However, once they had opened him up it was confirmed that he was suffering from stomach cancer.

Before the operation, Iant had suffered little more than mild discomfort. He had never had an enormous appetite, but he now found himself able to eat less. He stopped going down to *The Lion* almost entirely as the beer filled him so easily. Nancy had promised that she would quietly let it be known that he was waiting for a hospital appointment to see about his stomach ulcer. It was something that dated back to the poison he had inhaled in the mountains of Greece. Indeed, this is what the young doctor had suggested when he first saw him so it didn't feel like much of a deception.

As the tiredness became worse Iant did confide to John and Michael that he was not feeling as well as he might be and was waiting for an operation. He knew that they would cover for him without making a show of it. They had become friends of a sort through their time on the tiny station and had developed familiar patterns of behaviour that played to their strengths.

The family spent the Christmas before Iant's operation alone. Gwennie had urged them all to go to Wrexham, but Iant did not feel up to either the travel or a house full of people. He tried to persuade Nancy to take the children and tell everyone that he had special duties over Christmas. The children would have enjoyed being with their cousins and she could have visited old haunts. Nancy would not hear of it and neither would Ella, who half overheard their conversation.

As spring approached Iant knew that it would not be very long before he became too ill to work. This was what he had feared most and without Nancy knowing he had written to his sisters to ask them to look after Nancy and the children should

283

anything happen to him. They had both replied very quickly and it was with great mixed feelings that he had read a separate note from Gethin, promising to do everything he could and hoping that they could remember the friendship that they had once had.

Officially he remained at work, but Iant had been forced to rest for long periods during the day. As he lay, half in sleep Iant listened to the increasingly gloomy news bulletins. He didn't feel strong enough to be angry, but to those of his age, it seemed beyond belief that before their children had even been allowed to grow up some of them would be sent to fight and die in places that people had hardly heard of. It was barely twenty years since he had been fighting Bulgarians on a mountain in Greece. Nothing was mentioned of these places now. It seemed to be about Czechs and Poles, Danzig and the Sudetenland, wherever that was.

Iant was admitted to the hospital in Shrewsbury in late May and an operation was performed. To his frustration, he remained there for over four weeks. For Nancy to get to see him was a long bus ride through the back lanes or change of trains in Wellington. He longed to see the girls but didn't want them to see him as he was. They all came much more often than he thought they should, and he did not have the heart to argue. Sometimes Ella would come on her own after she had finished work, bringing some treat with her, though he rarely felt like eating much.

Finally, he was allowed home in an ambulance. The next day John Matthews called round and Iant could tell that his appearance had shocked his old colleague, though John tried to tell him to stop messing about and get out of bed instead of leaving all the work to them. They had sent a relief station master who John kidded was a far better worker than Iant, though later, as he was going, whispered that he wasn't a patch on him, though it was painful for him to say it.

There were days when Iant felt as though he must surely get out of bed and stop all this lying around. What had he been thinking, leaving all the worry and work to Nancy. He must get

284

up and see his girls. Help them with their homework. Who was seeing that they got on the train in time in the morning? But as soon as he began the walk downstairs he knew that his body wouldn't let him go further and that trying would just make Nancy's life more difficult.

Iant thought he was dreaming when he heard first Doy's voice and then Gwennie's. They were talking quietly as if they were a long way away. A little later, he thought he must have drifted off to sleep, they were in the room sitting beside his bed. He needed some more of the medicine as the pain was gradually returning but he didn't want to interrupt them.

Iant thought he heard someone talking about sending him back to hospital, and in his confusion, he was back in Salonika being nursed by Sara. He heard Nancy say firmly that she could manage. He was relieved but he didn't want her to be worn out and he knew the girls didn't like seeing him in pain. He tried to hide it when they were in the room, but it was becoming harder each day.

Nancy sat by his bed more now, which made him happy. She said that their neighbours were being kind and looking after Nia. Sometimes they brought round dishes of food. There were rumours in the newspapers of plans to send people out of some of the big cities, but no-one knew if they would be sent to Shropshire or not. Iant thought it would make a lot of work for the railways.

Iant passed away peacefully in his sleep at the beginning of August. Nancy tried very hard to see it, as some tried to call it, as a 'release'. Iant had been in a lot of pain and tried hard to hide it, but every bit of her just wanted him back and to hang on to him for as long as she could.

Despite all the difficulties Nancy was determined to take Iant back home. There was an insurance policy and Gethin had offered to make up the difference. Nancy had little inclination to argue. He would go by train, of course.

The Great Western railway sent flowers and a regional official wrote to Nancy, but a day later there was another letter

285

asking when the station house might be conveniently vacated.

On the 15th August 1939, Iant was buried in the cemetery at Glyndyfrdwy near to his mother and father. There were quite a few people there that Nancy had never seen before, but Gwennie and Doy knew some of them from when they were children.

In the days after Iant died Nancy had brought out the old biscuit tin from where Iant had stored it away. It had not been hidden in any way but was in a place that the children would not stumble across it. Iant had few possessions that were uniquely his apart from his clothes and a few old tools. This tin with its secret, a big secret in the scale of their small lives, Nancy thought, was the only thing of significance. She briefly thought of burning the letters and trying to sell the ring, though it would fetch very little she imagined. Then she wondered if she ought to write to the address on the letters and tell Sara what had happened.

Nancy did neither of these things. Though it would have been foolish to bear this woman any ill will, she had no desire to share this loss with her. Besides, her life would have taken many turns by now and why should it be disrupted in such a way? She would keep the tin and the ring though. She would bury it in her possessions and one day one of the girls would find it. One of them might even wear the ring. If they chose to look they would see something about their kind, gentle father, that would perhaps shake up their view of him. They should know that this was a man that was taken from the peace of Merionethshire and sent to face huge dangers in places that no-one had ever heard of. Though he had come back and settled upon a life that they would come to call dull, he had thought once of wandering back across Europe and marrying a woman that had nursed and loved him. A woman who had helped make him what he eventually became.

Nancy wondered if some might think her perverse for preserving this memory of Iant, but she had known and loved not just a man who was safe and kind and loving, but a man who was also this. She would hold onto that for herself and one day others would know this too.

Lightning Source UK Ltd.
Milton Keynes UK
UKHW050924081221
395183UK00010B/39